HASHISH KALEIDOSCOPE

"I remember someone passing me a small pipe and my happy laughter as I inhaled a few puffs of what I thought was tobacco. Then suddenly, I was floating in a dream world. I remember dancing, feeling certain that as I weaved to the strange music, I was obeying ancient rules imbedded in some part of my primitive brain. . . .

"I remember trying to thank Armand for a lovely evening, but the words coming out of my mouth seemed actually tangible; like butterflies they swooped around my head. Nor were Armand's eyes, as he followed me inside, just ordinary eyes. They filled his entire face. Giggling, I felt my dress take on a life of its own. It disappeared in a soft purple cloud over my head. I noticed that the chairs in the room were all smiling at me in delightful acquiescence. They liked my naked body. I held my breasts in my hands so they could see how lovely they were . . ."

ROBERT H. RIMMER'S
THE ZOLOTOV AFFAIR

Books by Robert H. Rimmer

🦅 THE HARRAD EXPERIMENT
THE REBELLION OF YALE MARRATT
THAT GIRL FROM BOSTON
🦅 THE ZOLOTOV AFFAIR

🦅 Published by Bantam Books, Inc.

THE ZOLOTOV AFFAIR

ROBERT H. RIMMER

BANTAM BOOKS
TORONTO · NEW YORK · LONDON

THE ZOLOTOV AFFAIR

*A Bantam Book / published by arrangement with
Sherbourne Press, Inc.*

Printing History
Sherbourne Press edition published May 1967
Bantam edition published April 1968

*Bantam Books are published by Bantam Books, Inc., a subsidiary
of Grosset & Dunlap, Inc. Its trade-mark, consisting of the words
"Bantam Books" and the portrayal of a bantam, is registered in the
United States Patent Office and in other countries. Marca Registrada.
Bantam Books, Inc., 271 Madison Avenue, New York, N. Y. 10016.*

PRINTED IN THE UNITED STATES OF AMERICA

"There is no place so high that an ass laden with gold cannot reach it."

ROJAS

Pb ← → Au

This book is dedicated to the few remaining people in the world who believe there is a pot of gold at the end of the rainbow.

One

Craig Barnett says that I am a come-what-may-girl. He may be right . . . but I am scarcely the type that takes *everything* that comes her way lying down. I do believe that if a person wants something badly enough he or she can shape destiny. Make it conform a little. I also am certain that most people have a potential for the inevitable. At least I do. And my potential may be greater than most.

It all shakes down to a basic fact. I was born poor, and I grew up poor. Oh, not poor starving, but poor middle class. A state of life that exists between low wages and high taxes. A place where most of us live on the fringes of existence. The only escape comes in tubes with shadows on them, bottles of high proof alcohol, tranquilizers, or stories about girls like me, Marge Wentworth.

So, I want to be rich. Most people, after they are sufficiently rebuffed by life and the indifference of the world, quietly die. They go through the motions of living but the wide horizons of youth give way to a narrow truce with necessity. Already at twenty-seven Craig had decided that an imitation of immortality could be achieved by eking out an existence in the suburbia of Midhaven, Connecticut, *with me* and whatever number of squalling children I was willing to hatch. I told Craig this was nothing but a perpetual, century by century, duplication of the salt of the earth, the great unknown billions who have lived and died and left no trace. I didn't tell him my occasional daydreams of being the mistress of a certain billionaire Greek shipping magnate. Since Craig believes in re-incarnation he left me with the food gagging thought that since nothing actually disappears in this world, the steak I was so daintily enjoying (at his expense) was probably only the bits and pieces of some former ancestor; like Croesus for

1

example. I laughed. Which proves I have some sense of humor.

Without going so far as to say that I was actually waiting for Horace Zolotov when he walked in the door of the Midhaven National Bank, it is obvious that the die was cast. What happened to me, Craig Barnett, Horace Zolotov, and ultimately every human being in what we now label the civilized world was as certain as death. The stage was set. The author of the whole bit could only stand back and watch, aghast, as his creations got out of hand.

Within minutes after Horace Zolotov peered down at me, hunched over my typewriter, my daydream potential received an injection of adrenalin. Behind Horace I could see Fred Chambers, the bank guard, grinning at me, his eyes rolling, to indicate that this strange looking man towering over my desk had probably walked right off the drawing board of some comic strip artist: the perfect earthbound visualization of the celestial mad scientist.

"He wants to see the President of the Bank," Fred said very straightfaced. "I think he wants to open an account."

"Mr. Wood, the Assistant Manager, can take care of that." I tried to avoid the unblinking stare of pale blue eyes surveying me through spectacles that looked like the bottom of jelly jars.

"Miss Wentworth," Zolotov said, reading my desk sign. "If you are secretary to Mr. Harold Nichols, will you please inform him that Horace Zolotov is here and wishes to talk with him." He rested his black satchel on the edge of my desk and extracted an old fashioned gold pocket watch from his vest pocket. The sunlight caught the shiny convexity of the case and radiated in my eyes. I shivered. I had the strange feeling that Horace Zolotov was trying to hypnotize me.

"Do you have an appointment with Mr. Nichols?" I

2

asked. I knew that Harold wasn't busy. It was fifteen minutes after one. Harold had dictated his last letter of the day. He was now probably scanning the *Wall Street Journal;* glancing occasionally at the clock on his desk. It was Wednesday and on Wednesday at 2 P.M. Pat Marratt, President of The Marratt Corporation, picked Harold up at the office to play golf at the Midhaven Country Club. If the weather was inclement, Harold still maintained this discipline. I guess they played cards in the locker room, or told dirty jokes to each other at the bar. At least I noticed on Thursdays, after rainy Wednesdays, that Harold had a new supply that he was anxious to test on my blushing ears.

"My dear young woman," Zolotov was by now a little aggravated at my indecision. "No one except the President of this bank can rationally discuss the business I have in mind. Will you please tell Mr. Nichols that I am here?"

I was certain that Zolotov didn't have an appointment. Since he was hovering over me I couldn't use the intercom and alert Harold. I asked Zolotov to wait. I walked into Harold's office, closing the door behind me.

Harold, one eye on the clock, listened impatiently. "It should be clear to you, Miss Wentworth, Mr. Zolotov wants to borrow money. His entire manner, as you describe it, indicates this. I have three vice presidents who are perfectly capable of handling loan requests."

"I am not interested in borrowing from your bank, Mr. Nichols."

I turned gasping. Zolotov had followed me in to Harold's office.

"Mr. Zolotov . . . this is an IMPERTINENCE!" Harold nervously harrumphed at him. He noticed Zolotov's bag. We both evidently had the same thought. Was Zolotov some kind of a nut with a bomb? "Miss Wentworth, tell Fred Chambers to come in here." Harold's voice was an octave too high.

I started for the door. But Zolotov had closed it behind him. He leaned against it. "Mr. Nichols, it is scarcely necessary to alert the entire personnel of your bank. I am carrying no weapons. I have no designs on your life. I simply have a private matter that I would like to discuss with you. Can this young woman leave for a few minutes?"

"Miss Wentworth is my private secretary." Harold tried unsuccessfully to stare Zolotov down. "She is present at all my conferences." This wasn't strictly true, but I could see that Harold had no intention of being left alone with Horace Zolotov. I expected momentarily that he would press the alarm in the floor under his desk. Just in case, I picked out the leather chair I would duck behind when Zolotov started shooting.

"Now, Mr. Zolotov," Harold was saying. "What is it you wish to discuss with me? I can assure you that your problems will remain in the confines of this office."

"I rather doubt that." Zolotov smiled. "But then, it probably doesn't matter. Within the next few days I am sure that you will wish to confirm the reality of what I am going to show you. I imagine that it will be somewhat difficult to keep this matter entirely confidential." Zolotov opened his black bag. Harold and I both drew back wondering if perhaps he had hari-kari in mind and planned to take us with him. But Zolotov lifted what seemed to be a bar of gold out of the bag. Using two hands he carefully placed it on Harold's desk.

"It's rather heavy," he said. "But then it's pure gold!"

Harold looked at it warily. "Where in hell did you get this?" He turned it over. "It has no markings on it."

Zolotov smiled at him. His eyes behind his thick glasses seemed abnormally large. Rather than softening his expression, the smile chilled his face. "This bar is the exact size of gold bullion, Mr. Nichols. It weighs twenty-seven pounds. It measures 6¾ x 3½ x 1¾ inches. Naturally, there are no U. S. Treasury markings on it.

4

I am not a counterfeiter. The market value of this bar at the present per ounce price of gold is fourteen thousand dollars. Because I am momentarily a little short of funds I am willing to cash it with your bank for ten thousand dollars."

Harold was obviously stunned. "Don't you know that it is against the law for a citizen of the United States to have gold in his possession? Moreover, in this form, I can assure you, Mr. Zolotov, that you had better be prepared to produce some certified information as to where you got it!"

"I *made it,* Mr. Nichols," Zolotov said calmly. The sepulchral, unemotional tone of his voice gave me goose pimples. "I don't believe that there is any law that states a private citizen cannot make gold."

"You *made it!*" Harold's New England dignity was shattered. He actually guffawed. "My God, if it were April instead of November, Mr. Zolotov, I would believe that you were giving me a little April Fool spoofing. Just how did you make it? Out of old iron and gold paint?"

Zolotov didn't respond to Harold's sarcasm. "I can appreciate your surprise, Mr. Nichols. But the truth is that I made it out of lead! I have discovered, after some years of hard work, the secret that defied the alchemists for years."

"Just what is this secret?" Harold asked. The tone of his voice was modulated for humoring someone who might have just announced that he was Napoleon. I guessed that Harold was enjoying himself. This was a story that would entertain his friends at the club for weeks to come.

"Your reaction is normal, Mr. Nichols," Zolotov sounded as if he was explaining a quite simple problem to a bewildered school boy. "I really don't blame you. In 1939 if a scientist had told the average citizen that an atom bomb was a reality, and that it could wipe out a city, I imagine that he would have invited a similar response. As a matter of fact, some of the principles of nuclear physics that were revealed in atom splitting have aided my discovery considerably. In essence, I have removed three of the protons from lead which carries an atomic number of 82. With a secret of breathtaking simplicity I have subtracted seven of the neutrons normally present in the nuclear structure of lead. If you are familiar with the periodic chart of the elements you will recognize that the result is pure gold. The surprising thing is that with a few hundred dollars' worth of equipment, *and my secret,* anyone in the world can make as much gold as he might wish. You can see, Mr. Nichols, the millennium is at hand. The common man can be as rich as Croesus!"

It was five minutes until two o'clock, I could see that Harold was getting fidgety. By this time I was wondering myself when the man in the white coat would arrive and put Mr. Zolotov back in the Midhaven Asylum for Disturbed people.

"You must realize, Mr. Zolotov," Harold said, "before I could purchase this bar of gold for ten thousand dollars I would have to have it tested."

"Naturally," Zolotov beamed. "You can take borings in my bar in any place you may wish. You will find that in every test it assays 100% pure gold. I will leave it with you until next Wednesday which should be sufficient time to make an assay."

Zolotov closed his black satchel, preparing to depart. I suppose Harold couldn't resist it. "Don't you want a receipt?" he kidded Zolotov. "Of course. I can't give you a receipt for ten thousand dollars, but I'll have Miss Wentworth give you a memorandum that you left an object of this size and weight with us."

"That's not really necessary," Zolotov chuckled. "I made it out of thirty pounds of lead. Lead is selling for about thirty cents a pound. I'm sure, Mr. Nichols, that

I can trust you for nine dollars. I will come back next Wednesday."

Two

On Wednesday nights I usually arrive at Craig's apartment about an hour before he comes home. After a day's work, my secretary-to-the-President-smile is wearing a bit thin. To get a new perspective on life and love, I usually make myself a scotch and water, take a leisurely shower, put on one of Craig's woolen shirts and nothing else. Then, trying not to think of how nice and snugly it was going to be burrowing in Craig's arms, feeling his chest against my breasts, his belly against mine, our breaths and hearts marching in unison, I happily prepare us a coq-au-vin or whatever else exotic happens to appeal to my culinary instincts of the moment.

Tonight both sex and cooking were taking a back seat in my mind to Horace Zolotov and his bar of gold. Wondering whether I had the right to tell anyone, including Craig, about bank business, I plunged into my Jambalaya recipe of shrimp, rice, and chunks of ham. Craig finally arrived from his job on the *Midhaven Herald*. He immediately shed his Society Editor, Ivy League image, by stripping and putting on an old sweat shirt. I suddenly realized that he was watching me prepare dinner with an expression that indicated why did we have to wait? Despite my carefully acquired sophistication, Craig has a way of discussing the physical *me to me* that makes me blush. In his words:

"I know that you are a good cook, Marge, but you really can't expect me to just sit here and watch. Beneath my shirt, the bottom of your behind is an undulating, fetching invitation to the joys of love. How can I keep my eyes off those soft curly hairs arching into your belly, and do nothing?"

"Love and sex should be savored," I chuckled. "Not rushed into haphazardly . . . and then there we are, both thinking: 'Ho-hum, now that's over with, what do we do next?' "

On this premise, while the back half of my mind kept steadily thinking about Zolotov, Craig let me ramble on with irrelevant chatter about art, music, politics, world events and just about anything that momentarily was unrelated to his obvious readiness to jump in the sack and spend the night there.

Craig is convinced that I am one of those new breed of self-sufficient women who never want to get married. "I do, Craig . . . really. Some day." I kissed his cheek when he managed to introduce the subject for the one-thousandth time. "But why can't we wait awhile? I promise when I finally decide to do it, it will be you."

I had stopped long enough in my peregrinations from table to sink to stove to permit him to dally his face for a second or two in the curve of my stomach. While I kissed his neck enthusiastically, he pushed up his old hunting shirt and tasted my breasts. His enthusiasm boded no good for the Jambalaya I had been slaving over.

"Do I have to get you pregnant before you will marry me?"

I kissed his nose and pulled away. "I think a shotgun wedding would be fun. Imagine mother's face when I tell her I need a maternity wedding gown."

"Marge Wentworth, you are bad. You will come to no good. It's lucky I am your paramour."

"Really," I told him. "When you finally persuade me to get married you'll wish you were back right here in your bachelor apartment. Think how much nicer this is than marriage. Wednesdays and Saturdays we sleep together. All the rest of the week we don't see each other. I never ask you too many questions. You don't ask me too many. If we were married, tonight I would have been waiting at the door. 'Why were you late?' I would say. 'Do you have to go out bowling with the boys again? I want to go to a moving pitcher! I've been cooped up in this rat trap apartment all day,' And so, on and on. This way we stay interesting to each other. It's not that I'm against marriage. But you are only twenty-seven. I'm only twenty-five. I've worked just one year. I love it. It's fun. Besides I managed to save enough to pay one third down on my lovely mink coat. You never could have afforded to buy me one. Even if you could have I would have felt unworthy of it. Oh, Craig, don't you see? I didn't slave to get to graduate school, and finally get a master's degree in economics, just to fiddle around with household budgets based on your meager salary. I love you, but I refuse to be a hot house plant. What would I do in suburbia all day with a brood of kids?" I shuddered. "Not right now, anyway."

"Just what are you learning about economics as secretary to Harold Nichols?" Craig murmured into my breasts. He had been there so long I wondered if he had smothered. I was dimly aware that his hands were playing havoc with the rest of me. He continued muttering: "Harold Nichols may be in his fifties. His dowdy wife may be President of all the Women's Clubs in Southern Connecticut. But I'll bet she weighs at least one hundred and ninety pounds. After seeing her stuff herself into a girdle week after week, Harold Nichols looks at you. Is he thinking about money and banking? Not at all. He wishes he was doing what I am doing. I'll bet he falls asleep at night trying to figure how to entice a skinny dish like you into the sack with him."

"That which you have your face against *is not* skinny!" I protested. "So far I'm lucky. I've grown plump in the right places. But that's no assurance for the long haul. Mother weighs one hundred and seventy-eight. What you're saying just proves it. Marriage is a dull business. Poor Mrs. Nichols. Just because she got bored hanging around and waiting for Harold to come home, she ate too much. Now Harold doesn't want to come home at all." I lighted the candles ignoring Craig's remark that he thought it was pretty dumb to eat in the dark. A little light would prevent him from jamming his fork into his cheek every time he took a mouthful.

"Just be careful your knife doesn't slip. You might puncture that thing near your middle that keeps staring at me. Then all your matrimonial desires would vanish forever."

Craig observed himself with too obvious male delight. "One of us will have to wear underpants."

"Here, pour the wine and get your mind on more prosaic things. Besides, I'm bursting to tell you what happened at the bank today." I filled Craig's plate with my ham and shrimp curry.

"If Harold propositioned you, tell him you can't. You really wouldn't enjoy it anyway. Tell him that you're frigid!"

I brandished my knife menacingly across Craig's gizmo. "I'll show you how frigid I am. If you don't listen to me, I'll cut off your weapon and eat it for supper." I quickly moved my chair to the opposite side of the table before this foolishness got out of hand. Slowly, still feeling an odd goose-pimply sensation, I told Craig about Horace Zolotov and his bar of gold bullion.

"He sounds like some kind of nut," Craig shrugged. "Tomorrow he'll be back in the booby hatch."

I looked at Craig disgusted. "You haven't got a romantic bone in your body." I suppose that wasn't quite fair, but all evening I had been bubbling with the thought of Zolotov and his gold. Didn't Craig have imagination about anything except sex?

"I don't see what you're so heated up about, Marge. So let's play it your way. Suppose some joker could

10

make gold. That's that! It wouldn't be worth any more than lead."

"Don't you understand?" I demanded excitedly. "If that bar was really gold and Zolotov made it out of lead for a few dollars, then you are right. Gold will be worthless. But there is more to it than that. The economic implications are fantastic. Did you ever hear about balance of payments? Most of the time the United States doesn't have enough gold to settle its international debts."

"I don't have enough dollars to settle mine," Craig said mournfully. "I never should have let you talk me into buying the Jaguar."

"Listen, maybe you won't have to worry. The whole damned world is going to be in an economic upheaval. It's beyond my master's degree in economics to comprehend it, but gold is the only thing most of the people in the world believe in. Only there's never been enough of it . . . When there's *too much* of it, what will take its place? Not the dollar or the pound. In Washington and London they can print too many of those!"

While I was talking Craig had led me into his bedroom. "What about all that gold in Fort Knox?" he asked. Flopping on the bed, he pulled me down beside him. He began kissing me rather passionately.

"Wait a minute!" I pulled away. "It's only ten minutes of nine." I was suddenly aware that Craig wasn't thinking about gold at all. "Craig, doesn't it bother you? Supposing Zolotov hadn't actually made gold? That bar would be all he would need to spread the rumor that he had. What if people believed him? The repercussions would be just as bad."

"It would be terrible," Craig was unbuttoning my shirt. Slowly he was kissing his way down to my belly. "I like the golden sheath growing between my true love's thighs," he murmured.

11

"It isn't golden, it's brunette."

"I was just trying to fit your golden mood." Craig chuckled. He teased me with his fingers. "You could dye it blonde. They say blondes have more fun."

Mostly, I react very quickly to Craig, but at the moment I didn't feel like playing his game that gave the middle of me an independent existence. I couldn't help it. Zolotov's bar of gold, sitting on Harold's desk, loomed larger than the feathery insistence of Craig's fingers.

Finally, disgusted, he got out of bed. "What in hell are you thinking about?" he demanded, as he turned on the television. "My God, Marge, sometimes I really think you are frigid."

"I'm sorry, Craig." Trying to shift the gears of my thinking brought tears to my eyes. I sobbed but I couldn't tell Craig why. Afterwards, I thought . . . afterwards I can probably think better. There must be some way! All I had to do was convince Horace Zolotov to make a few bars of gold for me!

Three

The next morning I arrived at the bank twenty minutes late. It was Craig's fault. I had slumped naked at the table unable to make breakfast. "I have been wrestling all night with a bear," I moaned. "Your beard must have grown while we made love. Look at me. I am sandpapered from stem to stern."

"You look as pretty and pink as the morning sunrise." Craig cheefully poured the coffee he had made.

"Well, I'm not. My bones ache, and I detest people who whistle and are happy in the morning. What's more, it is obvious that I am right. Marriage and a career don't mix. When Harold Nichols sees me this morning he's going to be sure that I was soliciting all night."

"Begging," Craig grinned. "Not soliciting. When you

12

finally tuned Zolotov and gold out of your mind, you put in a remarkably fine performance."

But Craig was mistaken. Most females can do two things at once, especially *some* things! I had spent a sleepless night, and had arrived at one conclusion. When Zolotov came back to the bank next Wednesday, somehow I was going to talk with him alone for a minute or two.

When I finally arrived at the bank and tiptoed into Harold's office I discovered him examining Zolotov's bar. "Do you really think Zolotov made it out of lead, Mr. Nichols?"

Harold sprang out of his chair. "Good God, Miss Wentworth, don't *ever* sneak into this office like that." He stared at me curiously. "You are *late*."

I blushed. Unaccountably I was wondering if he could tell. Just thirty-five minutes ago I had achieved one more impossibly unnecessary orgasm. Crazy thoughts like that are always flickering through one segment of my brain. On the other hand what was Harold Nichols doing thirty-five minutes ago? Probably sitting on his private toilet reading the morning newspaper. I wondered what he really thought about Zolotov's bar of gold. I sometimes think it would be a more interesting world if people were more confidential with each other. I was still feeling so limp that it would have been nice if I could have said, "Harold, I'm pooped from screwing last night. Would you mind if I lay down on your leather couch for awhile. If you want, you can lie down beside me while we talk about gold and economics."

Instead, I apologized for being late, and I promised never to be obtrusive again.

Harold stared at my blouse. "Miss Wentworth, you can't help it, I suppose, but parts of you are unavoidably obtrusive."

"Is Zolotov's bar really gold?" I asked, attempting to steer him into less provocative waters.

"Of course it isn't gold!" Harold's come hither smile gave way to his President-of-the-Bank-hard-jaw-look. "I have done a little checking, Miss Wentworth. Horace Zolotov teaches chemistry at Midhaven High School. He has been a respectable citizen and done his job well for more than fifteen years. I plan to talk with him privately in the next day or two. In the meantime, I am asking that you keep this entire incident private. A little secret between the two of us. We certainly don't want to make Mr. Zolotov look foolish, or give him a bad reputation. He has a wife and a young son, you know." Harold smiled. "These things happen sometimes, Miss Wentworth. When men like Zolotov and myself approach middle age . . ." Harold paused. His fatherly pink cheeks got a little pinker. "Well, some of us have moments when we think we are alchemists. Some of us probably get *even more* impractical ideas!" It was an invitation to naughtiness. Would Harold want me to sit on his lap? I was tempted to encourage him. Zolotov's bar might not be gold, nevertheless, I was sure of the assets of the Midhaven National Bank. But my middle class conditioning always saves my victims. I guess I am only a mental anarchist. Rationally, I know that the "rules" which protect pudgy Mrs. Nichols as she reigns over her Women's Clubs, were designed to save me some day when I, too, became old, and "hors de combat."

The gold bar stayed in Harold's office for nearly two weeks. Zolotov didn't return. I noticed, since I hadn't discouraged him, that Harold was sparking his conversation with increasingly titillating suggestions about love and sex. But he was careful to avoid any discussion of Zolotov's bar which continued to glitter on his desk. All that he would say was that it was too damned heavy to be a practical paperweight. One of these days if Zolotov didn't show up he would telephone him to come and reclaim his property.

As the days went by I nearly forgot Zolotov. While I hadn't revealed it to Craig I was beginning to think I might just as well face the inevitable and get married. I could still work. If I was going to continue to work in the bank, Harold's ideas with regard to me would have to be clarified. While he had made no overt proposition he had been hinting that on one of his monthly trips to New York, to attend a bankers' monthly meeting, he would take me along. As a secretary, of course. But, as he pointed out, his eyes growing moist at the thought, our evenings would be free!

At least, this month I hadn't succumbed. Harold left without me. The next day I noticed that Zolotov's bar of gold was missing. When Harold came to work the following Monday I asked him about it. I was sure that he answered too quickly; as if he had rehearsed the answer. His voice seemed a little tense.

"Zolotov came in Wednesday night, just after you went home for the day," Harold smiled weakly. "He's so absent-minded he forgot that it was two weeks since he had been here. I gave the bar back to him."

Harold waited for the assurance that I believed him. "Did Zolotov insist that he made it out of lead?"

Harold's face flushed. "Now look, Miss Wentworth, you are an intelligent girl. I presume that you have read all about alchemists. You probably know that old story about Paracelsus making gold. But the plain truth is that *it is impossible* to make gold in that quantity." He patted my arm affectionately. "I suggest that we both forget the entire matter. We shouldn't discuss it with anyone. Zolotov told me himself that he had been under severe mental strain."

I was certain that Harold was lying. Furthermore, he seemed to be unusually preoccupied, jumping when I purposely clattered into his office. He told me that he had a Special Directors' meeting. While he usually asked me to stay and pour coffee, tonight it would be

15

unnecessary. The nature of the business was strictly for the directors' ears.

"A change in bank investment policies, Miss Wentworth. Some of the directors may prefer to register their opinions privately." Harold looked at me as if I might try to contradict him. When I simply nodded he seemed relieved.

The next day when Harold was at lunch I searched in his private file and found a transcript of the meeting. Charles Nason, who is Vice President and Secretary of the Bank, had kept the minutes. Strangely, while in the past I had always typed up the report, Claire Gordon, Mr. Nason's secretary, had typed this one. I read the pages carefully trying to puzzle out what Harold was up to. Everything seemed quite ordinary. Harold had suggested that the bank should switch more of its investments from Government Bonds and various stocks into real estate. "As far as the law permits us," Harold had insisted. "I've been studying certain aspects of the economy. For the short term, in my opinion, this shift would be most advisable." The directors disagreed with him. Property was too over-inflated. They were well pleased with the bank's current portfolio.

Disappointed, I read the report twice. I had been certain that Harold had called the meeting to report the amazing fact that Horace Zolotov had actually made gold out of lead. Instead, it seemed like any routine directors' meeting. Then, two days later, Harold, who seemed quite distraught and was ignoring me completely, called another meeting. Again Claire Gordon typed it. Again, it was more of the same except that it was obvious that some of the directors were annoyed at what seemed like Harold's attempt to speculate in real estate. I was promising myself that I would ask Harold if the meetings were so private, why was Claire Gordon allowed to type them? Finally, it dawned on me. I was making scrambled eggs for Craig, waiting for him to return

16

from taking pictures of Midhaven matrons and their spouses. It was the night of the Annual Harvest Dance at the Midhaven Country Club. When Craig finally arrived at ten thirty, he was not in the best of moods. I only half listened to him. The real reason for Harold's odd behavior had begun to form in my mind.

"I've spent the best part of Saturday night with Mollie Bishop, female busybody of Midhaven." Craig ate the cold scrambled eggs with distaste. "Maybe you are right about marriage. If sex with a broad finally turns into rhapsodies on what old biddies are wearing it's a disillusioning prospect. Every damned one on the committee was angling to get her picture in the paper next week." Craig made himself a drink. "I took a picture of your competitor Penelope Nichols. One hundred and ninety pounds in her birthday suit. Harold wasn't there. He has been having a bout with an ulcer. Penelope left him home in bed. 'Poor Harold,' she said, 'He takes everything so seriously. He's making himself sick over the way the President is running the country, spending all that money . . .'"

"Craig," I gasped, as the two and two I was trying to put together finally added up. "I figured it out! I know why Claire Gordon typed those reports! Harold was afraid that if I typed them I would know the truth. Zolotov has really made gold out of lead! When Harold went to New York he must have had the bar tested . . . an assay made. That would explain everything. Don't you see? If Zolotov can really make gold, what would happen to the value of the dollar? Gold is selling for thirty-five dollars an ounce. If gold is worthless, what *would* have value? Not the dollar. Not government bonds, only things . . . things that people will always want . . . houses, land, buildings. That's why Harold has been having those meetings! If Zolotov's secret gets out, paper money isn't going to be worth anything!"

17

Craig looked at me astonished. "Marge, here I am telling you my troubles and you are still raving about gold. What the hell do I care about gold? I am just a useless newspaper reporter wishing he could write a column for the *Midhaven Herald* . . . or an editorial. Instead, I have to cover every stupid social event, making sure that I haven't missed getting pictures of the correct V.I.P.'s of the evening, or listing their foolish names in long columns in our silly society pages." Craig sighed. "If Zolotov has really made gold out of lead, the only thing I am certain of is that the rich will get richer and the poor poorer."

I tried to cheer him up. "Maybe I can figure out a way that *we'll* get rich. Anyway, it isn't too late to have a golden evening in the sack."

As he always does Craig turned on his television set. Without the sound. This is a compromise in lighting effect discovered after many evenings of disagreement. Just as Craig came into my arms, I whispered, "Tomorrow, let's you and I go to Zolotov's house. I'd like to talk with him."

Craig wanted to know why I couldn't leave well enough alone. What possible good would it do to waste Sunday with some nutty school teacher? But I wasn't listening to him. My eyes had caught a little newsband weaving its way across Saturday Night at the Movies. As I read it aloud to Craig, he collapsed on me with a groan of despair. "Just thirty minutes ago, after a terrific explosion at 1640 Brinton Road, the home of Horace Zolotov burst into a raging inferno. Fire fighters from Hadley Falls and South Midhaven joined with the Midhaven Fire Department to keep the blaze from spreading to adjoining homes. At this moment it is not known whether Horace Zolotov, who teaches Chemistry at Midhaven High School, and his wife and son were in the house when it erupted in flames."

18

The flaming red walls of Zolotov's house crumbled into the foundation as we skidded into Brinton Road. Craig flashed his newspaper card at the firemen blocking the street. He guided his Jaguar next to Bill Spanda's red Buick.

The turret light of the Chief's car flashed across our faces as Bill talked to us. "It's all over but the insurance collecting," he told Craig wearily. "Where have you been? Your buddy Jack Somers got the whole story for the *Herald*."

Craig explained that he had been covering a dance at the Country Club. "I always miss the front page stories," he said disgustedly. "Were the Zolotovs in the house when it caught fire?"

Bill shrugged. "If they were, they are now thoroughly cremated. This baby burned fast and hot. In a couple of days when it cools off we'll search the debris. My guess is that we won't find anything. This was deliberate!"

Trying not to choke from the acrid smoke that filled the street, I suddenly remembered that I had only taken time to put on a dress and my mink. I could feel the cold night air making goose pimples up my legs. I asked Bill what he meant by deliberate.

"There was an explosion in the basement. We understand that Zolotov had a complete chemical laboratory down there. Of course, the fire might have started with some combustible stuff and then ignited some chemicals that blew up. On the other hand, maybe Zolotov was broke. Maybe he set it himself."

"If Zolotov lighted the fire himself, then he wouldn't have burned to death." I was eager to embrace this theory. "Did any of the neighbors know whether the Zolotovs were home?"

19

"No one can say for sure," Bill was looking at me strangely. He could either read my mind, or he was aware that I was only wearing a dress and my mink. "The Zolotovs don't seem to have made any friends. They kept to themselves. One of the neighbors told us she thought she saw Manya Zolotov and the boy go off in a taxi a few days ago." Bill lighted a cigarette. "Just why is the Midhaven National Bank so interested in the Zolotovs?"

"Marge thinks Zolotov is an alchemist," Craig chuckled, and then winced as I kicked his ankle.

"Don't be silly." I tried to scowl Craig into silence. In another minute he would be telling Bill Spanda the whole story. "We were just driving around. We heard about the fire on a news broadcast. I love to watch a fire."

"So does Harold Nichols." Bill was still glaring at me. I tried to conceal my obvious surprise. "A few minutes ago your boss was wandering around here in an overcoat and pajamas. He looked as if he were in a state of shock. One of the boys in a cruising car just drove him to the hospital. All he kept mumbling was 'Poor Zolotov . . . poor Zolotov.'" Bill grimaced. "Maybe your bank has a mortage on the house?"

"Did Nichols say anything about gold?" Craig demanded. I could have socked him. He was obviously determined to blab the whole business to Bill Spanda.

"Gold?" Bill shook his head and then guffawed. "What has gold to do with this? Did Zolotov help himself at the bank?"

"Don't be silly," I said, trying to conceal how bewildered I felt. "We don't keep gold at The Midhaven National Bank. All the gold is in Fort Knox." I dragged Craig back to the Jaguar. "Please, for heaven's sake stop running off at the mouth about Zolotov's gold. I'm frightened. I think someone deliberately set fire to the house. Not Zolotov. Why would he want to collect insurance?

20

Someone who wants to make sure that Zolotov's discovery never sees the light of day." Shuddering I slid into the Jag. "Bill Spanda could be wrong. Maybe the Zolotovs were in the house. Maybe they were all murdered! Craig . . . maybe Harold Nichols set Zolotov's house on fire!"

"Marge, you're off your rocker!"

"Maybe," I told him. "But maybe not! Why wasn't Harold at the dance? I've worked at the bank six months. I never knew that Harold had an ulcer. Why was he wandering around in this part of town in his pajamas?"

Back in his apartment Craig persisted in his belief that Zolotov probably had set the fire himself. Maybe he wasn't trying to collect the insurance. Maybe he was just mentally unbalanced. Craig discarded my fantasy that Nichols, or anyone else had deliberately set the fire. What would they have to gain? I couldn't give Craig one good reason.

Somewhere in the middle of the night when Craig's spirit was still willing but the rest of him refused to respond to any cajoling, I curled into a ball beside him and whispered, "Tomorrow I think you and I should do a little digging in Zolotov's life." I guess that Craig thought it was easier to agree than argue. A sound principle with any female who, in this case, was so delighted with his easy acceptance of the idea that I quickly proved that a happy female, with the right tactics, can raise the dead!

Early Sunday morning we were at Charley Barnes' house waiting to interrogate him when he came home from church. Charley has a long memory. He recalled seven years ago when Craig and I were both in Midhaven High School.

"Principals of high schools spend most of their time worrying about the sex lives of the kids."

Charley chuckled. "I guess times haven't changed

much. The way you and Craig went smooching around I was sure you'd have a family long before this."

I finally steered Charley away from a discussion of my delayed marital life into the problem of Zolotov. Charley persisted in speaking about Zolotov in the past tense. "He didn't show up at school for the past two weeks." Charley flopped in a big rocker in his living room, obviously ready to pursue the problem of Zolotov until his wife announced Sunday dinner. "I finally drove around to his house. Zolotov was a queer fellow. I don't think he would set his house on fire. He was too fastidious, a martinet really. I am sure that most of his students heaved a sigh of relief when I brought in a substitute teacher. Only last semester I had my annual term discussion with him. Zolotov had flunked sixty percent of the senior chemistry class. Of course, this is impossible. For the tenth or eleventh time I told him that he would have to re-adjust his grading system. Zolotov has been with us at least fifteen years. Practically every marking period we've gone through the same problem. 'You expect too much,' I told him. Not every one can be a genius." Charley grinned. "Some genius. A teacher of high school chemistry making one hundred and thirty-eight dollars a week.

" 'I do not expect genius,' Zolotov told me testily. 'I expect competence and enthusiasm. Genius is simply a by-product of hard concentrated work. People in our society have forgotten that work is the only salvation for men. All they want is a welfare state where miraculously they all live like millionaires. When a student finishes my courses he may not know much chemistry, but he will know what work means. I do not spare myself. That's how I achieved what I have.' "

Charley chuckled. It was difficult for him to tell Craig exactly what Zolotov had achieved. But competent teachers are hard to come by, and Charley Barnes is not the type that would challenge a man's estimate of himself.

Charley told us that Manya Zolotov had greeted him at the front door with a worried look on her face. She invited him in for coffee. "I've been very worried about Horace. He never stops working. Night after night he works in the basement to all hours in the morning. He never did talk to me much, but lately he seems very far away. When he didn't go to teach his classes, I kept asking him what was wrong. All he said was that he had made an earth-shaking discovery. He needed time to think about it without any concern over the stupidities of teaching morons. He said that he had an appointment with Mr. Harold Nichols who is President of the Midhaven Bank." Manya thought that was ridiculous. She was afraid that something might have snapped in Horace's mind.

Charley agreed that this was a bit out of character. "Why would Zolotov want to see Nichols?" Charley shook his head. "Manya told me that they only had a very small mortgage on the house. Everyone in Midhaven knows that Nichols is one of the foremost authorities on banking and investments in the country. The strangest thing I discovered was that Zolotov had evidently been reading everything available on money, banking and economics. The living room was full of books." Charley shrugged. "Maybe Zolotov was planning to switch fields and teach economics."

Manya told Charley that Zolotov had decided to give up teaching. "It is nothing to worry about," Zolotov had told her. "We are leaving Midhaven for good. I am going to need a month to get organized then I'll send for you and Zoltan." Zolotov wouldn't tell Manya where he was going. He asked her to be patient. He left with a small suitcase. His last words to her were, "I've done it, Manya. All my life I have been flotsam and jetsam on

23

the tides of events that I, the typical average man, couldn't control. In a few months I will be in a position to topple the governments of the world. I have single handed made one of man's most sacred cows absolutely useless and ridiculous."

When Charley asked Manya what Zolotov had been working on in his basement, Manya didn't know. "The basement is full of all kinds of things you use in chemistry. But I don't know much about it," she confessed. "Horace has a Doctor's degree in Chemistry, you know. I only finished high school in Poland where I was born. I read a lot, and I like music . . . and that's about all Horace and I have in common. Whenever Horace used to talk Chemistry I couldn't understand him. After a while he never told me what he was trying to do. I think a few months ago he was melting lead. The smell was kind of sickening. Thank the Lord he stopped that."

Charley remembered that he had telephoned Manya to see if she had heard from her husband. "I am really not worried," she had told him. "Horace and I have been separated before. We were refugees in 1940. Horace finally ended up in a German concentration camp."

Craig asked Charley if Zolotov was a Jew.

"No, he's Russian, I believe," Charley said, "I was looking through his personnel file just last week. Not much in it. Just a few letters of recommendation, and his application for employment at Midhaven High School. On that he stated that he was born in Petrograd in 1924. He became a naturalized citizen in 1946."

That was the extent of the information that Charley Barnes could supply. He did remember when he was leaving Zolotov's house that he noticed Zolotov's son, Zoltan, sitting in a rocking chair on the front porch. Zoltan was watching a neighbor's girl playing hopscotch. "You looking for my old man?" Zoltan asked.

"He's gone. We'll all be gone soon. We're leaving this cruddy town."

After an attempt to see Harold Nichols at the Midhaven Hospital which got us involved in taking Penelope Nichols to lunch at Howard Johnson's while she repeated endlessly that I "was so nice to be concerned about my employer. Not like most girls who wouldn't be interested in anyone but themselves," we finally admitted defeat. No one could talk with Harold but his wife. All she could report was that Harold would have to stop taking things so seriously. "It would really be better," she said smiling at me, "if Harold knew how to relax." Why, Penelope wouldn't really blame Harold if he flirted with his secretary. But, of course, poor Harold would never do anything like that!

"It sifts down to this," Craig said, as he left me at my apartment. "A man named Horace Zolotov brought a bar that he claimed was gold into the Midhaven National Bank. A romantic girl watched this ploy and conjures a rags to riches story, in which she is the Princess and the elderly man becomes her benefactor." I tried to sock Craig, but he grabbed my arm and continued.

"The girl's boss knows that this man Zolotov is cracked. He tries over a period of a week or two to dispel her daydream. The real truth is that Harold Nichols discovered that your Zolotov was broke. He made a fake bar of gold and tried to con Nichols out of ten thousand dollars. All the rest was the imaginings of little Margery in Wonderland who tried to make two and two add up to a life of idle riches."

I listened to Craig babble on. Maybe he was right. Supposing the bar actually was gold? What would that prove? Certainly, it was unlikely that Zolotov had made it from lead. Thousands of daydreamers in practically every century of recorded history had tried to make gold and failed. If the bar really was gold (or had been gold . . . I was beginning to believe that it never

25

really existed) it was much more likely that Zolotov had collected old gold, melted it and poured it into a mold the size of bullion. But why? What would he gain? And where would an obviously poor school teacher get the money to purchase an equivalent of fourteen thousand dollars in old gold? A shuddering thought crossed my mind. Zolotov had been in a concentration camp. Was he a former Nazi who had extracted the gold from the teeth of his victims?

Somehow I fell asleep *in my own bed* with the growing conviction that if I had to spend sleepless nights worrying about such nonsense, I might as well marry Craig. At least, then I would have someone to torture.

Five

I must have left some doubts in Craig's mind. Monday he called Bill Spanda at the Fire Department. "I don't think you have a story," Bill told him. "There was no trace of human bones. Your friend Zolotov is alive somewhere. He'll show up one of these days, then we'll sweat it out of him."

Craig telephoned me at the bank. "I've got one other thought, I'll check it out and meet you for lunch. Did Harold Nichols come to work?"

"He isn't here." I tried to whisper and keep the tremble out of my voice. Mr. Nason had been poking his head out of Harold's office every five minutes demanding to know details of where and what Harold had been working on last week. "I can't talk on this phone, Craig. All I know is that Harold is still in the hospital under sedation. Don't pick me up in front of the bank. I'll wait down the street at Tracys."

At ten minutes past one I slipped into the bucket seat

of the Jaguar. I was bursting to tell Craig the discovery I had just made but first I had to figure out just how deeply we should get into the fortunes, or misfortunes, of Horace Zolotov.

"This will wrap the Zolotov business up for you," Craig said. "I checked at the Passport Office in the Federal Building. The Zolotovs applied and received passports six weeks ago. Their visas cover entry into practically every European country . . . *and Asia*. My guess is that friend Zolotov has gone back to Moscow."

I decided not to tell Craig about my discovery while we were on the verge of an argument. "I told Mr. Nason that I wasn't feeling well." I squeezed Craig's arm happily. "He said that I could have the afternoon off. I like this car. Aren't you glad that we bought it instead of getting married and settling down into a Mr. and Mrs. existence? With this car and my new mink coat I feel like the heroine in an Ian Fleming novel."

"Well, I am not James Bond and I have to work today, Pussycat," Craig said, puncturing my fantasy. "If we do get married, just how are we going to live in a house without any furniture? I'm broke."

"If and when that fatal day arrives, all we need is a bed. I promise to keep you happy."

Craig chuckled. "Okay, what about Harold?"

"His wife insists that he has had an attack of ulcers."

"How is she keeping it out of the papers? Nichols in the hospital would be on the front page of our greasy little newspaper."

"Mr. Nason, the Vice President, told me he spoke to Jim Prescott who owns the *Herald*. 'I know you will be discreet,' he said. 'Mr. Nichols has been under a great deal of stress the past few weeks, but everything is going to be all right. Many of our top depositors think a great deal of Harold. We don't want to cause them any concern.'" I started to repair my make-up using the sun vizor mirrior. "But that's not all, Craig . . ."

"Well, at least we can stop worrying about Zolotov. Neither he nor any of his family were in the house. My guess is that Zolotov is going to show up, collect the insurance for the fire he started and then beat it out of the country."

"That's silly. I've met Zolotov. He's too smart for anything like that. Why would he bother with chicken feed. Besides . . . there is something else." We had stopped at a cross light. I handed Craig a piece of paper. "That's Manya Zolotov's telephone number. It's a Miami telephone exchange. I checked the area code."

"Miami! What in hell is Zolotov's wife doing in Miami? Where did you get this number anyway?"

"Never try to keep a secret from me, amateur detective." I smiled at Craig. "I told Mr. Nason that I would straighten up Harold's papers and help him get oriented to Harold's work. Mr. Nason said that was very thoughtful of me. I found this paper with Manya's telephone number in Harold's personal file folder. There is something else on that paper, in Harold's writing: 'Try again Thursday.' That's today. Evidently Manya called and talked with him. Then Harold tried to telephone her back and couldn't reach her."

"So now where are we?" Craig demanded. He turned into a Red Coach Grill parking lot. "I'll buy you lunch, Marge. Let's forget Zolotov. I think he is just a crackpot. The whole business is just a series of coincidences." But it's not my nature to let well enough alone. Drinking a Manhattan, in the cocktail lounge, I finally convinced Craig to try and reach Manya at the Miami telephone number. Three drinks later, after five breathless attempts, as we squeezed giggling into a telephone booth, we still were unable to get an answer. I finally took over the telephone. After a lengthy discussion with the Miami supervisor she reluctantly gave me the street address. It was a pay station at the El Dorado Motel at Miami Beach.

Back at our table in the cocktail lounge Craig held the slip of paper with Manya's number over a candle on our table. When it flared he dropped it into an ashtray. "Don't burn it," I said, trying to snatch it out of the ashtray. "We'll keep trying."

"The number is etched on my brain. So what if someone had answered? Chances are it wouldn't be Manya. That's a pay station. If she is still there, we'll probably never connect. If we did, what then?"

"We would have found out why she was telephoning Harold Nichols." I sipped my third drink cautiously. I knew that I was beginning to feel quite bubbly.

Craig shrugged. "I'll tell you why she was trying to reach Nichols. Zolotov told her that he had left a bar of gold with him. Manya is trying to sell it now. Maybe she has reduced the price to five thousand dollars."

"Craig," I whispered, suddenly aware that a number of people in the cocktail lounge were busy watching us instead of pursuing their own business. "I *am sure* that Zolotov's bar was actually gold."

Craig grimaced at me. "My God, Marge, you are going to end up in a bed beside Nichols having *your* head examined. If it were gold, Zolotov wouldn't have left it in Nichols' office that easily. No matter how you slice it, fourteen thousand bucks is fourteen thousand bucks. No one is that rich!"

I shook my head. "Zolotov wouldn't give a damn if he actually made it for nine dollars. Craig, I'm going to ask you to do something quite crazy." When I saw the expression on Craig's face I crossed my fingers under the table. I looked at him soulfully forcing a tear into the corner of my eyes. "Please, Craig, say you will!"

"Say, I will what?"

"Just say you will."

"Okay," Craig grinned. "If I say I will, if I do whatever it is you want, then within two weeks we get married and stop this nonsense."

I was silent. Should I say yes? I guess that I loved Craig. I guessed the truth was that I would probably never find a man with the same drive for achievement that I had. But then I wasn't too sure what I wanted from life anyway. "You drive a hard bargain. I'm not certain that it is worth it. Oh, all right." I grinned and patted his cheek. "If you say yes, I'll agree to become a fat suburban non-entity."

Craig smiled. "Don't worry. When we get married, you'll have to keep working to pay for that mink coat. With your expensive tastes you'll probably have to work the rest of your life. That will keep you skinny. Besides, I don't trust you. I want it in writing."

"Here," I said, handing him a knife that was on the table. "Stab me. I might just as well write it in blood. We are going to drive to New York . . . to the airport and get a midnight flight to Miami."

"Listen, Marge Wentworth!" Craig tried to conceal the sagging expression of astonishment on his face. "I love you and all that . . . but what the devil business is this Zolotov affair of ours? If we ever locate Manya, what will she know? Charley Barnes gave me the impression that Manya didn't have the faintest idea what Zolotov was doing in his cellar. In the last analysis, if we find where Zolotov is hiding, if he actually did make gold from lead, what are we going to do about it? And on the strictly practical side, I am broke. I spent all but my last five hundred dollars on that Jag." Craig decided to drive the knife in a little deeper. "Moreover, if I hadn't been influenced by your crazy philosophy of living it up, before we settled down to the tranquil joys of marriage, I might have some money. What's more, since you just blew two thousand dollars for a down payment on that mink coat, I don't suppose you are rolling in dough and ready to finance this expedition."

"I have three hundred dollars," I said, unable to hold back the tears in my eyes. "I'll pay my way, if you pay yours. Even if nothing comes of it we will have a four day holiday swimming, in the sun, out of this damp New England climate. Please Craig. You said you would!"

It took me another hour to convince Craig. I finally succeeded by telling him that if he wouldn't come I was going to Miami by myself. From now on he could sleep alone on Wednesday and Saturday nights. The funny part is that all the time I was arguing myself into an emotional frenzy convinced that I simply must find Manya, another part of my mind was thinking Marge Wentworth, this is really quite mad. Craig is right. All we'll do is blow a lot of money on a lot of foolishness. What I refused to admit to myself, or to Craig, was the image of that bar of gold, and the happy daydream that I could persuade Zolotov to make a few of them for us.

By five o'clock Craig was waiting for me at my apartment. I tossed a couple of dresses, a bathing suit, and some underwear into my suitcase. I decided to wear my long-sleeved wool chemise with a plunging neckline for travelling, and of course my lovely mink coat. When I finally finished dressing Craig whistled happily at the effect. "You'd never guess that your sole resources were three hundred bucks." He grinned. "Okay, if I am going to be Big Daddy, let's have it!"

"Let's have what?"

"Your money. All three hundred of it. Remember, you are paying your own way."

Reluctantly, while Craig watched with amazed comments at my hiding place, I unearthed a box of sanitary pads from the closet. Digging underneath I finally handed him three packets of ten dollar bills.

"I thought since the pills you didn't need those things."

"Despite the pills my natural functions continue," I said. I still wasn't too happy about surrendering my last remaining money. "Anyway, you'll have to admit

31

that it is a good hiding place. No male burglar would ever look in a box of Kotex!"

Six

A cold November rain was beating against the Jag windshield as we left Midhaven. Had I any conception of what was going to happen to Craig and me, I might never have tried to persuade Craig to go to Miami. But even now I don't know whether that is wholly true. In the first place I wouldn't have believed that we were flirting with sudden death and worse. The truth is that our search for Zolotov slowly revealed to me aspects of my personality that even today I am not happy with. Am I essentially an evil woman willing to sacrifice anything for money and fame? There are a lot of people who think so. I argued about it most of the way to the airport with Craig.

"You see, Craig," I told him. "My family were poor. Not absolutely but relatively. My father was a life insurance salesman. He never was a top producer. He managed to sell just enough insurance to live a razor edge, middle class life. Like most men who have never had it, he believed that a college education was the solution to everything. Somehow, he managed to get my two brothers through college. When it came to me, Mother argued that a girl didn't need a college education. It was the same old middle class story you've heard all your life. I would finally get married anyway so why did I need an education? My mother with just a high school education had done very well thank you. But daddy was adamant. He mortgaged the house to the hilt. By the time I finished college he was in debt up to his ears. Daddy died a few weeks after I graduated. Mother blames me. She lives with my brother Danny in Chicago. I got through Graduate School on scholarships and mad penny pinching. I still owe Danny about two thousand dollars."

"Marge, you've told me all that, at least twice," Craig said. "What does it prove? I came from the same kind of family. Why don't you look on the bright side of things? A lot of kids don't manage to get to college at all. You owe your old man a debt of gratitude."

"I'm aware of that, and because of it I don't want to repeat the pattern."

"You mean marry me and live a life of genteel poverty?" Craig was getting a little angry. "For God's sake, Marge. There are other things in the world beside money. Your father and mother loved each other, I presume. They had a life together of shared joys and worries. I think we could have that. What else is there? Being a career woman, living alone, an old maid, with the money you have grubbed so that you can dress in mink coats and two-hundred dollar dresses isn't going to give you the satisfaction of raising a family. When you are forty you'll be sleeping alone every night."

"I'm not worried about finding a bed companion," I chuckled. "Even if you leave me and settle down with some nice little household drudge, I'll wager that after a few years of suburban misery, it won't be difficult to entice you for an occasional evening of soft dalliance."

We stopped for coffee at a Savarin's on the Turnpike. I knew that Craig was pretty exasperated with me. But he did have to admit, in all fairness, that the hundred and thirty dollars a week he was earning as Society and General Editor of the Seven Lively Arts on the *Midhaven Herald* was not the springboard to great wealth. "I don't intend to stay in a rut forever," Craig said when I brought the subject up. "I haven't told you, but I'm angling for a job as master of ceremonies, an afternoon radio program on Station WMBC. The Craig Barnett Show. If it comes through, I intend to be more

33

than a disc jockey. Gradually, I would give the show a wider perspective, commenting on local and national politics and the events of the world." Craig stopped talking. He looked at me angrily. "You're not listening to me, are you? You're thinking of that damned Zolotov."

"I am not," I protested, but it was true. "I heard every word you said. You are going to teach the kids who prefer rock and roll that current events are more interesting!"

As we were leaving the restaurant, Craig pointed out two heavily built men eating hot dogs at the counter. "Those two characters were at the gasoline station we stopped at half an hour ago," Craig whispered. "Do you suppose they are following us?"

I giggled. "Craig, you're getting worse than me. Everyone who races these turnpikes ends up stopping at the same places. Look, we passed that man and woman with the three kids at the last toll booth. Do you think they are following us?"

Less than an hour later I realized that I shouldn't have been so quick on the trigger. But even had we suspected, I'm sure neither of us would ever have guessed *why* we were being followed.

Back in the car Craig waited a minute but the two men didn't come out. Craig started the car and drove off. "We have been skirting an unpleasant subject," he said, settling back in his bucket seat. "I keep getting the message that your interest in Zolotov is somewhat more than just the story of his life and what he is up to."

I was silent. The light from the dashboard revealed the hard curve of Craig's jaw. He is very handsome. I wanted to stop the car and tell him to hug me. I wanted to reassure him that I really did love him. At least, even then, I told him exactly what I was thinking. "I can still see that bar of gold on Harold's desk, Craig. It was gold, and it was worth fourteen thousand dollars!

I am absolutely sure of that. A hundred or so bars like that, just think . . . we would be millionaires!"

"Oh, come on, Marge. You are daydreaming again," Craig laughed. "If you had a hundred bars of gold where would you sell them? Who would buy them from you?"

"Sure . . . bullion would be no good in the United States, but in Switzerland or Hong Kong I understand there is a free market in gold. You can buy and sell gold and no one asks how you got it or what you are going to do with the money."

"You've got to get it first," Craig said. "Let's assume that Zolotov can really make gold. Why in hell would he make a hundred bars of it for us? Who are we? We don't even know him!"

"I have a feeling that for a little while at least Zolotov may have decided to keep his discovery a secret. When Zolotov realizes that we know that he can actually make gold, he might be quite eager to avoid any further publicity until we all have a few million dollars in the bank."

Craig pointed out that I was too late. Zolotov had made no attempt to keep his discovery a secret.

"That was before his house was set on fire," I smiled. "Maybe now he will listen and I can point out to him the error of his ways. Zolotov isn't going to make a cent out of his discovery. More likely he will be the target for every government in the world. They will either want to eliminate him or make him an enforced, honorary citizen of their country. If Zolotov's secret ever becomes common knowledge the price of gold will sink below the price of lead . . . even lower. At least lead has industrial uses. What good is gold . . . really, except for decorative purposes? Another thing. Remember that Zolotov is poor, too. My guess is that he is pretty weary of living on a school teacher's pay. If we keep his secret, all Zolotov has to do is tell anybody who may be interested, that the bar he left in the bank was really a hoax. The truth was, he made one bar of gold from old gold that he had melted down. If Zolotov will say that, maybe we've got the cow back in the barn. When the furor has died down Zolotov and you and I can quietly make enough gold for the three of us. No one would be the wiser, and we could sell it without affecting the world price of gold. See," I grinned at Craig happily. "I'm putting my education in money and banking and economics to some use."

I could tell by the expression of shock on Craig's face that I was being a little too honest. "Honestly, Marge, you frighten me," he said. "Sometimes I'm certain that I don't really know you at all. You must have read too many fairy tales when you were little. What's more, you are willing to try and use Zolotov by any means, fair or foul, just to get rich. You give me the cold shivers."

I leaned over and kissed his neck and cheek. "Craig honey, don't be so literal. I know that you think I am a grasping female. But look at it as a kind of test of our love. If it just ends in a romantic and silly escapade, so what? So, if nothing comes of it? So, if Zolotov is really a faker? At least, we haven't been afraid to grasp at a moment of excitement. We will really have dared to live instead of being just content with existing. It's a kind of a romanticism that escapes most people. If we never have any money, I want to be sure that the man I marry at least tries to live life as if *anything* is possible. It's like putting a dash of pepper into the blandness of matrimony. *If* opportunity is knocking I don't want to think my husband would hold his foot against the door."

Craig sighed. "Okay, it's obvious I haven't got a bull by the horns . . . I have a cow by the tail."

Seven

In my wildest imagination I never realized how frightening it can be to walk through the looking glass, and find that "anything" can be mad hours of sheer terror.

We arrived at the airport at six-thirty. Craig parked his Jaguar in the Eastern Airlines parking lot. In the terminal, the clerk told us that all flights to Miami were sold out until 1 A.M. We could wait as standbys with a confirmed reservation on an early morning flight. Since we had a number of hours to kill, we decided to eat dinner in the terminal restaurant. As we were walking across the terminal, a man of about forty-five came up to us. He was wearing a homburg hat, and a chesterfield overcoat. He had heavy jowls and small eyes that were lost in creases of fat. He evidently hoped to compensate for his porcine look by an unfailing, obsequious smile.

"Pardon me," he said. I noticed as he spoke that his accent was British with a slight overtone that indicated it was not his original language. "My name is Sakin Nesterenko. I am a friend of Horace Zolotov. I believe you are Miss Wentworth, secretary to Mr. Harold Nichols."

I know I should have been suspicious. Craig was. I could feel his hand tighten on my arm, a sort of warning to watch out. How could this man, who had presumably never set eyes on us before, pick us out in a crowded airline terminal? How could he even know that we were looking for Zolotov?

Nesterenko continued urbanely, allaying my distrust. "I hope you won't feel that I am presumptuous, but some friends of Horace and Manya's telephoned me about two hours ago. They had heard about the terrible fire. Today, they saw you and Mr. Barnett in the Red

37

Coach Grill in Midhaven." Nesterenko smiled beguilingly. "Without meaning to be nosey, as you Americans might put it, they overheard a part of your conversation. They telephoned me. You see, my family are relatives of the Zolotovs. Manya has been at her wits' end. Two weeks ago Horace wired her to meet him in Miami. She flew down immediately but Horace had disappeared. Manya finally telephoned me knowing that eventually Horace would contact her through the family. Yesterday, in desperation, not having heard from Horace she flew back to New York. She's in my apartment now in Flushing. I'm sure if we could all get together and talk we might make some sense out of this. It's just a few minutes from here."

"How do we know this isn't some cock and bull story?" Craig demanded. "Why didn't your friends in Midhaven speak to us?"

"I realize that it sounds strange. The fact is that they thought you might feel that you were involved in some kind of insidious plot." Nesterenko smiled. "Americans are so pre-conditioned by their television to that sort of thing. Anyway, you can readily confirm that Manya is here in New York. If you prefer to talk with her by telephone from the terminal, I will give you the telephone number."

I was convinced. "See, Craig . . . all your moaning about the expense of flying to Miami was for naught." I smiled at Nesterenko. "We really would like to talk with Manya. Could you tell us how to get there?"

"My car is just outside in the parking lot. I'll be happy to drive you over and later bring you back to the terminal. Poor Manya, I know she will be happy to see you. I hope that we can put the pieces of the puzzle together and discover what Horace is up to."

We followed Nesterenko through the terminal out into the parking lot. It was still drizzling. I had a momentary feeling of regret over my aborted trip to Miami, especially with the cold wind piercing my mink and making me feel quite shivery. I wondered what we would accomplish, now. Obviously, too many people were aware that Zolotov had made gold. If we ever caught up with him, there were going to be too many splits in the pie.

The hundreds of automobiles in the parking lot, dripping wet and huddled together, row after row in the dim light, seemed particularly alone and deserted after the hubbub of the terminal. Nesterenko pointed to a black Cadillac sedan. "It's over there," he said.

As he spoke, two men appeared from behind the car. They were the men we had seen sitting in the Savarin Restaurant on the Turnpike. I screamed, "Run, Craig, something's crazy!" One of them clapped his hand over my face, hissing for me to be quiet. He dug his fingers into my cheek.

"What in hell is going on?" Craig demanded. "Let go of her, you bastard!" Craig grabbed my arm. Nesterenko, who was behind him, must have hit Craig with a karate blow on the neck. He crumpled to the asphalt, writhing in pain. I fought the men furiously but before I could save myself one of them snapped a large adhesive bandage across my mouth. The other forced my arms together behind my back. I felt the cold steel of handcuffs being snapped on my wrists. Nesterenko and one of the other men yanked Craig to his feet. They gagged and handcuffed him the same way. For a second I looked into Craig's eyes and saw furious anger and bitterness on his face. I knew he was blaming me, but I was too terrified to care. Who were these men? What did they want from us? My brain screamed but no sound came out. The bandage held my lips and jaw frozen together.

"In the trunk," I heard one of the men say. He grabbed me. "Ladies first!" I could see the trunk was empty even of a spare tire. I balked, but one of them picked me up and shoved me in. He crawled in after me forcing me to the back of the trunk. I tried to kick him in the face. He grabbed me my the hair and cuffed me across the face until I was dizzy with pain. I saw the other man suddenly slug Craig in the stomach. He slumped over and was pushed into the trunk. His feet were opposite my face. His knees were bent into my stomach. The lid slammed shut. It was pitch black.

I heard the Cadillac engine start with a roar. There was so little air I thought I would faint. I tried to twist a cramp out of my leg and realized that my shoes must be cutting into Craig's face. In agony, I tried not to move. I was terrified that Craig had been badly hurt. He was lying like a soggy lump against me. I couldn't tell whether he was breathing. For the first time in my life I knew a fear so intense that I thought my brain would burst. Worse, I knew that whatever was going to happen to us was all my fault. I was sobbing hysterically. Somehow I had to get a grip on myself. Where were they taking us? Who were these men? Were they Russian spies? What could they want with us? We didn't know anything. Or did we? I tried to force myself to review everything I did know. It didn't seem to add up to much, unless . . . The frightening thought occurred to me that Zolotov might be mixed up in this. Maybe he resented us prying into his business.

We were in the trunk for about forty-five minutes. I had the feeling the Cadillac was being driven at top speed, but it was impossible to tell. The first time we stopped for traffic lights, I was sure the inquisition was about to begin. About fifty stops later, with every bone in my body aching from being bounced back and forth against Craig on the floor of the trunk, I began to feel desperately sick to my stomach. I wondered if I had soiled my underwear from sheer fright. Finally the Cadillac came to a stop. The engine was no longer running. The trunk was yanked open. They pulled

Craig out and then me. Standing behind the car Craig stared dully at me, almost as if he didn't recognize me, a look so hopeless that my mind screamed "Oh, Craig . . . Craig, I'm so sorry!" But only a groan escaped from the gag that glued my lips together.

Nesterenko and the other two men shoved us away from the car. We were walking along a deserted pier. I could see the hull of a freighter, rusty with orange paint flicking off it. I guessed that we were somewhere along Twelfth Avenue near the Hudson River. The men pushed us toward a gangplank that extended out of the freighter onto the dock. The only light was an unshaded bulb that dangled from the deck of the ship and cast eery shadows into the darkness. The ship seemed to be unlighted, and deserted.

One of the men, carrying our suitcases, led the way up the gangplank. Nesterenko and the other man followed behind us. No one spoke. Our footsteps echoed hollowly on the metal plates of the ship. They pushed us down a ladder-way and below deck into a maze of dimly lighted corridors.

"Dump their bags in there, Sergei," Nesterenko said. He pointed to a cabin with an open door. I had a quick glimpse of a tiny room with double bunks. "We'll question them up above, in the Captain's stateroom. There's more space."

"Shall I search the bags?"

"Later. I think everything we want to know is in Miss Wentworth's head."

Our bags and my pocketbook were tossed into the room. They led us up a stairwell to the top deck, into the Captain's quarters. The room was deserted. A light was burning on a mahogany desk.

"Who do we work on first?" one of the men asked Nesterenko.

"The girl knows the most, Vasilev." Nesterenko shoved Craig on a bed in the corner of the room. "You can lie down, Mr. Barnett. We may want to talk to you later."

Nesterenko sat down behind the Captain's desk. He stared at me. "Take off her coat and those handcuffs." Vasilev ripped the gag off my face. I screamed with pain, certain that the flesh from my cheeks was attached to it.

"You can yell all you please, Miss Wentworth," Nesterenko said coolly. "No one can hear you."

"Please," I gasped. With my hands free, at last, I tried to rub life back into my face. "My mouth is so dry. I need water."

Vasilev went into the lavatory. He brought back a glass of water. I was trembling so much I could scarcely get it to my lips. "May I sit down?" I asked weakly.

"I think you will respond faster standing," Nesterenko said. "We haven't all night. Where is Horace Zolotov?"

"I don't know," I sobbed. I felt so faint that I was sure I was going to slump in a heap on the floor. Vasilev struck me across my face with an open palm.

"That's just to convince you, Miss Wentworth. We haven't time for amenities. Vasilev is a very rough customer. If you need further assurance that we mean business, Sergei here has a wealth of experience in handling females."

I looked at the other man called Sergei, and shuddered. He was staring at me lasciviously, his eyes slivered, a cruel grin on his face that accentuated a long white scar on his stubbly cheek. "I don't know where Horace Zolotov is." I tried to control my sobs. "You can do anything to me you like, but I don't know. I only saw Horace Zolotov once in my life."

"All right, Miss Wentworth. Let's you and I try another tack. Is it true that Horace Zolotov brought a bar of gold to the office of Harold Nichols, President of the Midhaven National Bank, about three weeks ago?"

I nodded dully, somehow I had to collect my thoughts.

42

I tried to anticipate what Nesterenko was searching for. "I don't know whether it was actually gold or not." Nesterenko smiled. "I'll bring you up to date, Miss Wentworth. We have our contacts in the Federal Reserve Bank in New York. Zolotov's bar was 100% pure gold. Where did he get it?"

"He told Mr. Nichols that he made it."

"Who else have you told about this curious idea beside Mr. Barnett?"

"No one else!"

Nesterenko got up from behind the desk. He grabbed me by the shoulders. "I want the truth!" His spittle flicked across my face.

"Please . . . let us go. I haven't told anyone else. If anyone else knows, they learned about it from Mr. Nichols."

Nesterenko slowly walked back to the desk and sat down. I could feel myself swaying. I looked at Craig. He was half propped on the bed staring at me. I had the feeling that maybe I was going to have a heart attack. I would drop dead right at their feet. "Please," I moaned. "I've got to sit down, I'm sick."

Nesterenko shrugged. "You'll be surprised how much you can endure, Miss Wentworth. If you can't stand any longer Vasilev will help you. Tie a rope around her wrists, Vasilev. Pull it over those pipes. If you can't stand, you can hang!"

"I'll stand by myself," I sobbed. But Vasilev disappeared. He returned with a coil of rope. He grinned happily at me as if in anticipation.

"Now, Miss Wentworth, before Vasilev hangs you I'll give you one more chance." Nesterenko's lips curved cruelly. "I'll bring you up to date. Harold Nichols brought Zolotov's bar of gold to New York with the comment that a customer had molded it from old gold as a joke. Since Nichols is in the hospital and we haven't got to him yet, we can assume that only you,

Mr. Barnett, Manya Zolotov, and Zolotov himself knows where the gold that went into that bar came from." Nesterenko paused. He stared at me again for a long time. "Why are you so interested in Horace Zolotov, Miss Wentworth?"

I had a feeling that he was reading my mind. "I wanted to find out if he had actually made the gold from lead."

"Why? Why does that interest you?"

I stared at Nesterenko unable to control the fright on my face.

"You wanted Zolotov to make some gold for you," Nesterenko shouted. "Isn't that right, Miss Wentworth?"

I looked at him shocked. I was aware that Vasilev had slapped my face again. I didn't know what to answer.

"Just why did you think that Horace Zolotov would make gold for you? Do you know him personally?"

"No, I don't!"

"Then why are you searching for Zolotov?" Nesterenko's words were furiously menacing. "I want an answer!"

I was petrified. There was no answer that would satisfy Nesterenko. I could feel my stomach quivering. I wondered, as I had heard about soldiers in battle, if I was going to lose control of my sphincter muscles. "All right." Nesterenko's face was mottled with anger. "You asked for it, Miss Wentworth." He motioned to Vasilev who quickly tied my hands together with the rope. Slinging it over a pipe that ran the length of the ceiling, he pulled me erect. My arms were over my head, my body stretched until I was nearly standing on tip toe. "Strip her, Sergei!" Nesterenko said grimly. I screamed. I saw Craig try to get off the bed. Vasilev shoved him back. I heard Craig's head bounce against the metal wall with a sickening thump. Sergei snapped

44

open a switch knife. Grinning, he stuck his hand into the V of my dress, fished out my breasts, and inserted the knife. With a sickening swish he slashed open my dress from neck to hemline. Then he ripped open the front of my brassiere. Inserting his knife in my panty-girdle, he hacked it off me. I watched him dazedly, unable to scream any more, as he sawed away at my clothing. Finally, I was stark naked, hanging from the overhead pipe, my stockings dribbling around my ankles.

Nesterenko had watched me being stripped with an amused expression on his face. "You are a very well made female, Miss Wentworth. I'm sure all of us here appreciate your femininity. I am sorry to have to subject you to this indignity, but we have discovered that a woman, naked as you are, in front of four men feels very insecure. I am going to let you hang there naked just as long as necessary. While Sergei and Vasilev may enjoy your physical beauty . . . what I want is straight, truthful answers to my questions."

I sobbed. I begged. No answers I gave him seemed to satisfy him. The cool air on my body which was dripping with perspiration made me shiver uncontrollably. My heart was beating so violently that I could scarcely catch my breath. "I'm going to throw up," I gasped, writhing helplessly, as the rope chafed my wrists.

I must have fainted. When I opened my eyes, Nesterenko was still staring at me. "This ship sails the day after tomorrow," he said grimly. "You and Mr. Barnett know too much already. If you cooperate with us, Miss Wentworth, I'll see that your life working in a labor camp is not so rugged as it might be."

"Please," I begged, suddenly aware that Nesterenko meant we were going to be forcibly taken out of the country. "Neither Craig nor I know anything. Please, for God's sake let us go."

"I'm afraid that is impossible. My country can benefit from Zolotov's discovery more than any other country in the world. You can thank your lucky stars that the Russians have not as yet discovered you. If Zolotov has actually transmuted lead into gold, the Soviet Union's vast supply of gold, larger according to our information, than your country has in Fort Knox, will be valueless. The truth is that no country, on the face of this earth, that has reasonable reserves of gold is going to be happy with your existence. Countries like mine with limited gold reserves will be much more amenable . . . but even if we have to dispose of you, your friend and the Zolotovs, we will actually be doing the people and the nations of the world a great favor. Can you imagine the economic upheaval that would result if Zolotov's secret is revealed? Trading between nations would cease. No nation now trusts another's paper money. The politicians can print too much of it. The world would be reduced to barter. Your knowledge and Zolotov's secret could destroy man's faith in the only value he has left in the world. GOLD!"

While he was talking, Nesterenko got up. He stood menacingly in front of me surveying my breasts as if he were going to touch them. "A woman like you should be in someone's arms, murmuring love words to him, Miss Wentworth. Instead, you are in mortal danger of rape!" He walked back to the desk and lighted a cigar. "I hope you understand why we need some fast answers. We have got to find Zolotov! Possibly, the whole thing is a tempest in a teapot. If that's true, if Zolotov is a faker, we will expose him rapidly. Actually, you and Mr. Barnett can pray that he is a charlatan. It could save your lives. Being kindly people, I am sure, in that event, we would eventually return you to your normal lives."

"I'm going to faint," I said weakly in a voice that

seemed no longer to belong to me. I could feel the room slowly starting to revolve. Just before I lost consciousness I heard Nesterenko shout "Get a pail of water." When I opened my eyes again I was dripping wet, my hair plastered against my face. I looked dazedly at Nesterenko who was still behind the desk. I suddenly realized that I was no longer a person. I was just a naked female body without much individuality or functioning brain left, trying dully to comprehend what was happening to this creature once called Marge Wentworth. Vasilev or Sergei, I don't know who, lashed me on the buttocks with a wet towel.

"I want some answers, Miss Wentworth. If you pass out again we'll keep reviving you." Nesterenko blew a cloud of smoke in my face. "The truth is that you *know* Zolotov can make gold from lead. That's why you think he will make it for you. That will be your price for keeping his secret. Isn't that correct?"

Had I said that? I no longer knew. I just nodded.

"Where is Manya Zolotov?" Nesterenko demanded.

"I don't know!" I cried. "Please, make him stop hitting me. I don't know."

"You were trying to telephone her from a telephone booth in Midhaven, Connecticut. What's her telephone number?"

Dimly, I remembered. It was an eternity ago. Craig and I in a telephone booth. Marge Wentworth, laughing, exuberant, about to embark on a wonderful adventure. There was a telephone number. What was it? Oh, God . . . please don't hit me again with that towel. "I can't remember . . . I can't remember!" I groaned.

Nesterenko was standing in front of me again. I choked from the cigar smoke engulfing my face, and then through the haze I watched fascinated, horrified as he pointed the glowing tip end toward me.

"The tip end of a burning cigar is very, very hot, Miss

Wentworth. Held against the nipple of your breast it would be excruciatingly painful."

"Please, God . . ." I screamed. "I knew the telephone number but I forgot it. I beg you have pity on me, I'm sick."

Dimly I realized that Craig had been struggling on the bed. He knows the telephone number, I thought. Oh, my God, I'm saved! Craig knows it! Please dear God, tell it to them, Craig. Stunned, I realized that for all his groaning with the gag over his mouth, he still couldn't speak. They evidently thought he was trying to defend me. Vasilev smashed him across the face. Craig lay still on the bed.

Nesterenko held the cigar as if he were holding a dart with a bright fiery point. He moved it slowly toward my breast. "Burning flesh smells very unpleasant, Miss Wentworth. What is Manya Zolotov's telephone number?"

Suddenly I had a flash of inspiration. "It's 202-393-6400." I screamed. "Don't burn me!"

"That's better," Nesterenko smiled. He wrote the number on a piece of paper and looked at his watch. "We still can catch the 1 A.M. flight to Miami." He walked over to Craig and fished inside his suit coat. "Ha, here's the tickets . . . just where I saw Mr. Barnett place them two hours ago. Come on, Vasilev, we have no time to lose."

"What about them?" Sergei demanded. "What do I do with them?"

"Lock Mr. Barnett in here for the night," Nesterenko said. He stared at me. Although I was shivering uncontrollably, I could read the crude sexual desire on his face. "Cut her down, Vasilev," he said finally. When Vasilev's knife released the strain, my body slumped. Still half hanging by the rope, I crumpled to the floor. "It's regrettable," I heard Nesterenko say. "But there's no choice. You can have her, Sergei.

Take her to your cabin. I envy you. If she doesn't want to cooperate I'm sure that you can persuade her." Groaning with pleasure, Sergei swooped me off the floor. I could feel his face loathsomely rubbing my body. I fought him feebly, but I knew it was too late. I fainted.

Eight

For the next few minutes until I regained consciousness and realized dimly that Nesterenko was lying on the floor, blood bubbling from his chest, with Vasilev beside him, his dead eyes still mirroring the terror and shock of his sudden death, and I, still naked, was being clutched around the waist by Sergei who was using me as a shield . . . for those few minutes I don't know what happened.

Craig told me later when Nesterenko walked to the cabin door about to leave with Vasilev, two men burst into the room with drawn guns equipped with silencers protruding menacingly from them. All Nesterenko and Vasilev managed was an amazed grunt. The guns went off with a quiet pop pop; Nesterenko shot through the heart, Vasilev hit directly between the eyes.

I saw one of the men walk toward me. He held his gun within two inches of Sergei's head. I heard Sergei blubbering. "Don't shoot! Don't shoot!" I felt his hands clutch my hips and stomach desperately. Then I heard another sinister pop. Sergei's hands slid down my legs. He was dead on the floor; his eyes ophthalmic in horror. I collapsed on top of him shuddering, too frightened even to scream or beg for mercy, waiting for my turn.

"Very clean, and swift!" I heard one of the men say. The other one pulled me to my feet. I was staring into a grinning Chinese face and slant eyes of a pleasant man about thirty years old. "I'm sorry we had to wait so long, Miss Wentworth," he smiled happily at me. "But Chang Yu and I thought you never would tell our very crude friends here Manya Zolotov's telephone number. Of course, the final reckoning for these very evil men would have been the same in any event."

Amazed, wondering if it still were just a matter of minutes before I was subjected to some form of Chinese torture, I realized that the other man was helping me on with my mink coat. I smiled at him gratefully, still unable to stop shivering. "This is Chang Yu," he said quietly. "I am Doctor Pao-lin. You have nothing to fear. Here, take this towel. Dry your face, and hair. We must not linger here. There may be friends of theirs who would not appreciate this mayhem."

Chang Yu had pulled the bandage off Craig's face. "Where are the keys to these handcuffs?" he asked. Craig gestured at Vasilev. Doctor Pao-lin quickly searched Vasilev's body, found the keys and unlocked the handcuffs. "Come on . . . we must get off this ship fast!"

Craig threw his arms around me. "Oh, my God, Marge," he said, kissing and hugging me. "I was certain they were going to kill you."

Chang Yu pushed us toward the door. I stumbled over Nesterenko's body. I was acutely aware that he was dead. "You murdered him!" I sobbed hysterically. "You murdered him!"

Chang Yu looked at me coldly. "Get a grip on yourself, Miss Wentworth. If we hadn't acted with surprise, you might right now be in the process of being raped. Had we given these men time to react, it would be a neat question whether it would be they or us lying on that floor." He kicked Nesterenko's body. "He was less than scum."

50

As they lead us down the corridors toward the gangplank, I tripped on my stockings which had fallen around my shoes.

"My clothes. I need clothes," I yelled, suddenly realizing that I was naked under my coat.

Chang Yu clapped his hand around my mouth. "One more sound like that, and I will be forced to kill you, Miss Wentworth. If anyone sees or hears us, we are all in mortal danger. You can worry about your clothes later."

Panic-stricken I stared at Craig. He stared grimly back at me and said nothing. Doctor Pao-lin was leading us, his footsteps light as a caress on the metal floor plates of the ship. Chang Yu was in the rear. I could still feel the biting clasp of his hand on my face. Shocked, I realized that we had been saved from the frying pan only to be thrust into the fire.

At the gangplank Doctor Pao-lin ran ahead of us, down it and off the ship. He stared into the darkness for a moment and then waved at us. On the dock, Doctor Pao-lin grabbed my wrist with an iron grip. Chang Yu held Craig's arm with one hand, his gun in the other. We ran wildly, clattering on the cobblestones until we reached Twelfth Avenue. Except for trailer trucks parked in rows, the street was deserted. Panting, and trying to catch my breath, I saw a taxi shoot out of one of the cross streets. It screeched to an abrupt stop in front of us. Dimly I wondered how the driver managed to stop so fast without the car turning over. Chang Yu pushed Craig and me into the rear seat. Doctor Pao-lin and he sat in the drop seats facing us. The driver quickly turned the cab around and drove across town.

"Deed accomplished," Chang Yu said to the driver, who was also Chinese. "Chou En-lai would be happy. I'm sure they did not truly understand Communism."

"We've got fifty-five minutes to get to the Eastern

Airlines Terminal," Dr. Pao-lin said to the driver. "Chang Yu and I, and our new friends are taking the 1 A.M. flight to Miami."

I heard his words but I couldn't believe them.

"The hell you say," Craig shouted. "Let us out of this cab!" He grabbed the door handle.

Chang Yu shoved him back in the seat. He pointed his gun at him. "It would be monotonous to make it five in one evening, Mr. Barnett. I advise you to do exactly what you are told."

"My God," I moaned. "It's all a bad dream. Tell me it's a dream, Craig!"

"Your bad dream is all over, Miss Wentworth," Doctor Pao-lin said. He was fumbling in a medical bag. Using a small flashlight he produced a hypodermic needle. "We Chinese are a more courteous, less excitable people than our Northern friends. Now, if you will both please push up your sleeves, I will give you a sedative. You needn't be alarmed. You have both had a terrible experience. This will permit you to have a good night's sleep on the plane. Tomorrow, in Miami, you will be as bright and fresh as oriental poppies in first bloom. You will be able to help us find Mrs. Zolotov."

It was useless to argue. I was in mortal fear that Chang Yu's gun would go pop pop, and Craig and I would be found dead in some New York City gutter. Craig winced when the needle went into his arm. I ached in so many other places that I scarcely felt it. We had lost all control over our individuality. We were nothing but slave puppets. Anyone who managed to get hold of the strings had it in their power to make us do anything they wished. Somewhere my mind warned me that I was still naked. "Please, please Mr. Chang Yu, I can't go to Miami without any clothes on," I said hopelessly. "Please! Everyone will wonder why I am naked. Please

52

let us go. We'll never breathe a word of what happened."

In the light of the passing cars I could see Chang Yu's face. Amazingly, it held a sympathetic expression. But maybe not. Maybe it was his unfamiliar Oriental features.

As we arrived at the airlines terminal I knew I couldn't wait any longer. I had to go to the bathroom in the worst way. I whispered my problem to Craig. "I can't walk through the terminal like this. My hair is a mess. I've got to go to the ladies room. Look at my stockings." They were still dangling around my shoes. Swiftly Chang Yu pulled off my shoes, removed what was left of my stockings and put my shoes back on. "No one will notice that you are barelegged," he said. "When you get out of this taxi hold your hand at the collar of your coat and make sure that you keep your chest covered. Doctor Pao-lin will take your arm. We will walk directly to the departure gate. Our tickets are purchased and everything is in good order. The sedative will be taking effect very soon. Doctor Pao-lin will explain to the stewardess that you are his patient. You have just left the hospital to visit your family. You are going to Miami for a rest cure. Mr. Barnett is your husband. When we get aboard the plane we will make arrangements for you to visit the lavatory."

Walking through the terminal, clutching my coat around me, I could feel the cold air blowing unpleasantly up my legs. In the back of my brain I kept thinking I am naked. I am naked. All I have to do is to fling open my coat and run screaming through the terminal. They wouldn't dare shoot me. Or would they? I wasn't sure. My God! What was going to happen to us? I knew that Craig had been beaten, that it was all my fault. But my arms ached, and my body felt stretched and mangled all at the same time. I was sure that my face

53

was swollen from being slapped. I kept thinking somehow we will be saved. The police will rush up and arrest these maniacs. Then, I realized dully that all my thoughts were far away not-now thoughts, distant . . . I was listening to the words but someone else was doing the thinking.

The plane was waiting outside the gate with the hatch open. A smiling stewardess saying "Good morning, welcome to our early morning Miami flight," guided us aboard. Doctor Pao-lin explained to her that I had just been released from a New York hospital. We were on our way to Florida for a sun cure. If possible we would like to sit in the lounge where he could watch over me. Vaguely, I realized that the plane was not crowded. A few passengers, here and there throughout the length of it, were asleep in their chairs. The lights were turned down; most of them were sleeping. The stewardess found us a circle of seats at the rear of the plane. Doctor Pao-lin sat on my right side, Craig on my left, Chang Yu completed the grim semi-circle.

"I have to go to the bathroom!" I moaned sleepily. "If I don't go soon the stewardess is going to have to mop up a great big puddle."

"Please control yourself!" Doctor Pao-lin hissed at me. "As soon as the plane takes off, Mr. Barnett can take you to the lavatory." He whispered across me to Craig. "Pull her coat together! Her legs are showing all the way to her crotch!"

The stewardess returned and told us we would be aloft in a few moments. She asked me if I would like to hang up my coat. Crazily, I giggled. I had an insane vision of me standing up, slowly taking off my coat, and standing there stark naked.

"Miss Wentworth is chilly," Doctor Pao-lin said quickly. "She'll keep her coat on. Perhaps you could find her a blanket."

At least the problem of my nudity was solved. When

the plane finally took off and the fasten seat belt sign was extinguished, I was so numb with the pain that I wasn't even sure that I could walk the length of the plane without urinating. Only the vague thoughts as to the ruin this would make of my mink coat made it possible for me to restrain myself.

"All right," Chang Yu said to Craig when the plane was finally aloft. "You can take Miss Wentworth to the lavatory. It's up at the front of the plane."

"I can go by myself!" I murmured.

"Your friend will go with you," Doctor Pao-lin said curtly. "We are taking no chances that you will lock yourself in or fall asleep." He shook Craig who looked pretty far gone himself. "Keep this in mind," he told him coldly. "If you don't return with her in ten minutes, you will not only endanger your own lives, but you will leave us no choice but to walk forward and shoot the pilot and the co-pilot. Everyone on this plane will die. It is not a choice that we would make for ourselves, but, in any event, we *cannot* fail." He emphasized the word cannot with his teeth clicking sharply. Craig guided me up the aisle. Somehow, he managed to squeeze me and himself into the tiny lavatory. I sank wearily on the toilet with my coat under me and fell asleep. I felt my coat being yanked up from under me. My bare bottom was on the seat. It felt chilly but I couldn't stay awake.

"Marge!" Craig whispered standing over me. "For God's sake, wake up and listen to me!"

I felt my face sting. "You slapped me." I moaned. "Oh, Craig. I am so sorry. It's all my fault. If I had listened to you we would never have gotten into this terrible mess. Now, we'll never know what happened to Zolotov."

"To hell with Zolotov!" Craig said crossly. He shook me roughly. "Listen . . . and listen good! I'm not going to be able to talk with you alone again. This is a propjet flight. It will take us five or six hours to get to Miami. Before we get off the plane they will serve us breakfast. When they do, keep drinking coffee. Force yourself awake, no matter what! When we walk into the Miami terminal do whatever I do. If there is a policeman or a crowd standing there . . . anywhere . . . be ready to run with me right to them. Start to scream, good and loud, that these goddamned Chinks are annoying us. It's our only hope. If it works these two birds will disappear fast. If it doesn't we'll be dead. We'll probably be dead anyway if we stay in their clutches. If we can scare them off, we'll rent a car and be gone before they can find us. Do you understand me?"

"I guess so," I said suddenly aware that my face had slumped against Craig's knees. "Turn around. I can't go while you are watching me. I've lost control of my reflexes!"

"There isn't room. I can't turn around." Craig said sharply. "Marge . . . concentrate! You've got to hurry up before those nuts go berserk!"

I grinned at him feebly. "Oh, dear. I have to go . . . so badly, but can't!"

I heard water running in the sink beside my face. Before I could protest Craig threw a cup of warm water on my belly. I yelled. But it worked! I sat there in sheer relief, staring at Craig's knees. Whether he dried me, or I dried myself, I'll never know. But even now I can't blush; Craig was familiar with the general area anyway. Somehow we shifted positions. With my face and body crushed against the door Craig managed to squeeze me erect and keep me from sliding to the floor in a heap while he did his business.

Back finally in the rear of the plane, my head on Craig's shoulders, I drifted in and out of sleep. Through the fog that enveloped me I heard Chang Yu carrying on a muted discussion with Doctor Pao-lin.

"This could be China's salvation," Chang Yu said.

"All that is necessary is to keep Zolotov's method a secret from the rest of the world. China will use this stupid metal the Western nations hold so dear. We can gradually reveal that fabulous gold reserves have been discovered in the Tibetan mountains."

Doctor Pao-lin chuckled. "In the meantime, in some remote area, carefully guarded, we will be manufacturing gold from lead. We will be able to purchase anything . . . from the entire world. Even the United States will sell to us by way of England and Canada. We will pay them all with Zolotov's gold. With such resources of gold, our paper currency will achieve an international value superior to the dollar or the rouble. The greedy Russians and Americans will be our slaves. They will produce and ship us their finest goods. All the material wealth of their countries will flow to China. We will give them in exchange yellow lead. It's a joke worthy of the gods!"

Nine

Their conversation droned happily on, an antiphonal rhythm to the hum of the airplane's engines. Remotely in the dim recesses of my mind I was terrified. I must do *something,* but I could no longer stay awake. Nothing seemed really important. I was a naked helpless prisoner being dragged through a jeering crowd toward a huge funeral pyre. I was being lashed to a cross made of faggots. My arms outstretched, gasoline was being poured on my naked body. The executioner, wearing a black mask, was coming toward me, a lighted torch in his hand. I saw myself scream, astonished that no sound came from my lips. I was Dido, Jeanne d'Arc, Rebecca. While the crowd groaned in approval I exploded in flames.

In a few hours I dreamed one horrible dream after

57

another. I was immersed in a pit of snakes. They were squirming up my naked body wrapping themselves around me, their tongues spitting greedily as they came toward my mouth and face. I screamed, and awoke to the grey reality of morning. Doctor Pao-lin was gently patting my cheek and telling me that the stewardess was bringing me a breakfast tray.

Before the tray was placed in front of me I was back in another dream. I was tied naked to the ground. Gold bars were being placed one after the other on top of me. I could feel their weight crushing my breast and stomach. I was being buried in a mound of gold! Harold Nichols, staring at me with a kindly expression on his face, placed one of the bars on my mouth. "You are getting your fondest wish, Miss Wentworth," he said. "You are being immolated in a golden shrine. Centuries from now all the world will come to visit the Tomb of the Golden Queen." I yelled. "I'm being smothered. Give me air! I don't want to die!"

This time I awoke to Doctor Pao-lin explaining to the stewardess that I had had a slight mental breakdown. I had been receiving shock treatments. He had great hope for my eventual recovery. The stewardess smiled at me sympathetically. I nodded in agreement with Doctor Pao-lin's story. I was pleased that he was taking such good care of me. Convinced that everything he had said was true, I stared dully at the toast and scrambled eggs on the tray in front of me. Half-heartedly I sipped my orange juice.

"It's five thirty, Miss Wentworth," Chang Yu said. "Eat your breakfast. We will be landing in Miami in twenty minutes."

Dimly, I wondered what I was doing on an airplane. I knew that my body ached. My buttocks were tenderly sore. Someone had been beating me. Was it part of the shock treatment that Doctor Pao-lin had been talking about?

58

I couldn't seem to bring myself into focus. Suddenly, I recognized Craig sitting beside me. I thought he looked quite rumpled. He needed a shave. I smiled at him vaguely.

"Why don't you drink your coffee? It will wake you up," he said tonelessly. I felt his foot press heavily on mine.

I put the coffee cup to my lips, and then with a feeling of shock I remembered! Coffee. Drink it! Lots of it! I've got to wake up! I finished the cup, poured another from the silver pot. I asked the stewardess for more. "I need to wake up," I told Chang Yu who was watching me curiously. "I'm groggy!"

Doctor Pao-lin smiled. "You can have all the coffee you want, Miss Wentworth. Now, please listen carefully. When this plane lands in Miami we will all walk through the terminal staying very close together. There are escalators that will take us to the ground floor where Chang Yu will rent us an automobile. Once we are in the car we will drive to a quiet motel run by some friends of ours. From this vantage point we will telephone Manya Zolotov. Eventually all of us will have a nice little talk together."

My God, I thought, if Chang Yu dials that telephone number, he's going to get the surprise of his life. I looked at Craig. He knew that I had given Nesterenko the wrong number. Craig's face was grim. I could see that he was furiously angry, but he didn't contest Doctor Pao-lin's plans.

The coffee was finally helping to clear my brain. When the fasten seat belt sign went on I shivered. How could Craig and I ever break away from Chang Yu and Doctor Pao-lin? They wouldn't dare let us escape. I have too much imagination. I could hear their guns go pop-pop. I could see Craig and me lying dead in the screaming confusion of the Miami airport. People were running in all directions to escape the maniacs. A few curious ones were staring at me lying on the cement floor, my mink coat wide open, blood pouring out of my naked chest.

The horrible picture was still in my mind as we walked down the stair platform from the plane. As we walked through the terminal I knew that Craig must be experiencing the same sinking sensation I was. At this hour of the morning, except for a few sleepy people waiting for early morning planes, it was practically deserted. It would have been foolhardy to attempt to break away and run from our captors. I caught the discouraged look on Craig's face as we started down the escalator.

Then, at the bottom good luck was with us! I could see the booths where Avis and Hertz rented automobiles. We were half way down the escalator. I saw a police cruising car and three state policemen, wearing skimmer hats, leaning against the fender of their car. Idly, they watched us descend. I was coming down behind Doctor Pao-lin. Craig was behind me. Chang Yu behind him. It was up to me! When we were about ten stairs from the ground, I screamed, and shoved Doctor Pao-lin as hard as I could. "You dirty, filthy man," I yelled. Doctor Pao-lin stumbled forward a few steps. Quickly grasping that the situation was out of his control, he leaped across the guard rail and ran up the opposite moving steps. When I screamed, Craig turned and lunged toward Chang Yu. The stairs reached the ground. I saw the amazed expression on Chang Yu's face, and his sudden indecision as he realized the policemen were below him. In a panic, with his gun drawn, he ran up the moving down stairs, two at a time.

Startled out of their early morning lethargy, the police belatedly rushed over to us. Although they had all drawn their guns they made no attempt to chase our Chinese kidnappers.

"What the hell are you two trying to do?" one of them demanded, pointing his gun at Craig.

"Those men were annoying my wife." Craig said glibly. "Thanks for being here."

"Who were they?" one of the policemen demanded.

"How do we know who they were? They've been following us ever since we got off the New York plane." For the first time in ten hours, Craig smiled at me. "My wife can't help it. She attracts the lunatic fringe."

"Not just the lunatic fringe!" One of the policemen was watching me pop-eyed. I suddenly realized that, unheeded, my mink coat was giving me a dangerously plunging neckline.

One of the policemen wanted to take our names and put the incident on file. Craig told him that we were on vacation and preferred not to get involved. Thanking them, he grabbed my arm. "Come on, darling, we are late. We'll rent a car."

At the Hertz desk, the clerk asked Craig if he wanted a Ford or Chevrolet. Craig told him we wanted a Cadillac convertible.

"Wouldn't a Ford do?" I whispered. "We haven't much money. I need clothes. First . . . fast . . . in a hurry!"

Flipping the credit cards in his billfold, Craig grinned sourly at me. "I have a feeling that we are living on borrowed time. We might just as well enjoy what remains of our lives, courtesy of American Express."

In a pale green Cadillac convertible I slumped wearily against the window and breathed the soft Florida air. I was still fighting a terrible lethargy; an insistent desire to just curl up and go to sleep. Determinedly, I refused to let my thoughts dwell on the past ten hours. I knew that Craig and I had both been close to death, yet the whole thing had the unreality of a nightmare. But Craig kept insisting on reviewing the gruesome details. "Right now that ape Sergei could be raping you . . .

while you lay there, a broken lump of female flesh."
Craig took his eyes off the road a second and looked
grimly at me. "I hope to hell that you have learned
something!"

I shuddered. "Don't worry . . . I have! Please, Craig.
I don't want to think about it. I'm exhausted. I feel as if
I had been mauled and man-handled by an invading
army." We passed a billboard with a large thermometer.
The temperature was 82 degrees. I realized suddenly
why I was so warm. I pulled open my mink coat, and
let the breeze from the window blow over my body.
Craig yelled at me to cover up. Passing cars could see
me.

"I can't walk around in this heat in a mink coat," I
told him. "I've got to buy a dress. Neither one of us
have a stitch of clothes except what we are wearing.
You are a lot better prepared to face the world than I
am."

"I don't know about that," Craig grinned. "That mink
coat is going to help us register at the most plush hotel
on the beach. Just you wait and see." He was about to
say something else but his words ended in a curse. He
swerved the car suddenly and raced up a side street at
seventy miles an hour. I was flung against the car door.
"You'll get arrested for speeding," I screamed.

"Maybe *they* will," Craig said grimly. "Look in your
mirror. Our Chinese friends are on our tail!"

Craig's sudden turn into a side street failed to elude
Chang Yu and Doctor Pao-lin. In a Chevrolet sedan
they were in hot pursuit of us. Screeching and squealing,
we whipped and skidded through a series of side streets
and turned into a cross street. Ahead of us I could see
a traffic signal. It turned red just as we arrived at an
intersecting boulevard.

"Hang onto yourself and pray!" Craig yelled.

Without stopping for the light, at sixty miles an hour, we
wove and twisted through the heavy boulevard traffic.

Miraculously, we didn't hit anyone. Still driving at breakneck speed Craig suddenly turned the car into a side street and sped in the opposite direction.

"Slow down," I begged him. "If we don't get arrested, we'll be completely lost."

"Better lost than dead!" Craig said. He wiped the perspiration from his forehead. "I think we have temporarily left our friends behind. But now they know this car. Look in the glove compartment. See if there is a Hertz directory. We'll turn this car in and get another one."

I fumbled through the pages of the tiny directory getting dizzy as I tried to read it. "There's an office at Miami Beach."

Still driving pretty fast, Craig smiled. "I've got a better idea. We'll check into the Fontainebleau. I'll give the car to the doorman. We'll get rid of it there."

"You're crazy. We can't go to an expensive hotel like that. I'm still naked under this coat, remember?"

"That coat is going to do it for us!" Craig grinned at me. "Your hair is a bit messy, but you look like a million dollars."

Twenty minutes later we were standing at the registration desk of the Fontainebleau. Craig explained to the room clerk that we had flown down to Miami this morning rather unexpectedly. Our luggage was on another flight. He had asked the bell Captain to turn our Cadillac back to Hertz, the engine had a bad knock in it. We preferred a Corvette, anyway. Would the desk clerk see that the transfer was made. The clerk listened patiently, an expression on his face that gave the impression he thought Craig was one level above a Bowery bum.

He was sorry, while it wasn't the height of season, the hotel was fully booked. Then he spied me. The mink coat must have done it. "Just a minute," he said, his eyes widening. I wondered if he was looking right through the coat. "We do have a suite that was vacated unexpectedly this morning . . . overlooking the pool. It's one hundred and twenty-five dollars a day." He looked coolly at Craig, gauging his reaction.

My mink suddenly failed me. A hundred and twenty-five dollars a day! I didn't feel sophisticated any longer. I grabbed Craig's arm whispering to him that we could go somewhere else. But Craig calmly told the clerk that was fine . . . we might even stay a month!

Registered, and in the room at last, I exploded. "Have you gone completely crazy? We can't afford this. And a month we are going to stay! Some joke!" I looked around the room. Wall to wall broadloom that you sank into up to your ankles. Modern chairs and lighting. Wide sofas and exquisite pastel colors everywhere. "We can't afford to stay here even for an hour! What do we do now?"

Craig wandered into the bedroom and flopped on one of the wide twin beds. "We are going to do absolutely nothing, sweetheart . . . except sleep, make love, sleep, make love, until Monday night when we will reluctantly take a plane back to New York, get my Jaguar, and drive peacefully home to Midhaven, Connecticut." He looked at his watch. "Unbelievably, it is only ten minutes past nine. We have a wonderful expanse of hours before us. But let us not waste a minute." He pulled back the sheets and started to undress. "Don't look so astonished. Take off your mink coat, my lovely filly, and let me feast my eyes on your delectable body!"

I sat down on the bed opposite him. "Don't be insane. Do you think I can just jump in the sack after what I've been through? Besides, I am not staying holed up in this room for two days. What about Manya Zolotov? What are we going to do about her?"

Lying naked on the bed Craig stared grimly at me. "We are going to begin right now and forget that we ever heard the name Zolotov . . . now and forever. We

64

are going to stay in this room, with the door locked, for the next forty or so hours. We'll call room service for meals. Right here in this hotel, in the middle of all these tourists, we are safe. If we start poking around Miami, God knows who might be looking for us. The Russians may even send out their first team. You can stay bundled up in that mink or not, as you please, but neither of us is going one step out of this room until Monday."

"Craig," I said seriously. "You are overlooking one thing. When we get back home, we still are in deep trouble. If we are the only persons who know that Zolotov has made gold from lead—and besides the Zolotovs themselves and Harold Nichols I think we are—then the agents of every country in the world are going to be after us. They will never leave us alone. Zolotov's secret is only good just so long as it is kept absolutely secret. The country that can keep it a secret is going to make billions of dollars or roubles, or sterling, or what have you out of it. We are never going to be free of Zolotov until we either find him ourselves . . . or until the truth leaks out. Then everyone in the world will know that gold is no good anymore."

"Fine!" Craig said snatching the telephone book from under the bedtable. "I'll telephone the F.B.I. They can come down here right away. We'll tell them the whole miserable story."

"No," I yelled grabbing the telephone book away from him. "You can't do that!"

"Why the hell not?" Craig demanded angrily. "Oh, I get it! Marge Wentworth still has dreams of owning her own private Fort Knox. She sees Horace Zolotov, her slave, grinding out an endless stream of gold bars. You must be insane. You won't be happy until they've strapped both of us to a butcher's table, and sliced us up into prime cuts!" Craig jumped off the bed. He yanked off my coat, and forced me back down on the mattress. "Now, won't these tasty titties look just charming wrapped in cellophane. I can see them now. The week-end special in the supermarket. Breast of Virgin, $2.00 a pound!" He tried to rub his face against my breasts. I yanked at his hair. "Maybe not virgin," he yelped, burrowing his stubbly cheeks against my chest. "But there's at least ten dollars of meat in each tit!"

I fought him furiously. "Let me go, you rapist! You haven't shaved. You feel like a porcupine!"

Craig released his grip on me. I scuttled away from him and sat puffing on the other bed.

"Pardon me," he said coldly. "I was wrong. Those titties are pure gold! Hard as a rock, with a calcified heart underneath them. Go ahead, call Manya Zolotov. Use the telephone number you gave Nesterenko, when he nearly branded you. What a joke! He would have discovered he was stamping out his cigar on solid gold knockers!"

I was crying hysterically by this time. Maybe Craig was right. Maybe I was willing to sacrifice anything for money. Maybe I was a heartless bitch. But after all we had been through, I felt certain that since we were so deeply involved, the only logical thing to do was to follow the affair through to the end.

"I can't remember Manya's telephone number." I sobbed, wiping my eyes on the pillowcase.

"What was the number that you gave Nesterenko?" Craig asked curiously. "You sputtered that out fast enough."

"It was the telephone number of the United States Treasury Department in Washington." Between sobs I couldn't help laughing. "It flashed into my mind from a directory on Harold Nichols' desk. When Chang Yu and Doctor Pao-lin try that telephone number, good heavens . . . are they going to be surprised!"

Craig's mouth sagged in amazement. "You mean when

you were about to be branded with a cigar, when you knew that you were in danger of being raped, you had the cool nerve to give Nesterenko that number?" Craig shook his head. "If you are a typical female, this is where I came in. Women should be running the world!" "Damn you anyway!" I was so exasperated and furious with him by this time I started to pound his chest. I was angry enough to maim him for life with fingernail scratches. "Everything I say to you, you twist it! You are trying to make out that I am nothing but a money mad cold-blooded female monster."

While I socked the air around his chin, Craig held me at arm's length. A naked harpy, I kept flaying at him uselessly. "I had to give Nesterenko some number . . . any number. He would have burned me if I hadn't. Let me go, you rat! I still can't remember Manya Zolotov's number. You know it! Tell it to me! I'll call her myself." I could see that Craig still didn't believe me. He thought I could really remember Manya's number, but I had been so determined to reach Manya myself that I wouldn't have given the number to Nesterenko if he tortured me until I was dead.

"Why that number?" he kept insisting. "It's just too cute. The Treasury Department, no less!"

My hands finally connected with his vulnerable part which was pointing at me altogether too eagerly. "Let go," he squealed. I held it harder and looked at him defiantly. "All right!" he yelled. He tumbled me over his shoulder back on the bed. "You asked for it!"

"Go ahead," I screamed, fighting him desperately, trying to bite him. "Go ahead. I'm smelly. I need a bath. Please. Please wait! Please, Craig . . . Oh, damn you anyway!" I held his face hard against me and kissed his bristly cheeks.

"This is ridiculous," I murmured. "How can we make love when just a few hours ago we were praying for our lives?"

He didn't answer. The big ape. He just continued the happy business of getting me so excited that I finally forgot everything. Well, not quite everything. "Listen," I told him. "If you want me to co-operate, you've got to promise that we will try to find Manya Zolotov."

Craig groaned. "How can you do this to me? At a time like this? You are the absolute living end, Marge Wentworth!"

I chuckled. "My end will really be living if you say yes!" So I won another round. Well, almost. When we both lay back, in complete utter exhaustion, it suddenly occurred to me that I had forgotten to take my daily pill! They were in my pocketbook. God alone knew where that was. Maybe on its way to Russia for all I knew. "Do you know what you have done?" I asked Craig indignantly. "You've probably gotten me pregnant. From now on . . . until I get a new supply, you can just keep away from me!"

Craig accepted the news altogether too cheerfully. He took a shower, with me still heckling him about Manya Zolotov. Finally, he agreed to go downstairs to one of the shops in the hotel and buy me a size twelve dress. Once I was wearing at least that much, I could finish my own shopping. "But I can promise you," he said grimly. "We are *not* going to Manya Zolotov's motel together. You can wait here. Those chinks may have found her. They may be there already. If they are, at least they won't get both of us." He looked at his watch. "It's quarter to twelve. I'll pick up a car, drive to the El Dorado Motel and see if Manya is there. If I'm not back by five, you can call the police and tell them to look for my corpse. It will probably be floating in Miami Bay."

No amount of arguing would convince Craig that I should go with him. I had temporarily lost my power over him. I gave up and begged him to be careful. Besides, I had to admit that after our mad lovemaking and our Walpurgis night with the Russians and Chinese I was more than just exhausted. I was a limp and aching sack of bones held together by bruised flesh. Even the thought of a million gold bars didn't interest me, not until I regained my strength.

I was half asleep in the bathtub when the telephone rang. Dripping wet I nervously picked it up.

"You are going to have to wait for your dress," Craig chuckled. "At the prices of dresses in this hotel I couldn't afford to buy you underwear or a garter belt, let alone a new supply of pills. I'll find a middle class dress store and be back. Get yourself all pink and shiny for me!"

Ten

Waiting for Craig, I lay down on the bed and tried to relax in the luxurious room. I tried to close my eyes and enjoy the warm air floating in, caressing my naked body. But I couldn't let go enough to fall asleep. I was desperately exhausted. My eyes actually ached to stay closed. But just as I would drift off into sleep, I would be immersed in mad dreams, even worse than those I had on the airplane.

I knew I should have gone with Craig. I didn't really trust him to find Manya Zolotov, to even *want* to find her. He was quite willing to call it quits. Really, the truth was, I agreed with him. We were lucky to be alive. But some remote area of my brain kept insisting that I couldn't stop midstream. Even if the search for Zolotov came to nothing, I had to know the truth. Did Zolotov really know how to make gold from lead or was it just a mad hoax?

Then I began to worry about what kind of dress Craig would find for me. It was ridiculous. Had I stopped to think about it there was no reason why I couldn't have walked into a store myself. Without taking my coat off, I could have picked out a dress, underwear and what not. Then, I could have come back to the hotel room and dressed. Whatever had possessed me to think a sales clerk would know whether I was naked under my coat? And if she did know? What the hell. I had come all the way from New York, registered at this hotel, and was here in this room without anyone knowing that I was in my birthday suit.

I got so exasperated at myself for getting trapped alone in a hotel room without a damned thing to wear except my mink coat that I began to get angry at Craig. He couldn't possibly pick out a dress for me. I could see it now . . . probably something an old dowager would wear. Fretting, certain that he had gone to look for Manya Zolotov without me, cursing him for not returning with the dress, I suddenly realized that, even worse, he had all my money. My last few dollars were in my pocketbook which by now was probably on its way to Siberia. The rest of my worldly wealth (three hundred dollars, less the plane fare to Miami which I was sure Craig would exact from me as tribute) was in his billfold.

I was registered in the swankiest hotel in Miami with no luggage whatsoever. Except for a pair of shoes and a mink coat, I was a naked vagrant. It was the height of madness. If Craig didn't come back, no one would possibly believe me. I could see the headlines in the Miami paper. Marge Wentworth hustled off to a sanatorium, yelling insanely, trying to convince the police that I was really me, prim and efficient secretary to a bank president.

Attracted by the happy laughter drifting up to the room from the hotel pool, I wrapped a towel around me and watched the glamorous men and women, ten floors below, sunning and swimming, joyous and carefree, in the warm Florida sun. Then I had one of my unfortunately brillant ideas. I tried to convince Craig later it proved that he never should have left me alone. Yon, Margery, hath a lean and hungry look! . . . She thinks too much!

Using the room telephone, I located one of the hotel's fancy women's shops. I explained my sizes, ruminated with a very obliging sales girl about the most attractive colors, agreed that a spun gold lycra bathing suit, a white lace pool coat and thong shoes would be just fine. Within fifteen minutes they were delivered to my room and duly charged on the room bill. Quite elated with the affluence that money (or at least the semblance of having it) can bring, I quickly decided that since American Express was going to be nice and pay the bill, after a quiet little swim in the hotel pool, and a rest in the warm sun to improve my color, I would finish my shopping, *in person, in style!*

While I was a little shocked when I signed the charge slip and noticed that the total purchase came to ninety-three dollars and thirty-seven cents (I knew in case we lived to pay the bill that Craig would be furious) I put aside all grim thoughts and took the elevator to the pool. In my lovely golden swim suit I discovered the sheer joy of appearing at poolside, cool and sophisticated. I noticed my new bathing suit immediately provoked the sun inebriated males to a new interest in life, and studied disinterest from their less spectacularly attired females.

Knowing that I would probably further stupefy the kohl-eyed, mascaraed women who couldn't possibly venture into the pool without turning into cosmetic blobs, I discarded my lace coat and shoes and coolly walked to the diving board. I stood poised for a second ready to execute a graceful swan dive. To my horror, at the far edge of the pool, completely out of place, in black business suits, searching from one group of sun bathers to another, I saw Chang Yu and Doctor Pao-lin! My dive turned into an ignominious belly flop. Without looking back, I swam rapidly to the far end of the pool, praying that they hadn't seen me.

With a feeling of panic in my stomach I gathered up my shawl and sandals, I tried to walk calmly back to the pool elevator. The elevator indicator showed that it was on the top floor. I waited in agony wondering whether I should run up the ten flights of stairs. If I could only get back to the room and lock the door. I would sit close to the room telephone ready to dial for help if there was a knock. If only they hadn't seen me!

The elevator finally arrived. It crept slowly up to the tenth floor, with me its only occupant. The door opened and I breathed a sigh of relief. The corridor was deserted. I was safe! I ran down the hall toward my room. Just as I arrived trembling, trying to insert the key in the lock, Doctor Pao-lin and Chang Yu, not even puffing although they must have run up the ten flights of stairs, appeared behind me.

"Let me open it for you," Doctor Pao-lin said gently, taking the key from my paralyzed hand. "That is a very attractive bathing suit you are wearing, Miss Wentworth. You seem to have an affinity for the color of gold." Gently he shoved me into the room. Although it was warm I started to shiver. I stared at them like an escapee from an insane asylum who has suddenly been caught by understanding guards. I was, in truth, so terrified that I couldn't speak, let alone scream. Chang Yu bolted the door after us.

"Please, there is nothing I can tell you." I pleaded. "Neither Craig nor I know anything about Zolotov."

"Please calm yourself," Doctor Pao-lin said smiling at me. His face assumed a fatherly expression. "We are not going to harm you, Miss Wentworth. Really, have we ever hurt you? Think about it. You and Mr. Barnett owe your lives to us." He gestured toward one of the

72

French Provincial chairs in the room. The back of the chair was facing to the balcony overlooking the pool. "Sit down there, Miss Wentworth. I want to talk with you for a few minutes alone. Chang Yu will leave us." I noticed that Chang Yu had gone into the bedroom. "Please, Miss Wentworth," Doctor Pao-lin insisted, gently. "Just sit down!"

Still shivering I collapsed in the chair. I was unable to conceal the feeling of complete despair that over-whelmed me. If only I had listened to Craig. If I had stayed in the room these damned Chinamen would never have found me. I couldn't stop trembling. "Please," I moaned. "My bathing suit is wet, I'm cold."

Doctor Pao-lin smiled. "You may take your bathing suit off, Miss Wentworth," he said, his voice deeply reassuring. He ignored my look of amazement. "Chang Yu, bring Miss Wentworth a towel so that she may cover herself."

Chang Yu re-appeared with a bath towel. He handed it to Doctor Pao-lin. As if there had been some silent communication between them, he disappeared into the bedroom.

"Now, Miss Wentworth," Doctor Pao-lin said in a voice that left me no room for discussion, "I will turn around for five seconds. Take off your bathing suit and wrap yourself in that towel. You will feel much warmer." He turned around and looked at the wall. "And please do not attempt anything foolish like running out on that balcony and screaming. It would only cause all of us a great deal of unnecessary trouble."

Frightened at the easy way that Doctor Pao-lin was anticipating my thoughts, I hastily unzippered the clammy gold bathing suit, dried myself with the towel, and clasped it around me. I thought my heart would pound its way right through my breastbones.

As I finished Doctor Pao-lin pulled up a chair, and turned toward me. He sat down about ten feet away and stared at me appreciatively. "Now, isn't that more comfortable, Miss Wentworth? If you will just sit down once again in that chair, we will have a nice little talk. The answer that you will give to my questions will solve all our problems."

With my back to the balcony the room seemed darker. The sunlight flickering into the room danced on the planes of Doctor Pao-lin's face. I was thoroughly frightened by Doctor Pao-lin's quiet manner. Thinking this is the calm before the storm, I tried to brace myself to be evasive. It really was silly. Evasive of what? I really knew less about Zolotov than Doctor Pao-lin did. If I was going to be subjected to some kind of subtle Chinese torture what could I tell him? Where was all this going to end? I started to cry.

"Please," I sobbed. "There's no use just sitting there staring at me." A large diamond ring on Doctor Pao-lin's left hand caught a ray of sunlight and reflected it in my face. "I'll tell you anything I can. Please, I beg you let Craig and me go home. I met Horace Zolotov only once. Honestly, I think that Mr. Zolotov is just playing a huge practical joke. Anyone with a grain of sense would know that it's impossible to change lead into gold."

"You may be quite correct, Miss Wentworth. In any event, all your fears are completely unnecessary." Doctor Pao-lin's voice was as soft as a caress. "You really have had a terrible experience. You must be quite exhausted." He chuckled. "My goodness, you and Mr. Barnett left the airport as if you were being pursued by the devil himself. Don't you realize that we Chinese are gentle people? I, myself, grew up in the shadow of the Himalayan mountains, in a valley town called Kunming. My father and mother were farming people. I had four brothers and three sisters. My entire youth was spent in an atmosphere of warm tenderness and kindness. Ah, those wonderful days of Chinese summer,

74

with the sunlight filtering lazily through the leechi trees. On days very much like this one I used to wander beside flowing brooks bubbling with water that had been cleansed by its long trip down the mountain side . . ." Doctor Pao-lin's voice droned on, affecting me like a soporific. Only half hearing him, I kept watching his diamond ring flashing the rays of sunlight on my face. I kept wondering when he would come to the point and start hammering questions at me. But his words glided on like a lullaby.

"You are relaxing, Miss Wentworth," he said. "You've been awake for hours. Your eyelids feel heavy. They just want to close. You know that Doctor Pao-lin likes you. He wouldn't possibly want to harm you. Relax your muscles. Let your body sink into a soft white cloud. There now, your tense feelings are rushing away from you. Your eyes are growing heavy. Your eyes are so tired now. It's a real effort to keep your eyes open. If only you would let them close, you would feel so much better. Your eyes are closing now. Your whole body feels so much better now."

Doctor Pao-lin's voice, confident, easy, like flowing music, rippled pleasantly across my mind. I stopped staring at his ring. I felt my eyes closing. Then, dimly I realized what was happening. Doctor Pao-lin was trying to hypnotize me! I giggled. I didn't care. How silly could he be? No one could hypnotize me! I was Marge Wentworth. I wasn't some moron a hypnotist could tell to go to sleep and make lie suspended between two chairs while someone from the audience stood on her.

"You can't hypnotize me," I heard my voice saying from a great distance. "When I was in college, the psychology professor tried. He tried and tried and tried and tried. . . ." I knew that I was laughing at the way my voice drifted like that and repeated the word "tried." And then I stopped laughing. My brain couldn't seem to escape the wonderful, blessed monotony of Doctor Pao-lin's musical words; words that caressed my tired eyes and aching muscles.

"You feel lighter now, Miss Wentworth," that voice without a body kept saying, "You are falling into a deep sleep. You are slowly drifting through white clouds as soft as cotton. You can hear me counting now. With each number you are sinking into a lovely, warm embracing mist. When I reach ten you will be fast asleep. *One.* You really feel warm and peaceful, now. You are falling asleep. *Two.* You are drifting into an even deeper sleep, now. *Three.* You are in a deeper sleep, now. You hear nothing but my voice."

I listened . . . happy, warmly delighted at the lilting cadence of his voice. I had such a nice floating feeling. Oh, God, I was tired. It was so nice to relax.

"*Five.* You are drifting deeper and deeper into sleep. All you can hear is the sound of my voice. *Six.* You are very comfortable, now. Your mind is free. All you hear is my voice. All you want to do is what I say. *Seven.* Never before have you felt so relaxed. You are almost there, now. *Eight.* You are floating off into a deep, deep sleep. You don't want to do anything unless I tell you to do it. *Nine.* You are deep in a warm sleep. Soft as a caress. All you can hear is my voice. *Ten.* There, NOW! *You are fast asleep!* All you can hear is my voice. Now, Miss Wentworth, nod your head. Tell me by your nod that you understand me."

I knew that I was nodding. I was sure somehow that soothing voice was not a voice outside me. The voice was my own thoughts. I knew I was vaguely aware that Doctor Pao-lin was telling me to do things. But it didn't matter. Everything the voice of my thoughts said were things that I really wanted to do.

"Miss Wentworth," the voice said beguilingly. "You have been swimming this afternoon in the hotel pool. You swam a little and the sun felt warm and good on your body. But now you have just come back to your room. Your bathing suit felt cold and clammy. You have just taken off your bathing suit. You have dried your body. Now you feel so good. So warm and comfortable. In a moment you will hear a noise in the bedroom. You will know that is Craig. *He has come back to the room!* He went out to look for Manya Zolotov but he has come back. He has forgotten her address. He can't remember her telephone number or where she is staying. You love him very much. He is so silly to have forgotten. You are not anrgy. You will run into the bedroom. You will kiss him and tell him the telephone number. You will tell him to hurry back, that you will be waiting for him. When Craig leaves you will go to one of the beds. You will pull back the sheets and get into bed. You will immediately slip into a blissful relaxing sleep. You will not hear any sounds. Nothing will disturb you. You will not even hear my voice until I speak directly to you again. There . . . now, *you hear the sound in the bedroom! You are so pleased! It's Craig!*"

I know now that I must have rushed into the other room. Naked, I must have thrown my arms around Chang Yu! I must have told him where Manya Zolotov was staying . . . I must have spilled out the forgotten telephone number which Doctor Pao-lin had released from the depths of my subconscious mind. What else I did I will never know. I understand enough about hypnosis to realize that before Doctor Pao-lin woke me from my trance, he must have told me exactly what I could remember of my actions. Everything else remains buried or forgotten forever.

As I think about it now, nearly nine months later, I have an uneasy dread. Within a few weeks my baby will be born. I suppose it is possible believing Chang Yu was Craig that I might have gone to bed with Chang Yu. Right now Chang Yu's child could be in my belly. Or even more likely the baby could be Carlos Fernanda's child. The only thing *I am sure of* is, it is not Horace Zolotov's baby. When I finally met Horace it was too late for that . . . thank the lord!

But all I was aware of then, was Doctor Pao-lin's voice, speaking mellifluously to me: "Miss Wentworth. Do you hear me? Nod your head if you hear me. That's fine. You have been blissfully sleeping. The telephone has just rung. It was Craig. He has found Manya Zolotov. He is very happy. Manya wants to tell you and Craig all about Horace's discovery. You are going to the El Dorado Motel and meet Craig and Manya. You are going to get out of bed now. You are going to put on your shoes and your mink coat. You are going down the elevator. You are going to walk through the lobby of the hotel. You will not see anyone. There will be no one in the lobby. You will not hear anyone. At the entrance of the hotel there will be a Chevrolet waiting for you. You are going to get into the back seat and sit quietly there. You will be riding for sometime but you won't worry about it. You will see nothing when you look out the window of the car. You will know that you are on your way to see Craig and Manya. You won't see anyone else, nor will you hear anyone else. All right, Miss Wentworth, you are going to open your eyes. When they are open they will be bright and clear. Open your eyes! Put on your shoes and coat! You are ready to leave."

Incredibly I must have obeyed Doctor Pao-lin's commands. I have no memory whatsoever of walking through the Fontainebleau lobby, naked except for my mink coat, nor do I remember the automobile ride to the El Dorado Motel. The next thing I remember was Doctor Pao-lin's voice like a distant echo of my own thoughts.

"In a few minutes I am going to wake you up, Miss Wentworth. You will be outside Manya Zolotov's room at the El Dorado Motel. It is seven o'clock in the evening. Manya is not here. She has gone away. But Craig is inside the room. He is safe and sound and will be joyously happy to see you again. When I wake you up you will open the door and go inside. You will throw your arms around Craig and kiss him. You will find that we have brought some food in the room for you to eat. You will sit down with Craig and eat it. You are ravenously hungry. All you want to do is eat. You do not want to talk about Manya Zolotov or gold or anything. *All you want to do is eat.* When you have finished eating you will tell Craig that you are feeling very sexy. You are actually overwhelmed with love for Craig. You want to do nothing but be in his arms and make love for the rest of the evening. You will tell him that as soon as you have gone to the bathroom and prepared yourself for the evening *all you want to do is make love.* You will tell him that you know things about making love that he never dreamed existed. Tomorrow morning when you wake up you will remember Doctor Pao-lin told you to make love to Craig. You will be happy that you spent the night so pleasantly. When you see Doctor Pao-lin again he will look directly at you and smile. *You will want him to tell you to go to sleep again.* When he says to you: 'You look sleepy today, Miss Wentworth,' you will feel your eyelids grow heavy and you will fall into a deep sleep. All right, Miss Wentworth, I am going to wake you up, now! When I count to five you will wake up fully, completely! You will feel marvelously alive! Your eyes will be bright and clear! *One.* You are waking up now! *Two.* You are feeling wider awake! *Three.* Wider awake! *Four.* Wider awake! *Five.* You are wide awake, Miss Wentworth!"

Quite assured and smiling, I opened the door. I ran into the room, threw my arms around a bewildered Craig and kissed him breathlessly.

Eleven

I awoke the next morning vaguely aware that Craig's
arms were around me. I was snuggled against the soft
hairs on his chest. For a moment I had lost continuity.
I was still in the room at the Fontainebleau. I must have
fallen asleep after we made love. Then I remembered
that Craig had gone to look for Manya Zolotov.
"How the heck did I end up in bed with you again
so soon?" I demanded sleepily. "When did you get
back? Did you find Manya Zolotov?" I jumped out of
bed naked, aware finally that we were in a different
room. The place was a mess. A trunk in the middle of
the room had been spilled open, the drawers ripped
out. Dresses and underclothing torn to shreds were
scattered around the room. A cosmetic case and a
pocket book had been emptied in a heap on the floor.
Dozens of books with the bindings and pages torn apart
had been flung together with clothing that evidently
had once belonged to a boy about twelve years old.
The room looked as if it had been ransacked by a
maniac.
Shocked, I stared at Craig and the rubble. "What's
been going on here? Who did this? Where is Manya
Zolotov?" I felt the goose pimples run up my back. I
suddenly knew this had been Manya's room. This
jungle of ripped and desecrated clothing belonged to
Manya Zolotov. Dimly, I realized that much more
time had elapsed than my conscious mind had grasped.
Slowly, I remembered Doctor Pao-lin talking to me. I
remembered incessant words winding themselves
around my brain. I remembered rushing into this
room. My body told me that I must have spent an
athletic night performing bedroom gymnastics. But
there were strange missing gaps in my memory. I knew

80

that I was trying to avoid the frightening reality that Craig and I were once again captives of Chang Yu and Doctor Pao-lin.

Still lying in bed, Craig watched me with a half grin on his face. "My God, Marge," he said, leaning on his elbow. "I've known you two years. We've made love at least a hundred times. But in my short amorous life I've never known a woman like you were last night." He chuckled. "For the first time in three days you didn't mention gold once. What in God's name did they do to you? I figured that they must have told you that today is execution day. Your dying wish was to spend your final hours in a sexual explosion." Grinning, Craig kissed me. "Not that I minded. I'm just a little awe stricken at the hidden talents you've never before revealed."

"You're crazy." I told him. "I'm a passionate woman. That's all."

"Never before that passionate!" Craig chuckled. "I think they must have given you an aphrodisiac. Every two hours or so you entered the fray with renewed vigor. Everytime I began to hope, hooray, at last Marge is exhausted! She must be just one gasp away from sudden death. (I had long since passed into a nacroleptic stage). Then, by gosh, you'd revive and decide that we could invent some new exotic way. Finally, about two a.m. when you were experimenting with a Hindu technique, lapping me from head to toe, all I had strength to do was laugh. You got so peeved you started to bite and scratch until I'm darned if I didn't come alive again in self defense!"

I listened to Craig, blushing a little, gnawing my knuckles and trying to figure what the devil had come over me. "You don't have to repeat the whole gory business," I told him indignantly. "I was hypnotized. I couldn't help myself. Doctor Pao-lin gave me a post-hypnotic suggestion."

Craig choked with laughter. "Hypnotized? You? Impossible! No one could hypnotize Marge Wentworth! You're too damned practical. Unless Doctor Pao-lin thumped you on the head with a mallet first I'd take odds that you'd hypnotize him before he got to first base." Craig started to look for bruises on my head. I didn't think he was very funny.

"Okay, laugh like a damned fool. You think I'm a dominating female, but the plain shuddery truth is that Doctor Pao-lin hypnotized me. Just wait until he starts on you!"

The more I thought about it the more uneasy it made me. Being tortured and nearly raped by Nesterenko was one thing. Then, I was tied and physically helpless. But to know that a complete stranger could reach into my mind, and make me do things that I didn't intend to do, was terrifying to me. I read somewhere that a hypnotist couldn't make you perform acts that violated your moral beliefs. Doctor Pao-lin had made me do things that I didn't want to do by suggesting actions to me that were in the framework of things I would normally do. Even now, after hundreds of attempts to force myself to reconstruct in detail what happened to me, I can't account for approximately three hours when I must have been in bed in the Fontainebleau. The truth was, if Doctor Pao-lin had made me believe that Chang Yu was Craig, I would have made love with Chang Yu! Oh God, this baby kicking in my middle just better not have slant eyes!

I didn't tell Craig the grim thoughts that were rushing through my mind. At the time, I didn't even remember the unhappy fact that for forty-eight hours I hadn't taken any pills. While I wouldn't admit it, I was aware of every minute of my compulsive love-making. It was hungrily delightful. I knew that I had been the aggressor. Craig's absolute disbelief at my transformation into a nympho girl friend was funny beyond description.

Among a hundred other things, I remember deciding that Craig was a nice horsey. I told him I was taking a canter through Central Park. Both of us were yelling giddyap . . . whoa! Then we fell off the bed clutching each other in hysterical laughter.

But the predicament we were in precluded laughter. Whatever reality is, as distinguished from dreams, Craig brought me back to it when he told me what had happened to him. When he left the hotel he decided that my dress could wait. The El Dorado Motel was only about ten miles from the Fontainebleau. He would find Manya Zolotov first. Halfway between Miami and Fort Lauderdale he located the motel. A heavy set Cuban greeted him at the entrance to the motel's office. At first he pretended not to understand Craig. There was no Manya Zolotov registered at the motel. Craig persisted. Finally, the Cuban told him to wait in the office. He didn't understand English too well. He would get the manager. Craig sat in the office of the motel nearly fifteen minutes. Finally the Cuban re-appeared with another man who seemed to be more receptive.

"You wish to see Manya Zolotov. Very good. She is in room 1730. Through the courtyard. Down to the end of the second row. Fidel will take you."

Manya's room was at the rear of the building. As he followed Fidel through the courtyard, Craig noticed that the motel seemed to be deserted. Although the sign in front was lighted NO VACANCIES, there were only two automobiles parked in the driveways. When they arrived in front of the room Fidel produced a key. "Mrs. Zolotov not here right now. Come soon. We wait inside."

The room was dark with curtains drawn. Fidel snapped on a light. Craig found himself staring at a forty-five revolver. "You sit down. No make noise. Try big funny beezness. I keel you queek!"

"So there we were," Craig told me bitterly. "I didn't

83

know whether to curse you, Marge, or just start praying for us both. I could see that the room was in shambles. Manya Zolotov may have been there once, but she's probably dead by now. Every bit of her clothing, and the kid's clothing had been ripped to pieces. The rug was torn up. The mattress was sliced down the middle, the pillows slit. I thought at first it was those two damned Chinks. They must have gotten there first, abducted or murdered Manya and the kid, and then searched their effects thoroughly to find a clue to Zolotov's whereabouts, or maybe even his secret. I couldn't figure where the Cubans fit into the picture. We sat here nearly an hour with Fidel propped against the door pointing his gun at me. I wondered if I dared to tackle him. Obviously, if I didn't get out of here quickly I was going to be dumped into a grave with Manya Zolotov and her kid. Smiling Cubans and Chinks would rake sand over us. Then they would plant a palm tree on our grave before they offered our souls up to Mammon." Craig shrugged. "I hoped they would be nice and wait until they found you. Since you had gotten us into this mess I couldn't think of a more fitting ending than your carcass rotting in a grave too. Manya underneath. Me on top of her. You on top of me. One male and two females. Archaeologists would find us some day, a delirious pile of bones."

I shuddered. "If your after-life thoughts were sexual, forget it. Zoltan would be there."

"Very funny. Anyway, not having the stamina of a TV hero, I kept deliberating whether I dared rush Fidel. Since his arm muscles were larger than my leg muscles it wasn't an easy decision. Just as I was thinking, what the hell, I had better try it, there was a knock on the door. Fidel opened it and there was Chang Yu. With him was the manager of the motel . . . looking quite unhappy. Fidel didn't have time to express surprise. 'What the hell ees . . .' he shouted.

Chang Yu's gun went pop-pop. Fidel slumped to the floor, a red bubbling hole in his chest.

" 'I have saved your life again, Mr. Barnett,' Chang Yu said grinning. 'You owe much to the People's Republic of China.'

"By this time," Craig went on, "the other Cuban was on the floor begging for mercy. Chang Yu looked at him as if he were some kind of Cuban cockroach. 'You have a few hours of life left. Stop sniveling my friend,' Chang Yu told him. 'Just sit there on that bed. We will all wait until Doctor Pao-lin arrives. He will have some interesting questions to ask you.'

"And that's all I know," Craig told me. "Except that right now there are two new Chinks sitting on the walk in front of this room playing mah jong, or some damned thing. Just before you woke up, I opened the door. They politely gestured at me. They have those damned guns, equipped with silencers. I gathered it was nicer inside here than outside."

"What happened to Fidel and the other Cuban?" I asked. A hopeful thought penetrated my mind. If Chang Yu had been so busy at least he hadn't been dallying in bed with me. That, of course, still left the possibility of Doctor Pao-lin. What had he been doing while he waited at my bedside to hear from Chang Yu? Craig shrugged. "Before you burst in here with your titties palpitating, a quivering dream of unrequited love, Doctor Pao-lin arrived. The manager, who by now had turned to jelly, was told to remove his deceased friend. I was locked in the room, and informed that soon now the lovely Marge Wentworth, bollicky bare, would be frisking with me like a lamb in heat."

"You're not taking this very seriously," I said. "It's not funny. I don't know about you but I'm scared to death. You might have at least bought me a dress. If I don't get some clothes on pretty soon I'm going to forget how they feel." I tried to banter, but beneath the flippancy I was close to tears. What were Chang Yu and Doctor Pao-lin going to do with us? Had they discovered Zolotov's secret? What had happened to Manya?

We didn't find all the answers for three days. We were prisoners in the room. Each morning, one of the Chinese guarding us brought us a breakfast of oranges, toast and coffee. Every night they brought frozen chicken dinner partially warmed through. When I complained that they had other things in the super-market besides chicken dinners he just grinned: "Cold-chicken dinner very good. Lot less in China."

With a towel wrapped around me I cleaned up the mess of Manya's clothes. I tried to find something left that I could wear. Manya evidently was a big woman. Her brassieres would have held both of my breasts in one cup. I tried on the remains of a dress that had been ripped apart at the seams. There was room for Craig in it too. Having nothing better to do we put it on together. Finally, I found a pair of scissors, a needle and thread in Manya's effects. From the pieces of a cotton dress splashed with printed flowers I made myself a diaper and a brassiere. A large red rose flowered on each of my breasts.

By the end of the second day with nothing to do but argue and commiserate with each other, Craig was so enraged with our enforced leisure that he was blaming me for the whole misadventure. We were finally speaking to each other only in monosyllables. The only happy thought he expressed was that in my diaper outfit I looked like Tondelayo . . . with an accent on the last two syllables.

He kept pulling back the curtain and staring disgustedly at the Chinese who grinned at him and continued playing their interminable game. "I think we should make a break for it, Marge. They don't seem to have their guns with them today." He looked at me morosely. "Even if they do, it's better than staying cooped up here."

"You have every man's dream," I told him, trying not to let him see how frightened I really was. "You are incarcerated with a warm, willing female who is not your wife."

That, of course, was the wrong thing to say. It led us into an interminable discussion of the benefits of a dull life in suburbia compared to this. I tried to kiss him but he shoved me away.

"Marge, for God's sake, how can you think about sex? Not a soul in this whole damned world knows where we are. When your friends or mine finally get around to thinking about it, they will assume that we finally decided to get married. They'll think we have gone on our honeymoon. By the time anyone begins to wonder about us weeks will have gone by. You and I will be nothing but rotting corpses."

"If co-habiting has anything to do with a honeymoon," I said trying to cheer him up. "Then we are fulfilling the requirements."

But Craig had lost his sense of humor, and in truth all I was doing was whistling in the dark. I was quite ready to forget what Craig called my money mad motivations. I was praying that we would live to tell about our adventure, months from now, at some quiet cocktail party for friends in our mortgaged home in surburbia! On the second night Doctor Pao-lin and Chang Yu finally paid us a visit. I was electrically aware of Doctor Pao-lin and very much afraid to look directly at him. He was very courteous, and expressed regrets over our poor accommodations. He was pleased that I managed to make such a charming outfit from the debris in the room.

"It really is too bad that we lost almost ten hours," he said. "If we had come here directly from the airport we would have found Manya Zolotov. Unfortunately, she and her son were abducted. They have been taken to Cuba in a high-powered motor launch. It really is a shame. The poor woman will obviously be subjected to a terrible interrogation. Chang Yu and I are going to have to leave you. Working with certain Cuban defectors we may be able to liberate her before it is too late. While Cuba could use Zolotov's gold, the Spanish are such an emotional people they would never be able to keep the discovery a secret."

"You can let us go, then," I said quite elated. Despite appearances, I am somewhat naive. "Really, Craig and I appreciate that you saved our lives. All we wish to do is go home and forget this whole business."

Doctor Pao-lin looked directly at me, a kindly expression in his eyes. "You look sleepy today, Miss Wentworth." He said. I stared back at him unable to pull my eyes away from his. "Your eyelids are quite heavy. You are falling into a deep, deep sleep."

I suddenly realized that he was right. I was very tired. In a second without preliminaries, Doctor Pao-lin had put me into a hypnotic trance.

Craig was so amazed that he momentarily forgot he was angry with me. "I never saw anything like it in my life," he told me later. "You were completely in his command. He gave you a post-hypnotic suggestion. All he has to do is walk right back in here now, and put you back to sleep in a second or two."

Lying in bed, amazed to find myself naked again, I grimaced at Craig. I was really trying to hold back a flood of tears. I was thoroughly frightened. What kind of pin brain was I? All that man had to do was look at me, and he could put me into hypnosis! It destroyed every image I had of myself as a cool self-possessed woman. I was really an incapable idiot, a reincarnation of Candide's girl friend Cunegonde. I could be raped, disemboweled and Doctor Pao-lin with a few words could convince me that I was having the time of my life. Right now, I knew he had done it again. He had given me another post-hypnotic suggestion. I was determined to resist the feeling edging around the circumference of my brain. I would defeat Doctor Pao-lin by not looking at Craig at all.

"What did he make me do?" I demanded angrily. I stared at the ceiling.

Craig laughed hollowly. "I don't know why in hell I am laughing. While you were asleep Doctor Pao-lin told me that he was quite fascinated by your personality type. If it weren't necessary to force us to go to China because of our knowledge of this Zolotov business, he would in any event be compelled to bring you to the University of Peking for detailed study. He feels that you are a typical American. It is so easy to lead you by suggestion. You could open the door to an entirely new form of psychological propaganda." Craig patted my hand. "Don't worry, Marge. It's not because of your low I.Q."

"My low I.Q." I exploded. "Damn all of you. I have an I.Q. of 175."

"That's just it," Craig grinned. "You are the perfect subject . . . a composite of the vivid imagination that is an American characteristic. Because of this you are extremely suggestible. That's probably why you bit hook, line and sinker for this Zolotov business. Doctor Pao-lin tried to hypnotize me, but he couldn't! I am too pragmatic."

I looked at Craig incredulously. Damn him! I was having a hard time resisting the compulsion to kiss him. "I don't believe it! You are a snap. I hypnotized you. Else why are you here?"

"Because I am an easy going male in love with an impossible wench. And believe me . . . no matter what crazy thoughts are percolating in that head of yours, you better forget them. We've got to concentrate! Unless we figure out a way to escape, we are going to be sailing on a fast boat to China!"

"What else am I supposed to be thinking?" I demanded. "What did Doctor Pao-lin make me do beside get undressed and get into this damned bed?" I figured that I might just as well have my suspicions confirmed.

Craig shrugged. "He told you that you were alone in this room. You couldn't see nor hear anyone else. While he told me what a wonderful subject you were, and how fortunate we were to be going to China and see the People's Republic first hand, you sat in that chair like a petrified mummy. After about fifteen minutes he told you that he was going to wake you up . . . that you were to take off that diaper and bra and get into bed . . . that you were not to listen to any of my worries about what was going to happen to us . . ." Craig stopped. He grinned at me.

"Yes . . . and what else?"

"He told you that you were to look at my wristwatch. At eight o'clock, you were to start kissing me passionately. He told you that until tomorrow morning at six o'clock you would only have *one thing* on your mind."

Grimly I refused to look at Craig. I got out of bed and ran into the bathroom determined to stay there all night. I wouldn't do it! I wouldn't! But finally, it was impossible to resist. I dashed back in the bedroom.

"What time is it, Craig?" I begged him meekly.

It was two minutes to eight!

"My God, Marge . . . NO!" Craig yelled. "Don't you see? It's a new kind of Chinese torture! He wants you to kill me in bed! He wants us to be nothing but copulating morons!"

I knew that Craig was right. But damn it, I couldn't help myself . . . and after awhile neither could he!

Twelve

But Doctor Pao-lin's compulsive suggestion spent its force rapidly. The reality of what was about to happen to us was too frightening. Unless we concentrated on how to save ourselves, Marge Wentworth and Craig Barnett were going to be listed on a roster of "Missing Persons" with absolutely no clue left behind that might save us.

With the uneasy feeling that we were being watched, we turned all the lights out except the bathroom light. In the dark Craig prowled the room looking for some way of escape.

The Chinese guarding us had put a padlock on the door. Craig pushed back the sliding glass window at the front of the room. He tried to open the screen. But it had been built into the window. It would be impossible to force it out without making considerable noise. Staring into the night we could see a row of empty motel rooms across from us. On an angle, across a sandy hill, the Atlantic Ocean gleamed restlessly in the moonlight. We were obviously the only "guests" of the motel. But just as obviously we were under close surveillance. If we tried to break out we would probably find ourselves surrounded by grinning Chinese. Instead of being in a Miami Beach motel, we might just as well have been in the middle of Red China.

Craig slowly probed the wall. He had an idea that if he could rip out a section of it it might lead us into another room on the opposite side of the motel. With no other tools but coat hangers and a pair of Manya's scissors he finally gave up. There was a connecting door to the next room, but it was locked. There was no keyhole. Craig peered under a slit in the door and detected a light.

We guessed that Doctor Pao-lin and Chang Yu, or our

Chinese guards, were sleeping in the next room. They may have even bugged our room and were listening to us. Hopelessly, for the hundredth time, Craig tried the telephone in the room but he could get no sound out of it.

Craig finally flopped on the bed. "It's no use, Marge," he whispered. "What we've got to do now is anticipate them. If they are planning to put us on a boat to China, they can't do it here. United States doesn't trade with Red China so it won't be a Chinese boat. They'll have to drive us to the docks in Miami. Miami is at least twenty miles from here. Somewhere we'll have to make a break for it. I've got Manya's scissors . . ."

Craig's voice trailed off waiting for an answer, but I couldn't stop crying long enough to encourage him in his wild hopes. All my trumped up bravery had vanished. I hugged him and tried to stop sobbing.

"Oh, Craig, I'm scared. We haven't got a chance. You know it. When they take us out of here to a boat we'll be tied and gagged. Even if they don't find those scissors on you, what good would they be against those damned guns? If you try anything Chang Yu will most certainly kill you. They may decide to kill us anyway. From their standpoint the very fact that we know about Zolotov is sufficient reason to murder us."

Craig didn't say it but I knew that he was convinced that being prisoners of the Chinese could actually be worse than chancing immediate death to save ourselves. Grimly, I wondered if we should kill ourselves. There were razor blades in the bathroom. I couldn't do it myself, but maybe Craig would be willing to slit my throat, and then take his own life. God knew he had reason enough to want to kill me. I blubbered my thoughts to Craig but he didn't answer me. I didn't blame him. What was there to say? Our pitiful fund of ideas circled uselessly on each other without resolution. Words between us disappeared into a hopeless vacuum.

We lay on the bed staring at the shadows on the ceiling. A ray of light from the bathroom created insidious daggers on the far wall.

The only thoughts that I had left were endless self-recriminations. It was all my fault. Poor Craig. He must have loved me very much to get himself into such a jam. What good was I to him, anyway? Now, surfeited with love-making, facing death or worse, all I could possibly be to him was a mercenary female. Except to be an occasional obliging bed mate what had I ever done for Craig anyway? Even our love-making had been far from altruistic. I had enjoyed it as much as he. Why did a man want to marry a woman anyway? Especially a woman like me. If we had married and stayed in our little Midhaven, Connecticut rut, would I have been a good wife? . . . A home maker? A mother? Probably not. I had been bitten by the gold bug. I was an inveterate end of the rainbow chaser. I wanted the life and the luxury of the rich. Whether it had been Zolotov, or just constant pressure on Craig "to be someone in the world," I would have put the same noose around his neck.

Lying beside Craig in the darkness, knowing that he was exhausted from our insane love-making, knowing that his thoughts about me could only harbor sexual disinterest, knowing that I couldn't explain my motives to him or ever have him understand my mad drives for success, I just couldn't stop crying. There was only one decent thing I could do. Somehow, I must persuade Doctor Pao-lin to take me to China, and let Craig go. I would promise Doctor Pao-lin anything. I would consent to be his eternally hypnotized puppet. I would be a sexual slave giving myself to a hundred million Chinese in a mechanical lifetime orgy. Anything . . . only he must let Craig go home and find a nice loving suburban wife. I hated her already, but I had to do it! I was deep in my paranoid thoughts when Craig nudged me. "It's probably quite mad," he whispered excitedly. "But do you see what I see?" He pointed to the top of a wardrobe cabinet on the far side of the room. Pushed back against the wall was a box of sanitary napkins, barely visible in the dim light.

"What one woman does another might do!" he muttered. Getting swiftly out of bed, he stood on a chair and reached the box. I couldn't help smiling. Poor Craig was obviously losing his mind. Because I hid things in a Kotex box Craig was assuming that Manya Zolotov might have done the same thing.

I followed him into the bathroom. "Talk in whispers," he said tossing the box at me. "They must have missed this when they searched the room."

I looked at the box discouraged. "It's full. The box has been opened but nothing has been taken out." Disgustedly, I pulled out the pads letting them fall on the floor in a heap. "Nice try," I grinned at Craig. "Let's fill the tub with water and drown ourselves."

I kicked the pads and noticed something peculiar. Three of them stuck together! They seemed heavier than normal. I noticed threads where they had been sewn together. Squealing with joy I ripped them apart. Carefully inserted between the cotton padding were Manya and Zoltan's passport, and a long hand-written letter on airmail paper from Horace Zolotov!

We spent the night in the bathroom. Forgetting our troubles, Craig sitting on the toilet, me lying in the bathtub, we read and re-read Zolotov's letter . . .

Thirteen

Dear Manya (Zolotov wrote)
Only with such a trusting and dedicated wife could I have dared to move so fast. I am mailing this letter to

you from Paris, but when you receive it I will have left France. Continue to have patience with me. Even though in our marriage we have never achieved full communication, your ultimate confidence in me is appreciated. As a man, who less than a year ago was as nearly a complete failure (in relation to his ambitions) as it is possible to be, I want you to know that despite my seeming pre-occupation I have recognized and admired your devotion and patience.

While I was unable to wait for you in Miami, a fact which I am sure you will understand has nothing to do with my concern for you and Zoltan, I promise you, now that I have nearly sifted out the consequences of my discovery, we will be together soon.

When a humble man, in poor circumstances, makes a discovery of such consequence he often is at a loss which may be the best way to proceed. During the weeks that I actually produced pure gold from lead, and perfected the process so that gold can be made relatively simply in large quantities, I was only partially aware of the implications and magnitude of the problem I had created.

I now realize that our limited financial resources made greed my original motivation; combined, undeniably, with an overwhelming sense of ego at my accomplishment. Had I carefully considered my emotions I would never have made the impulsive mistake of contacting Mr. Harold Nichols. Worse, I, at the time, was so dominated by my own superiority feelings I compounded my error by not only telling him that I had made gold from lead, but I demanded that he exchange a bar of gold bullion for dollars.

The only justification and excuse I can make for myself was that immediate cash money seemed to be the only way I could accomplish my objectives which, I must admit, were only dimly perceived at that time. In retrospect, I know all that was really necessary was to use caution; convert my gold into dollars by selling odd pieces from time to time and thus eliminate any danger or suspicion.

All this is water over the dam. I made a mistake. Fortunately, I recognized the folly of my ways in time. Perhaps, some higher power was watching over me. But once out of the bag, the story I told Mr. Nichols must have travelled rather swiftly. A few days after I left my bar of gold with him, I was returning home from school, when two men who identified themselves as employees of the United States Treasury Department, introduced themselves to me. They told me that I was not under arrest, but they thought I might be willing to come with them to the Midhaven Courthouse where we could have the use of a room to talk privately. For an hour or more I was given a very thorough questioning. Fortunately, I was sufficiently alerted to be evasive. I tried to give these men the impression that the whole business of the gold bar was a huge practical joke. The truth was I had been buying old gold for many years at low rates, melting it, and re-selling it at prevailing rates. Since any activity of this kind is regulated by United States law, I soon discovered that I was digging myself into a deeper and possibly more dangerous hole. The conversation proceeded, still on a friendly tone, but I had the impression that not only would my income taxes be investigated, but it was not improbable that a warrant would be issued to search our home.

This was not the only rude awakening I received that day. A few minutes after I was released by the Treasury Department officials, I was accosted by two men who forced me into their automobile. I surmised they were either Russian agents or connected with some Communist government. Their apparent friendliness held an insincerity they were unable to conceal. When they offered me an immediate cash payment of 100,000 dollars for my secret I was hard put to hide my amazement. Having just previously perfected my story, I repeated it with new verve insisting that the whole business was a hoax. I said I was in reality a dealer in old gold, and was very alarmed that my unregistered activities would ultimately land me in a federal penitentiary. When this failed to thoroughly convince them I took an opposite tack, I admitted that I had dabbled in alchemy. I told them I was positive that I was actually a re-incarnation of Paracelsus, but so far my efforts to transmute lead into gold had been unsuccessful!

They finally let me out of their car in front of our house. I knew the respite was only temporary. I would have to move swiftly. That night I destroyed all the records that led to my discovery. Unfortunately, there was certain heavy equipment in our basement that might have provided a clue to any knowledgeable nuclear chemist. There was no choice. I knew that I couldn't consult with you. The entire business was really too beyond belief. Once I was certain that you and Zoltan were safely in Miami I returned to Midhaven and very thoroughly set fire to our house. I know this must shock you, but realize that it was done of necessity. Had I discussed it with you I am sure that you would most certainly have considered it an act of madness.

Again I pray you remember . . . we have survived much together. Back in Europe once again after all these years, the memory of the terrible suffering that we, and thousands like us, experienced floods back on my consciousness. I am now convinced that my discovery was not granted to me by God for idle misuse or for my own personal aggrandizement. I have in my power a secret so devastating to the false nationalistic practices of this world that I am forced by my own conscience to use it for the betterment of mankind.

So now, Manya I have made my decision. Within two

months I shall be ready. I have within my power the means to destroy the present economic systems of the world. I can create international havoc by wiping out the myth of the gold standard that men live by. I do not wish to hurt the little men. Very soon now I will tell the leaders of the world of my discovery. I will give them fair warning: "Use all means at your disposal to immediately end wars and hate in the world, or I, Horace Zolotov, will plunge the world into economic chaos from which it will take years to emerge."

Your loving husband, Horace.

P.S. My plans are now definite. If you do not hear further from me, you and Zoltan will fly to Brussels and meet me in the Hotel Westbury on January 12th. I will wait for you in the lobby at exactly twelve noon.

Fourteen

I have often wondered what might have happened to Craig and me if we had never found Zolotov's mad letter and Manya's passport.

While it didn't change our immediate situation I was beginning to feel like a record placed on a moving turntable. Once the needle of events crept into the groove it had to play through to the end. Only God could have stopped it. At the moment I guess He wasn't looking.

I didn't tell Craig that I was sure from Zolotov's letter that Zolotov had crossed over the bridge into a never-never land of his own. But whether Zolotov was suffering from a mad delusion, or not, didn't answer our present problems. Craig wanted to use the letter to buy our freedom. He insisted that he could convince Doctor Pao-lin to take us back to the lobby of the Fontainebleau. I finally convinced Craig that once Doctor Pao-lin knew that I knew Zolotov's address we would be really sunk. All he had to do to get it was hypnotize me!

Since we didn't see Doctor Pao-lin or Chang Yu until many, many months later, Craig never got the chance to prove whether he was right or wrong. The whirlpool we had ventured too closely to finally sucked us inexorably down into worse horrors.

Sitting in the cramped little bathroom, both of us naked, we used Manya's scissors to trim the postscript off Zolotov's letter. When we finished it looked as if Zolotov had just used a half sheet of paper to finish the last page. If the letter were found on us, our persecutors still wouldn't know where to find Zolotov. Craig insisted, since I had no place to hide it, that he should keep the letter. I wanted to destroy it, but Craig argued that it was the only evidence that proved we weren't completely mad . . . that Zolotov actually did exist and had stated in his own handwriting that he had made gold from lead. If we ever escaped, we could bring the letter to top government officials. We could reveal the whole monstrous business.. Maybe then all the international spies in the world would stop demanding a pound of our flesh.

I suppose I rejected the unappetizing idea that we both might be dead by morning. The thought was trickling through my mind that if we could escape, perhaps I could meet Zolotov in Brussels. I could show him the letter he had written to Manya, and tell him what we had been through. Maybe then I could persuade him that we should be silent partners to his wealth. Because, while Zolotov's letter revealed two things to Craig: that Zolotov had actually made gold, and where Zolotov would be two months from now; it told me something else in addition. That in some ways Zolotov was very much like me, that he had achieved the dream of all the poverty-stricken people in the

99

world . . . He, the serf, could thumb his nose at kings. He, Zolotov, could be more powerful than anyone. The rich and the wealthy living their lives on inherited wealth; the aristocracy of money, peopled by morons in Palm Springs, São Paulo, the Riviera, Paris, London, Rome; the conniving politicians and rapacious dictators were all victims of his discovery. But, of course, after years of impecunious frustration poor Zolotov was quite mad. He needed me, Marge Wentworth. I would convince him to use his discovery for his own power. To hell with equality and fraternity. We would enjoy the unfailing liberty of money!

I was quite certain, at this juncture—knowing that we were walking the edge of a precipice, about to slip and plunge into a boiling hell below—that Craig would only have one thought in his mind; exposing Zolotov's secret to the world. It took some doing, but I finally persuaded Craig, since I had no other clothes except my improvised diaper and bra, that if we were going to be kidnapped I could probably persuade our captors to let me keep my mink coat. Before he could change his mind I quickly sewed Zolotov's letter and Manya's passports into the lining of it. They scarcely created a bulge.

We waited drearily through the next morning. Our Chinese guards didn't arrive with breakfast. By noontime we were reduced to sharing one orange left over from yesterday's breakfast. From the window the motel seemed to be quite deserted. Craig had almost convinced me that we should force the screen out of the window and make a run for it. I was helping him put pressure on it, hoping we could push it out of the frame without too much noise when a closed panel truck lettered on the side DING HOW, CHINESE LAUNDRY, backed swiftly into the courtyard and stopped in front of our room. Three grinning Chinese climbed out of it, took the padlock off our door, greeted us with smiles, and no obvious weapons of warfare. "Lie down on floor." A big paunchy one grinned at us. "No talk back. Hands behind back, please."

Craig must have thought it was our only chance. With a snarl of anger he slugged the fat one in the stomach. Almost simultaneously, he swung at his jaw. God knows how he expected to take them all on. But the big fellow didn't need any help. Craig's blow only made his grin grow larger. While his skinny compatriots watched the fat one lowered his head and butted Craig in the middle. In one simple jiu jitsu movement, as easy as flopping an egg, he stretched Craig flat on the floor. I screamed, positive that he must have broken Craig's back. Stunned by the impact of his fall all Craig could do was stare up at the grinning Buddha. Cursing, he lay on the floor helpless. My body ached for him.

Agreeing with our captors that it was too warm, I scrambled into my mink coat. Fighting furiously with one of the skinnier ones I pummeled him while he tried to yank it off me.

"Not need," he kept insisting. "Very warm. Too hot." I knew what the rat had in mind. He was going to give my lovely coat to his girl friend or sell it. The more he tugged the more I yelled. I hung desperately onto the coat. They were going to have to knock me out to get it. Finally the fat Buddha intervened. He stared at my rose covered breasts approvingly. For a second I thought he was going to snatch off my bra. Then he said, "Okay, you keep. Only shut damn mouth. Lie down on belly."

In a few seconds they tied us hand and foot. Tearing up what was left of one of Manya's dresses, they gagged Craig first to stop his cursing. Then they forced the cloth into my open mouth, and bound it around my head. This not seeming to satisfy them they blindfolded us. I felt myself being swung into the air. We were being carried to the truck. Craig was dumped beside me on what seemed to be an old mattress. It was permeated with the smell of sweat and urine. I heard the doors slam.

The truck jerked to life. I was a blind and tongueless creature rolling from side to side as we swerved onto the highway. We were in the truck for nearly eight hours. Where they took us I can only guess. Probably to the docks in Miami. The actual ride wasn't too long. But then they parked the truck in the direct sunlight. It took only a few minutes to know that being imprisoned in this steel casket was equivalent to slow cremation.

The damned Chinaman was right. I certainly didn't need my precious mink coat. I could feel rivers of sweat running down my armpits. Slowly the coat turned into a stinking sponge of hot wet fur. I fought at the ropes around my hands and legs. The more I pulled the tighter they gripped me. The saliva in my mouth had dried up. My tongue felt huge and swollen. My wracking sobs produced no tears. The water in my body was slowly boiling out. Were Craig and I being left to die in this black hell hole?

As my body lost its water I began to feel dizzy. I prayed that I would faint or just die. I could hear Craig fighting at his bonds. His body thrashed against mine. I tried to nuzzle my face against his and discovered to my horror that he had evidently been tossed in feet first. Somehow, I got to my knees and bumped against Craig who had managed the same feat. Blindly we rubbed our dripping faces against each other, grotesquely trying to rub off our blindfolds so that we could at least see each other. It was hopeless. The cloth had been tied too tight. I tried to mumble, I love you . . . I'm sorry, but I knew that no sound came out. We were blind and dumb slave creatures, groveling in an insane sweat dance. I crumpled against Craig, felt him stiffen trying to hold my weight and then he collapsed sideways.

When they opened the truck I was delirious. I felt the cool night air on my legs and face. But I was so nearly unconscious that I only have faint memories of the sound of voices, the throbbing of a powerful marine engine, and the dim realization that I must be on a fast power boat bound for God knew where. Blessedly someone tore off my gag, and water, cool water, was poured on my face. Someone pulled me erect by my hair and held a cup of water to my lips. I drank it greedily and retched until my throat ached. Finally I must have lost consciousness.

I have recollections of Craig, stripped to his shorts, spooning food into my mouth, and moments when I was suddenly aware that I must be in the cabin of a ship. In a tiny room, I was on a lower bunk, stretched out, naked. Flat on my back, I was screaming. I could hear myself but I couldn't make myself stop. Craig was leaning over me, his face unshaven. He was wiping my forehead. And then as if the fog had blown away in a cool wind, I finally recognized him.

"Oh, my God, Craig," I moaned. "Where are we?"

"Searching for pots of gold," he said bitterly. "You damned near died of dehydration."

"What about you?"

"We both damn near died. You've been like this for a day and a night. I guess it's night. It's continual night in here. They painted the porthole black."

I sat up slowly in the bunk and stared at my new surroundings. The cabin we were in was about eight feet wide and fifteen feet long. An upper and lower bunk, a chair, a washstand and a toilet was all it contained.

"First class accommodations to hell," Craig said following my glance. "You better eat. The Captain himself brought it in a little while ago. Cold rat meat stew. On the other hand maybe you should wait. After the interested way that he examined your naked corpse he may be a necrophiliac. He muttered in Pidgeon English that you looked as if you might live. If you survive, our jailkeeper may invite you to a more personal repast. Sliced Marge Wentworth, served live and flopping, with hot blood sauce on a platter. There's enough of you left to feed the crew for a day."

I was in no mood for Craig's ghoulish humor. "Are they taking us to China?" I asked, not really caring. My head ached too hard for interest in anything.

Craig shrugged. He flopped in the chair. I saw my diaper and bra hanging on the towel rack, and realized that I was still naked. Was I ever going to have clothes again? I guessed not. They never dressed captive animals in a zoo. "Who undressed me?"

"How in hell do I know?" Craig sighed. "When I finally realized that I was still living, I discovered you were in the bunk, naked but not very interesting sexually. Being male I have evoked no interest whatsoever. They dumped me in here still wrapped in my sweaty clothes. I undressed myself." Craig pointed at a hook on the wall. "Anyway, you saved your mink. It's still damp with perspiration. Zolotov's letter probably melted."

I tasted the cold stew trying not to gag at the thick grease floating on it. It trickled, like thick molasses, down my throat.

"In case you hadn't noticed," Craig said, wiping the sweat from his forehead, "we must be on a southern cruise. After you have eaten, we'll go up on deck to the pool, and bask in the sunshine with the other tourists."

"Very funny." I groaned. "You said that the Captain was Spanish. Maybe they are taking us to Cuba."

"Marge, this is *your* party, remember," Craig said nastily. "You tell me where we are going."

It was obvious that Craig was silently cursing his fate for ever having wanted to go to bed with Marge Wentworth. But I no longer cared. What did it matter? Even

Zolotov was forgotten. I read a play once called *Outward Bound*. All the passengers were on a vacation ship. Slowly as the play progressed they awoke to the fact that they were all dead. They were really on a final crossing to the next world. Somehow, this seemed much the same. I had died. I had boiled to death in my own fluids. The only reality left was an excruciating headache. Worse, my skull was throbbing, and none of it, not even the salty taste on my lips, was me. I no longer existed. I belonged to anyone who wanted to use me for any purpose.

Slowly I washed my face scarcely recognizing my reflection in the cloudy mirror over the basin. My eyes were sunken. With no make up, I was pale and ghastly. My hair was snarled; an uncombed, tangled mess. I was a picture of a female Dorian Gray . . . deteriorated, ravished by her own greed.

Craig was lying on the bunk, and I was sitting on the toilet, no longer even embarrassed by the fecal functions of this robot woman, when I heard the key turn in the lock. The cabin door opened. A massive chested man, well over six feet tall, wearing a Captain's hat and a well washed navy blue shirt, open at the neck, stared at me. A grin spread slowly over his face, lifting his bushy black moustache over clean white teeth, making his full lower lip a leering, jack-o-lantern curve.

Unperturbed, he waited. He didn't even have the good grace to turn his back. Hopelessly, I just sat there and finished my business. A far call from the Marge Wentworth of less than a week ago who would never have tolerated any man in a bathroom with her. Something in me had snapped. I was no longer a unique, private person.

"You come with me, now," he said finally. He took my mink and threw it over my shoulders.

Craig had been watching him dully. "Where in hell are you taking her?" The sound of his voice revealed his disinterest. The Captain probably could have said I was going to be fed to the sharks. Craig would have simply agreed that it was a fitting denouement to this morality play.

"You sleep," the big man said to him. He shoved me into the hallway and locked the cabin door after him. "I am Captain Fernanda . . . Carlos Fernanda," he said, leading me along the passageway and up a narrow companion way. We emerged on the sunwashed deck of a freighter. Squinting, trying to adjust my eyes to light again after hours of darkness, Fernanda led me up to the captain's bridge. Below us I could see a few men, near the prow, scraping rust and painting the deck a patchwork of bright orange. The throb of the engines vibrated the metal floor plates beneath my feet. We were moving slowly across a pale blue ocean. Lightly rippled by a hot wind, it extended to the horizon on all sides of us.

Fernanda led me up to the bridge. An unshaven man with bloodshot eyes stood at the helm. He stared insolently at me, then spoke angrily in Spanish to Fernanda. I listened uncomprehending, dismayed by the man's sheer ugliness. My eyes were rooted to a livid hairless scar that looked as if someone had once attempted to slice off one side of his face. Fernanda's answer to him was brusque. Angrily, the man turned back to his work.

Fernanda opened a door behind the bridge. Grinning he led me inside to what I realized must be the Captain's quarters. "El Cuchillo, ees preety mad," Fernanda said. "He say you half heese. I tell heem, money half heese. Moca, all mine."

I looked at him puzzled.

"Moca ees girl in Portuguese." Fernanda chuckled. "El Cuchillo means the knife, in Spanish. He preety bad fellow."

I didn't know whether I was shivering from the coolness of Fernanda's quarters or the apparent fact that I was some kind of spoil that would have to be divided between the two of them. Given the choice I voted overwhelmingly for Fernanda who at least looked as if he washed himself once in a while. After the sunlight Fernanda's quarters were a black, musty cave. Walled in dark mahogany with worn leather chairs, a couch, a desk, and a bed in the far corner it was permeated with the lion's odor of male sweat and cigar smoke. The lion, who inhabited this cave, tossed his cap on the bed, picked up a fifth of whiskey, and took a long swallow. He stared belligerently at me, his expression saying, let's not waste time. He shoved the bottle at me obviously wishing to warm me up.

I shook my head, refusing the offer.

Fernanda took another swallow of whiskey. "Take off coat, please," he said, grinning. In anticipation he wiped his moustache on his sleeve.

"I'd rather not," I said. I tried to keep my voice from quaking. From the look in his eyes, and the spittle forming at the corner of his lips, I half expected that he was going to rip it off me. I knew I could scream and put up a token fight, but the thought occurred to me that he might suddenly decide to give me to El Cuchillo. At a wave of his hand he could make me the ship's whore. If I was going to be raped, it seemed the better part of logic to encourage Fernanda to take a proprietary interest in my sexual organs.

I still hugged my coat around me. I tried to stop trembling. Surprisingly Fernanda made no move. "No one say no to Carlos Fernanda!" He chuckled and took another swallow. "Eeef Carlos say yes, you not argue." He shrugged. "Seet down. Be comfortable. You my guest. Two weeks we leeve together, right here."

"Get your guest something to wear," I suggested. I tried to ignore the implication in his accent on "leeve." "Mocas don't like to be naked."

That made Carlos laugh. "No clothes for girls." He opened a closet and produced a cotton shirt the same color as his. It looked cooler and more practical than my coat. There was no alternative. I took off my coat and put on Carlos' shirt, ignoring his wide-eyed interest as I buttoned it over my breasts. I rolled up the sleeves. The shirt hung just above my knees.

"Very preety. Very easy to take off." Carlos picked a large guitar off a hook on the wall. He sat down behind his desk, planked his feet on the edge, and strummed chords idly.

"Will you tell me where you are taking us?"

"Thees sheep ees on way to Chile."

"Chile!" I looked at him shocked.

It wasn't possible. "What happened to the Chinaman who kidnapped us?"

Carlos accompanied his answer with soulful chords. "Carlos feel vairy bad. Carlos sell hees soul for damned Yankee dollar. Twenty thousand, they geeve us. Five for El Cuchillo, five for Carlos. Take thees two prisoners to Valparaiso. When you deliver, get ten thousand more. Een harbor Chinese sheep waiting." Carlos put the guitar down on his desk. "Why thees Communists want you in China?" He took another swallow of whiskey.

Slowly the pieces of the puzzle were coming together. For the moment, so far as Carlos Fernanda was concerned, Craig and I were just a business transaction. We were on our way to Chile. It would take two weeks. Time at least to figure a way to escape. We had two weeks before we were irretrievably on our way to China. There was another ray of hope. Carlos had not attacked me. He was drinking considerably for a man in charge of a ship. Did he feel guilty? Could I convince him to free Craig and me at some port along the way? What would be the price? What did I have to offer? A mink coat? My body? Zolotov's letter? I soon found out that

Carlos had only one thing on his mind. A complaisant female!

Fifteen

The first night Carlos took the midnight watch. Far below us the prow cut a glittery white path through the dark water. Silently, I watched the evening stars moving across the sky. For an hour or two we said nothing. Carlos seemed lost in his thoughts. I was worried about Craig. I wondered how I could get him free from the prison below. Finally, I invented a story about Craig and myself. Attempting somehow to evoke Carlos' sympathy, I told him that we worked for a newspaper syndicate. We had uncovered an international spy ring operating out of Miami. We were about to expose the whole set-up to the F.B.I. when they kidnapped us. I told Carlos that I loved Craig, and we were going to be married.

All the time I was talking I kept trying to fathom what was going on in Carlos' mind. If he even had a mind. He fiddled with various instruments and charts, only half listening. Did he know more about us than he had told me? Did he even understand me? I had tried to keep my English simple.

"You are Spanish, I think," I said.

He spat on the floor. "Spanish ees peegs. Carlos ees Portugese." Carlos looked at me grimly. "That peeg El Cuchillo, my mate. He ees Spanish. He vairy mad. Lock you up, he say. Keep out of beeg trouble when we get to Valparaiso. Carlos tell heem, go sheet himself! Carlos do what he do!"

At six o'clock in the morning El Cuchillo reappeared on the bridge to take his watch. He stared angrily at me but said nothing. Carlos spoke to him briefly, evidently giving him instructions.

Back in Carlos' quarters a grinning Spanish seaman brought us a breakfast of melon, eggs, cereal, coffee and toast. Although I was starved, I refused to eat. "Please Carlos," I pleaded. "Bring my friend up here. Let him eat with us."

Carlos chewed his toast. He grinned at me as if I was quite silly not to realize that three is a crowd. "Your fran get plenty to eat. Not worry. You leeve here. He leeve down there." He thumped the floor ominously to prove he meant it.

I finally ate my breakfast while Carlos watched, delighted with my appetite.

All through the night I had fought to keep myself awake. I was certain that I would have to somehow keep Carlos at bay. I had to keep him in control while I figured some way to get Craig out of his prison. I had learned from the freighter's navigation chart that in less than a day we would go through the Panama Canal. As I ate I cajoled Carlos, offering him a simple plan. Just before we entered the Canal at Colon, he could lower a rowboat in the Bay of Limon, and let us go. He could tell the Chinese that we had jumped overboard. "Please, Carlos," I begged. Seeing this had no effect I tried a new tack. "You are a good man. I know you are. You hate this filthy business. I can tell. Maybe somewhere you have a wife, a girl friend, a mother. If I were your sister, would you want me sold to the Chinese? . . . I would be put in a whorehouse, tortured! God would never forgive you!"

Carlos listened without comment. "We sleep now," he said, locking the cabin door. "Seex hours we stay een bed." He quickly undressed down to his shorts, and pulled back the cover on the bed. "Get een first please. Carlos have no wife. Carlos girl fran, she not wait for heem. Carlos teenk God not geeve a damn. Make man

110

to feet woman. Make woman so she like eet. God be very happy. Two parts together feel much better!" He took off his shorts and smiled beguilingly at me. "Take off shirt, now. Please not to be damned seely."

I looked at him dismayed. Carlos was in a state of enthusiasm that was going to be hard to deflate with words alone. I shivered. Should I let him? Should I just lie down and get it over with? Where was the sophisticated Marge Wentworth now? I knew that I had given Craig the impression that I was an experienced female who knew the facts of life. The truth was that the only other man I had ever made love with was a boy named Elmer in high school. That episode had lasted about five minutes. I remember crying for a week over my lost virginity. Neither Elmer nor I ever attempted the unhappy business together again. Craig wouldn't believe it, probably. All the time I've known Craig, I've never been sure that the image of the worldly sophisticated lover that he thought was Marge Wentworth wasn't actually the lure that had kept him attached to me for the past two years.

Perhaps, if any females read the Misadventures of Marge Wentworth, they will think that I am altogether too pragmatic. In my place they would have preferred to die than to submit to Carlos . . . or at least they would have protected their virtue to the bitter end. But really, when you have made the mistake of grabbing a bull by the horns, it does seem unrealistic to let go. You could be gored to death before you managed to tame the beast.

Factually, Carlos looked manly enough to please any female. A bit hairy, with a ruddy complexion, a heavy chest, that tapered into slim hips and muscular calves and legs. Although he hadn't yet forced me, it was apparent that he was either going to have me, or burst from internal combustion. No matter what happened it couldn't be quite so bad as it might seem to be in the

111

telling. Still, it's the better part of female valor to offer whatever resistance a female can muster.

"I'm filthy," I said demurely. "I need a bath."

"Carlos not geeve a damn how you smell." He grinned invitingly at me and lay on the bed waiting for me to join him.

"I give a damn!" I said. "Furthermore I'm not the kind of girl who just jumps in the sack with any man. I have to love a man to want to do that with him."

"Carlos luv you already," he said seriously. "Een a little while you learn to luv Carlos. Everytheeng can be vairy nice."

I shook my head, still hoping I might squirm out of this contretemps. "Please Carlos, let me bathe first." I thought that Carlos might take the hint and decide he needed a bath too. A dash of cold water might extinguish the flame.

Reluctantly, he got off the bed, put on his shorts, grabbed a towel, and with a disgusted look at El Cuchillo, as we passed him, Carlos led me below to what must have been the boat shower locker. In a few minutes he turned the place into a steaming inferno. With much laughter and obvious enjoyment, ignoring my screaming as I was blinded by the spray that plastered my hair against my head, Carlos soaped me from head to foot. He stopped here and there, washing parts of me with assiduous interest and too damned much enjoyment. I could see by the state he was in that my plan had miscarried. Since he didn't seem to care whether he washed himself or not I returned the favor, making sure that this hairy, male statue of a man was scrupulously clean as a newborn baby. While the water poured over him and I scrubbed, the big oaf kept kissing any part of me that got within his reach. Evidently my laundering was altogether too effective. Carlos finally couldn't stand it any longer. With a groan of sheer pleasure, making a scissor out of my legs, he lifted

112

me off the slippery shower floor, and in a gigantic convulsion that swept me along with him, he finished his business.

Still holding me, spreadeagled, he grinned at me appreciatively. "Vairy long time Carlos not have woman." Slowly he put me down. "Now, you marry Carlos! Take bath every day. Carlos decide . . . not geeve you to damn Chinese."

In tennis you would call it "my advantage." If I was going to continue to play this love game, I had to serve well and fast. A few minutes later, lying in bed with Carlos, his arm around me, his hand fondling my breasts, I tried to keep him awake long enough to exact something in exchange. Desperately, I tried not to think about Craig. I knew without asking what he would think of me. The conventional morality would condemn Marge Wentworth to purgatory and hellfire forever. To me (and I think a great many females would agree with me) what I had done with Carlos more or less willingly was only what I was going to have to do ultimately, agreeable or not. It certainly lacked cosmic significance. Carlos' lips on mine, or his genitals inside mine, were simply the response of a healthy male to a female. It was not an experience I would have chosen. I felt no love for Carlos. On the other hand I felt no great dislike for him. I simply had avoided being raped. I was now in a position to trade favors.

I make this point, not only for Craig who will probably read this book and never understand, but also for any male novelist who may chance on its pages. Females in their hearts are considerably more amoral than the moral or immoral fantasies of our book club selections would suggest.

Of course, I didn't know what was going on in Carlos' mind as he listened sleepily to my proposals. If he would let Craig go, set him free in Colon or Panama City I would become his mistress. Yes, I would even

113

marry him and travel around the world with him on a freighter. (What the devil is it about me that I bring out the protective instinct in males who seem bent on legally eliminating my freedom?)

Carlos fell asleep, a happy smile on his face, without making any effort to participate in my monologue. But around noontime, when he awoke, rediscovered his sleepy bed companion, and began to ply me with renewed ardor, I was more adamant.

"Can't do," he kept insisting. "Plenty beeg trouble now weeth El Cuchillo. Money we get half hees. Besides we not dock at Colon or Panama City. Not stop anywhere unteel Valparaiso."

"And then you are going to turn us over to the Chinese?"

Carlos shook his head violently. "Not you. Carlos keep you. Find Priest. Get married, presto." He shook his moustache happily over my breasts.

"Not on your life. No more," I said indignantly. I jumped out of the bed. "You don't love me. I don't believe you." I put on his shirt, and tried to stare at him with a poker face. "If you expect to marry me, you've got to let Craig go." This was pretty kooky conversation. Did he really believe that in less than a day of knowing him, after being forced to make love with him, that I would even consider marrying him? I crossed my fingers hoping that somehow I was getting through to the big grinning grizzly bear. "When you go through the locks in the Canal you can lower a boat somewhere. Put Craig on it. He has enough money to fly home. The Canal Zone is a United States protectorate."

Carlos grabbed my arm, and dragged me back on the bed. "Let heem go! He tell poleece!" Carlos looked at me suspiciously. "You theenk Carlos one dumb bastard?"

I silently admitted the thought was on my mind. "Carlos," I said soothingly. "Craig doesn't even know where he is. He doesn't know what the name of this ship is, or what your destination is. For that matter I don't know the name of this ship. It you blindfold him and row him ashore, he'll never know where he has been."

Carlos started to fiddle with me under my shirt. "All right, Carlos not promise. He theenk about eet."

It was still my advantage . . . but Carlos' serve. For such a fierce looking opponent he was remarkably gentle, preferring a pleasantly extended volley to a blitzkrieg attack. To my amazement he started to whisper to me erotically in French as well as Portuguese. "J'ai apprais le francais dans l'ecole en Lisboa," he said. "Apprendre L'anglais, j'etudais les livres 'sexy.' " Carlos gestured to a pile of paperback books on his desk. "Je ne le parle pas, tres bien . . . mais quand tu m'epouseras je te promettrai apprendre au lit avec toi." While I could understand him very well, I quickly discovered that his limping English was less dangerous. Finally, he hastily dressed. He apologized for locking me in the cabin. "Not to keep you een . . . to keep El Cuchillo out. Carlos be vairy beezy today." He grinned. "Tu dors ma jolie amour, ce soir Carlos te baisera de tete a pied. Ah, ces bonnes bossoirs!"

I was left alone with my wild thoughts and tears for the rest of the day. Sobbing until I had no tears left, I tried to figure how I was ever going to escape from my mad Portuguese captor who seemed bent on spending a large portion of his life making love to me.

Less than two weeks ago I had been a proud woman; my own mistress, with my own body, my own person. I could give myself or not as I chose. What had happened to me? What flaw in my personality was responsible for turning me into a slave-whore? If it hadn't been Zolotov and his damned gold would I have discovered some other means for my own self-destruction? Was I really the mercenary that Craig thought I was? Even if I managed to get poor Craig free what would happen to me? Instead of sitting on the control end of the see-saw, was I destined to live suspended in the air, a perpetual victim of my own greed? I hated myself. Walking aimlessly around the cabin, naked . . . what was the use of even putting on Carlos' shirt? . . . I noticed a calendar. What day was it? The past eight, or was it ten days, had run together so insanely that time had no meaning. But suddenly it did! Frantically, I counted the days. Over and over again. No amount of arithmetic would change the facts. I should be having my period right now! I knew that I should have taken those pills for at least four more days than I had. I had always been very regular. There was no doubt about it! if Craig hadn't got me pregnant, or if I was delayed (God knew that I had been through enough to change the cycle of a female elephant) then Carlos had most certainly sealed my fate.

Hopelessly, I ripped off the page of the calendar and started to count days all over again. There was no escaping the gruesome fact. Nine months from now in late July, I would be the mother of somebody's child. Discounting Chang Yu . . . or Doctor Pao-lin (they just couldn't have!) the father was probably Craig . . . but if I were delayed it could be Carlos. I couldn't be sure until I discovered whether the poor thing would have slant eyes or a moustache!

To get my mind off the dreary subject, I tried peering out the one porthole in the cabin. I could see only pale blue water and sky merging. It was unbearably hot. Even naked, perspiration kept dripping off my face. I tied Carlos' shirt underneath my breasts and knotted it behind my back. Lifted, they felt cooler underneath. In a mirror in the cabin I decided, with my hair stringy and uncombed, with my face freckled and shiny, my breasts in a crude harness, I was the acme of unvarnished, uninteresting female. The trouble was, Carlos the

116

primitive man, didn't seem to care for cultural refinements.

The thoughts of how I could . . . solicit? . . Craig's freedom, and whether I was pregnant circled wearily in my brain. Finally, in desperation, I took a couple of swallows of whiskey from the bottle on Carlos' desk. Listlessly, I picked up one of the sleazy sexy paperbacks on Carlos' desk. The hours passed drearily. I had a sensation that the engines on the freighter had stopped. There was a lot of shouting. From the porthole I could see we were in some kind of berth, but I could see no people. I guessed that we were in one of the locks of the Panama Canal.

I finally immersed myself in a book called *Sex Thieves* . . . trying to discover both how Carlos had learned English, and what males in general found exciting about females. Here was a girl named Leah in this book by a male author, . . . "She felt her entire body aflame. (Maybe she had poison ivy) Leah had never seen a man nude. (Poor thing) How marvellous, she thought, that someone (God-almighty!) had designed such a perfect matching. She was soft and rounded with a well for his love (well, well!) and he was hard and angled (ye gods, I hope not right-angled) and ready to fill her need (so that's what men called it). He lay next to her. She breathed him in (through her nostrils, I hope) warm and clean with a nice strong male odor. (He, whoever he was, forgot to use a deodorant) He dropped his hands to Leah's hips, and pulling, he pressed their bodies together for the initial contact (position number six, rear entry, dog style). Then he rolled her back, crouching over her. "Leah, I don't want to hurt you." (Ha, a gentleman!) "I'm not afraid," Leah said. (Silly ass . . . wait until nine months from now) He smiled down on her. "It'll hurt just a little at first but after that it will be nice" (Now, how in hell does he know?) Leah arched her body and he was crashing through the barrier (A

117

virgin, quel mess!) He set loose the emotions inside her. (Get out of here with that horrible thing) It was a wild, wild ecstasy. She clung to him curling about him (a gymnast, no doubt). She cried, crooned as he made love to her (I'm in love with you, Sunny!) driving against her (A rough go, old boy) and making her soar higher and higher like a bird with wings spread full, sweeping with the current. (Yipee!) His love lifted her up, up up (The man should be at Cape Kennedy) Leah realized in that moment was the essence of her existence (to be a penis deflator . . . some essence) that this was the reason for being a woman. She thought it was the most wonderful knowledge in the world. (Why the hell go to college when you can learn the whole business on your back) They went higher. (This was a secret weapon that would beat the Russians to the moon, for sure) He loved her with yet harder drive. (Love is a rocket engine) Thrusting, plunging, pushing her to her peak. (This guy never studied the female anatomy) where her soul surveyed everything (The poor thing must be at the pearly Gate) the whole scope of creation, the male and female of each living thing. (Ah, I get it, he was lubricated with LSD) She was at a sacred moment, a place where each woman comes, (X marks the spot) an experience that never can be shared with another being except the man who brings her there. (Well, this guy is trying, I suppose) Then, poised on the edge of oblivion, their bodies met in a final heaving sigh of fulfillment, and with a cry of passion, completed and satisfied, Leah went limp against him." (and he rolled over and snored)

I flung the silly damned book across the room just as Carlos opened the cabin door. It hit him in the stomach, and he grunted. "That's a hell of a way to learn English," I said. "Reading feelthy books ees vairy bad!"

"Not blame you be mad. Carlos preety beezy. Look out. Now we in Gatun Lake."

I looked out the porthole. Against the afternoon sky I could see a green mountain and small islands. "Where's Gatun Lake?"

"Panama Canal. We go up in the air eighty feet. Through the Gatun Locks."

I scowled at him. While the engines had been turned off and we were passing through one of the seven wonders of the world, I was reading sexy books. I suppose this was what they meant when they said join the navy and see the world. The engines were vibrating again. We were moving under our own power. Eight or nine (or was it ten) days ago Marge Wentworth had been a sober, unpregnant secretary to the President of a Connecticut bank. Now, in some kind of fantastic nightmare, she was the mistress of a Portugese sea captain . . . on a forced honeymoon through the Panama Canal.

"Please," I pleaded, suddenly feeling quite tipsy from the whiskey I had drunk, "This is educational. I've never been through the Panama Canal. Can't I go on deck and watch?"

Carlos shook his head. "Not now. On return treep. Then we married. You see everything, tout le monde."

I wanted to laugh. This was so damned unbelievable. At least my baby would have a father. But what about Craig (the real father . . . I prayed)? "You haven't let Craig go. Are you going to put him ashore or aren't you?" I hoped Carlos understood the equivocation. If he insisted on playing this marriage game, there had to be some dowry.

"I do eet. Tomorrow. After we go through the Miraflores Locks. We be in Pacific."

Carlos pointed to a map on the wall. "See . . . thees Panama Ceety. Here ees Las Perlas. Leeve your fran there."

I looked at the tiny chain of islands on the map about fifty miles from Panama City in the Gulf of Panama.

119

In the middle of the ocean they looked tiny and deserted. "Why not Panama City? He could fly home from there."

Carlos shook his head. "Your fran can find poleece from there. Too queek. We leeve heem here in rowboat . . . take no chance. He twenty miles from Panama . . . row here." Carlos pointed at the map. "From here back to Panama Ceety about seexty miles . . . all jungle. Take a week . . . maybe more to get back. Not worry. Plenty nice Chocos Indian girls een jungle . . . wear no clothes . . . make your fran vairy happy. By time he find poleece . . . we in Valparaiso," Carlos chuckled. "Priest, he say to you . . . you take thees man, leeve happy ever after!"

I listened to Carlos astonished. It was impossible. He couldn't do this to Craig. But no entreaties prevailed on him. He didn't really trust me. Beside there would be trouble enough with El Cuchillo.

"He theenk, Carlos soft in head. Say eef Carlos must keep girl, then stick knife een her fran's back. Toss heem overboard." Carlos looked as if he might be weighing the idea. "Maybe, he right. El Cuchillo not like thees beezness."

I shuddered. It was quite obvious that if I pushed Carlos too far, prudence might replace his sexual starvation, or he might even begin to think that bachelorhood had its merits.

I finally persuaded Carlos to let me say good bye to Craig, but not until I had given him further tangible assurances that I really was "hees moca."

Feeling like a captive doll, almost embarrassed to see Craig again, trying to convince myself that what I was doing was our only hope, I let Carlos lead me below deck. He unlocked the cabin door, shoved me in, with the warning that he would be back soon.

Craig hugged me, trembling, with tears in his eyes. "My God, what has that bastard done to you?" he demanded.

120

Then he recognized Carlos' shirt. "I see you have given up mink." Craig's voice was bitter. "You always *were* the practical one . . . when in Rome . . . What in hell else did you do to accommodate the Romans?"

"Craig, for God's sake," I sobbed. "What could I do? We are slave prisoners. No matter what I did, I love you. I've persuaded Carlos to let you go."

"Let me go . . . *your* Carlos is going to let me go?" Craig looked at me angrily. "You little bitch. I suppose you've talked Carlos into filling the gap. You've told him that Horace Zolotov is somewhere at the end of the rainbow waiting with his pot of gold just for Carlos and you." Craig squeezed my arm menacingly. "Just how did you persuade Carlos to let me go? I can't wait to hear the sickening details."

"You are hurting me," I said, squirming out of his iron grip. "Don't be a damned fool. No matter what I have done, or what I have to do, I am at least trying to save your life. Carlos is going to put you overboard in a life boat in the Gulf of Panama . . . near some islands called Las Perlas. No matter what happens to you, you won't end up in a Chinese prison for the rest of your life. If you can get back to Panama City, before the Chinese get me. . . ." I decided not to tell Craig that Carlos had other plans for me. "Well, anyway if you can reach the authorities in Panama in time you may be able to save me."

The truth was that I was beginning to wonder whether I should be saved from Carlos or from the Chinese. All Doctor Pao-lin wanted to do was hypnotize me. I had an idea that Carlos had visions of me on a farm in Portugal, jumping up and down barefoot in a wine barrel, with our nineteen children, as we pressed our harvest of grapes while Carlos played the guitar and gathered strength to plant the seed for the twentieth brat.

Craig listened to my somewhat censored story sullenly.

I was tampering with his life again. How did I know that being dumped into the sea in a rowboat, trying to find his way back to Panama City through jungles and insects and man-eating alligators wasn't even more dangerous than accepting fate and going with me to China? What the hell right did I have to decide? All I was really doing, once again, was trying to save my own neck at his expense.

I tried to suggest to him that if he really loved me, he would want to do it. "You do love me, don't you?" I said. I hugged him and kissed him through his forest of whiskers and told him that he looked very masculine and rugged.

"I don't know whether I love you or not," Craig said mororsely. "I loved Marge Wentworth, ten days ago, B. Z., Before Zolotov. Now I realize that there are aspects of you that I never realized existed."

I silently agreed with him. But, no matter what, I knew that I had to convince him to leave the ship. "Please, Craig. I'm no different . . . please," I murmured. "Make love to me."

I suppose that this was fiddling while Rome burned. I suppose that, practically speaking, coming from the arms of Carlos to the arms of Craig makes me appear promiscuous and pretty cold blooded; not to say downright immoral. But I did love Craig. The embryo gathering strength in me was in all probability part of his doing. He had been so damned determined to get me pregnant. While I was determined to keep this fact a secret for a while, surely he might as well continue to have the enjoyment—a small recompense for the mess I had involved him in.

Some females must have an amazing capacity for the pleasures of the couch. In the past six days, I had, as the author of *Sex Thieves* described it, travelled "up, up, up, up," more times than I cared to count. Strangely

122

the trip never got boring. My only fear at the moment was that Carlos might attempt to reclaim me in the middle of things. If that happened there would be no doubt that Craig and I would both spend our declining years in China.

Fortunately, Craig and I were talking dispassionately when he returned. Well, not quite dispassionately. Craig was angry with me all over again. He insisted that he would refuse to leave the ship. Then suddenly he had a better idea. If I thought it was such a breeze to make a sixty mile trek through the jungle, why couldn't I persuade Carlos to put us *both* overboard in the rowboat? I was trying to figure out how to explain to Craig that it was too late, "the guests were met, the feast was set," and I was willy nilly going to be snatched up by my hairy Lochinvar when Carlos terminated the discussion.

"She not go weeth you," he told Craig, bursting into the cabin with a happy grin. He shoved me into the passageway. "No worry. Carlos not geeve her to Chinese. Carlos geeve her bath every day. She geeve Carlos plenty love every day."

"It's not true, Craig!" I wailed as Carlos slammed the cabin door shut. I can still see the shock and utter disbelief on Craig's face. I wondered if he would ever trust me, or any female, again as long as he lived.

El Cuchillo was at the helm when Carlos returned with me. Before either of us realized what was happening, El Cuchillo grabbed my arm, yelling at me in Spanish. Angry spittle leaked out the corners of his mouth as he shook me. Screaming, I saw him slip a long, thin knife from a scabbard in his waistband. From the look on his face, I thought he was going to shove it through my chest. I was going to die. God knew I deserved it. But the knife whizzed by my cheek. Carlos had wrenched him so fast and quickly away from me that I wondered if El Cuchillo's arm had come loose at the socket. Off balance, El Cuchillo skidded across the bridge and landed on a table piled with navigation charts. Carlos didn't wait for him to recover. He grabbed El Cuchillo by the throat and squeezed. I think he would have strangled him on the spot if I hadn't screamed. The sight of El Cuchillo's ugly face with his eyes turning blood red and popping out of their sockets made me sick to my stomach. I retched over the side of the ship. When I finally dared to look back El Cuchillo was on his knees, crossing himself and begging for mercy. The white pressure marks of Carlos' fingers were deep and livid on his throat. With a disgusted grunt and finally heeding my pleas, Carlos shoved him off the bridge. Terrified, I watched El Cuchillo limp away. I wondered if maybe it wouldn't have been wiser to have let Carlos murder him. At the same time, I suddenly realized, as I swallowed the bitter juices in my mouth, that Carlos Fernanda might be gentle enough in bed, but he was no man to tamper with.

"Hees a damn greedy one," Carlos said, picking up the maps scattered over the bridge. "He want hees money. Say, all right . . . eef he not got another five thousan, he want hees turn damn queek!"

"His turn?" I shivered. "What does he mean?" I really knew, and I was very much afraid that if Carlos didn't watch out El Cuchillo would get "his turn" whether Carlos or I were agreeable or not.

Carlos shrugged. "Not worry. Carlos take care of heem." And then, as if to reassure me, Carlos switched to French. It was interesting that in a language over which he had command, Carlos' personality seemed to change. He was no longer the heavy handed Captain of a freighter. He was a suave, debonair adventurer speaking mellowly to his lady fair. It was difficult for me to re-orient myself. While I had developed a good speaking knowledge of French in college, it had been

124

three years since I had spoken it much. Whenever I begged him "lentement" Carlos agreeably repeated for me.

While I had been with Craig, Carlos explained, we had passed through the Miraflores Locks. The lights in the distance, on the portside of the ship, were Panama City. In about an hour we would be off Las Perlas. A life boat was ready to be lowered. The boat was stocked with sea rations, a compass, a portable searchlight, and a thirty-eight calibre revolver, with plenty of ammunition. He would give Craig a chart of the waters. Getting Craig aboard, lowering the lifeboat, while the freighter's engines idled, would take not more than ten minutes. While this was being accomplished, since El Cuchillo would be at the helm, I would be locked in Carlos' quarters.

Frightened, I asked him a torrent of questions. It would be dark in an hour. How would Craig find his way? What would happen to Craig? Could he possibly get back to Panama City? I guess I was sobbing because Carlos took the end of my shirt and used it to wipe my eyes.

"Je sais que tu aimes Craig. Ne pleurs pas, ma cherie. Cette experience fera un homme de ce garcon. Si, il meurt . . . c'est mauvaise fortune. Prends, moi, aussi . . . souviens, si je ne t'ai pas apporté a Chile, les Chinois trouveraient une autre personne faire la besogne. Je risque ma vie, parce que je t'aime." Carlos grinned. "C'est la vie, qui sait quand on mourra."

By the time Carlos had finished his disquieting philosophy I was crying even more. If Craig never managed to get back to the United States his death would be my fault. Now, Carlos was telling me that he, too, was risking his life for me, and so what if we all died? I wondered if, somewhere, Horace Zolotov, muttering abracadabra over his pot of lead, realized all the trouble he had caused.

125

Sixteen

According to Robert Burns "the best laid schemes o' mice an' men gang aft a-gley." Locked once more in Carlos' cabin, with El Cuchillo back at the helm, I couldn't understand why Carlos was so confident that he could continue to hold "the knife" at bay. When Carlos changed watches with El Cuchillo I guess he explained in Spanish that he was putting Craig overboard. El Cuchillo listened to him expressionless. The obvious fire may have gone out but I was certain that underneath El Cuchillo's pathetic manner a seething volcano was ready to erupt.

Perhaps females don't underestimate their adversaries as easily as men, but nothing I could say to Carlos about my fears disturbed his supreme certainty that El Cuchillo was a "dumb peeg."

"Not leeve you alone weeth heem," Carlos said, grinning, when he returned to the cabin. "Nevair mind El Cuchillo. Come look, now. See! Your fran gone overboard!"

On the bridge he handed me a telescope. About a half mile over the stern the rippling wake of the ship ended in a small dot on the ocean. In the early twilight, with the sun a red glow on the ocean, I could see Craig rowing for the shore of what looked like a deserted island. My eyes blinded with tears, I gave the telescope back to Carlos, and ran back into his cabin. Carlos rushed after me. He tried to put his arms around me. "You are a rotten bastard," I screamed at him. "I hate you!"

He looked at me puzzled. "Thees, you ask me to do. I do eet!"

"You could have taken him to Valparaiso. You could have saved both of us from the Chinese."

Carlos shrugged. "Why should I do thees? Carlos not

luv heem. Carlos not even sure he save hees own neck."
He unlocked his desk drawer and threw packets of
money on top. "See thees. Ten thousand dollars. Eeen
Valparaiso, the Chinese waiting. We arrive there weeth
you and your fran get ten thousan' more. Not deeleever
you, your fran, not get more money. Worse. Get plenty
trouble. Chinese be damned mad. Who knows? Me, El
Cuchillo, we get our throats sleet." Carlos drew his
finger across his throat. "Carlos damn lucky eef he save
you, and not be dead. You damn lucky Carlos ees boss,
and not El Cuchillo. So please not worry about your
fran. He not worry about you . . . be too busy in
jungle."

With that take it or leave it explanation Carlos shoved
the money back in the drawer, locked the cabin door,
and started to undress. Like it or not I was going to bed
again. I don't know how long Carlos had been without
a woman, but he certainly had stored up a tremendous
amount of energy. "Come een bed," he chuckled.
"While you hug Carlos and kees heem, he tell you
beeg plan."

I shrugged and joined him. What choice did I have?
"Vairy nice thees love beezness," Carlos said, embracing me enthusiastically. "Please not to worry. When
sheep get to Valparaiso we anchor in harbor. Chinese
come queek, but we be queeker. Power boat ready.
Get to docks fast. Today, Carlos radio to owners of
thees sheep, Carlos vairy homeseek. Have month leeve
coming. Chinese geeve us plenty of money. We fly to
Lisbon. Get married queek."

"Doesn't some of that money belong to El Cuchillo?"
I asked trying to restrain my eager suitor.

"What he do?" Carlos leaned over the edge of the bed
and found a bottle of whiskey. "You want to make love
slow? Dans l'amour lentement est douce." He took a
slug from the bottle and handed it to me. "When Chinese not find you, not find your fran, not find Carlos

127

. . . just find El Cuchillo weeth empty bag . . ."
Carlos laughed until I thought he would choke. "El
Cuchillo not need money. Where he going, El Cuchillo
make feesh very happy." Carlos pulled me on top of
him. "Carlos vairy happy. Make you vairy happy now!"
And so began my six day enforced honeymoon. I suppose it really was an ancient form of marriage. The
big chief just picked out the most likely looking babe
in the tribe and took her, or if he had been on a hunting expedition and his men had captured a few ladies
from a neighboring tribe, the bigwig had his choice.
As for the female, she knew eventually it was going to
be one man or another. What did she have to argue
about? Later on, as time went by, the big chiefs went
through the formality of arranging things with mom and
pop. Maybe some money changed hands, or a cow or
two (more valuable than the wife anyway), and the
female got a man. According to Carlos, in his village
in Portugal, the female was introduced to her future
husband by her family. She didn't protest. Females
belonged to males. It was as simple as that. So what
could I expect from a man who had the cool nerve to
not only be certain that I was delighted with him as a
bed mate; who was not only calculating enough to go
on a honeymoon with the money he had received for
abducting the bride, but at the same time had figured
a way to let his partner in the kidnapping take the rap
for the whole business? Craig would probably say that
at last Marge Wentworth had met her match. I wasn't
sure he wouldn't have been right.
I suppose if I hadn't spent a good part of the next five
days wondering how I could escape from Carlos, and
if I had been able to forget that my idyllic bed companion had given me no choice in the matter, it would
have been possible to like Carlos . . . or in another
world, and in another place, have fallen in love with
him. In many ways he was the perfect male; approach-

128

ing me as a warm affectionate lover . . . exalting my femaleness. In the act of love and its prelude, Carlos abandoned any attempt to dominate me. If it took hours, he never hurried until he finally achieved a mutual capitulation.

Nights, when he took the watch he spoke softly to me in French, telling me about himself and the joys of his youth in a small village a few miles outside Lisbon. How his girlfriend whom he loved, as only a young boy can, was married by her father to an older man. How he, bitter and lonely, had left his father's few acres of land and joined the merchant marine. In the songs he sang, accompanying himself on the guitar; songs he called *"fados,"* songs of fate, love and homesickness, Carlos made love to me.

With the warmth of the Portuguese language (which he painstakingly translated for me so that I would understand his music); with the balmy nights and the ocean pale green with white topped ripples extending to the horizon; with the clean smell of the Pacific air in my nostrils; with the joy of wandering the decks of the freighter in the bright sunlight (no longer confined as a prisoner . . . my only fear to stay clear of El Cuchillo); with the smiles of the sailors (I guessed there were about twenty-five men on the ship) and their grins as they maintained their distance but greeted me enthusiastically in Spanish, delighted with my costume, perhaps hoping that Carlos' shirt would blow away from my knees revealing more of me to them; with the freedom of just being a lazy human being, sitting and staring at the sea; with all these emotions adding up the fact that I was really quite insignificant from the standpoint of man or history or the cosmos, I simply abandoned myself to being nothing. I was a Zen Buddhist creature, no longer striving, no longer trying to shape events, finding myself a little by participating in the "not-me" in the world.

One night I tried to explain the feeling to Carlos. He had just finished singing a fados "Porque Te Quero" (Why do I love you?) "Nunca pretenda saber, A razao por que te quero. A razao deste meu querer, Nasceo dum armor sincero". Not knowing what impelled me, feeling lonely and as lost as people anywhere in the world who sang about love that escaped them, I kissed Carlos and in a torrent of words that I was unable to restrain, I told him the real story of Horace Zolotov.

I have to admit that it wasn't quite spontaneous. Lurking in the back of my mind was the thought that if I could get Carlos interested, I might even convince him to fly to Brussels to meet Zolotov. Carlos had the money (really my money when you stop to consider it) given to him by the Chinese for abducting Craig and me. In truth hadn't I earned it, in more ways than one? Also, not to be overlooked, was the fact that if I finally managed to get some clothing to wear, I would become my own person again. When that happened Carlos Fernanda was going to find that he no longer had a suppliant bride to contend with.

Listening to me rattle on about Zolotov, Carlos seemed to be interested. At least until he had finally engineered me into the sack again. But once there, with me being most co-operative, he finally confessed, that for him, a life where one day flowed blissfully into another (with the routine broken only by frequent couplings with me) was far more enjoyable than having all the gold in the world.

"Your Zolotov can keep hees gold," he said, burrowing into my breasts. "Gold ees not soft and warm like thees teets."

While I tried to convince him that these "teets" and all the rest of me was going to be much happier "reech" than poor, Carlos just grinned. "Marga, you vairy much like Carlos . . . All hees life Carlos chase, run, look

130

everywhere for soft, hungry, warm moca who loves heem. You chase after gold. Gold not love you. Soft, hungry mocas nevair geeve a damn for Carlos. Nevair find . . . maybe best . . . keep looking, best way to be happy!"

I finally gave up. All during my teens, my mother taught me a girl's mission was to catch her man; that men were natural bachelors and had to be persuaded to give up the easy job of just supporting themselves. But the world must have changed. First Craig and now Carlos couldn't wait to snare me into their dreams of married bliss.

If I couldn't divert Carlos' wedding intentions with the intrigue of finding Zolotov I was going to have to find some other way of escape. The day before we arrived in the harbor at Valparaiso, I noticed that a number of the crew who had always carefully kept their distance, but seemed friendly enough, were now leering at me and following me with an entirely different expression in their eyes. From being the unattainable chattel of the Captain, I suddenly had the feeling they were planning a division of the wealth program.

I mentioned it to Carlos. "Nevair mind," he scowled, "Eeen seex hours we will be in the harbor. Carlos has the sheep's power boat all ready." He fished a piece of paper out of his pocket. "Radio message thees morning from Chinese sheep, *Yanghu*. She waiting for us een harbor. Soon as we anchor they come aboard fast to get you and your fran." Carlos tossed the paper overboard, and patted my cheek. "Not worry, Marga. We be gone. El Cuchillo be here." Carlos chuckled. "Carlos radio *Yanghu*. 'Very sorry, Captain Fernanda leeve sheep in Panama. Vairy seek. But not worry. El Cuchillo, first mate, in charge. Take care of everytheeng.' "

Carlos explained to me that just as soon as it was dark, I would climb into the power launch which was sus-

131

pended on the portside, midships. I would lie on the floor and wait until he joined me.

"Long drop. Thees sheep empty. Carries nitrate when full. Not worry. We be een water queek. Feefteen meenutes later we be een Valpo."

But Carlos had underestimated El Cuchillo. An hour before we reached the harbor I saw El Cuchillo standing near one of the hatches arguing with five of the crew. I was too far away to hear their words but a heated discussion seemed to be going on. Just as I pointed them out to Carlos, El Cuchillo and the men started to walk menacingly toward the bridge. Carlos started yelling at them in Spanish to go back to work. But they ignored him and quickly climbed to the bridge. With big grins on their faces, two of them and El Cuchillo pointed guns at Carlos and me. El Cuchillo spoke rapidly in Spanish. He made it clear that he was taking over the ship. Unheeding, Carlos tried to yank the gun out of El Cuchillo's hand. Just as he did two of the crew leaped on Carlos. One of them hit Carlos on the back of his head with a blackjack. He slumped unconscious to the floor.

They quickly tied Carlos' arms and legs, carried him into his cabin, and dumped him on his bed. El Cuchillo pushed me into the cabin after them. Shoving me against the wall, using the barrel of the revolver, he lifted the shirt over my breasts, exposing me naked to the crewmen. An excited discussion ensued in Spanish. I wondered if I was going to be raped by all of them. I watched their grinning faces, too terrified to scream. I knew that it was hopeless to beg for mercy. The rage bubbling in El Cuchillo's mind had boiled over. He was going to have his revenge on Carlos. Unfortunately, I was the convenient, coveted object.

"Money?" El Cuchillo said, pressing the gun against my breast. "Dollars, pronto."

I pointed at Carlos' desk. The drawer was locked. El

132

Cuchillo kicked it viciously until it finally opened. Quickly he counted the packs of hundred dollar bills. Then he counted out three one hundred dollar bills for each of the crewmen. Coolly, he shoved the rest in his pocket. Grinning at me, he took my mink coat off the hook on the cabin wall and tossed it at me. It was obvious, like it or not, dressed in high heels, Carlos' shirt and my mink, I was ready for disembarkation.

Ignoring Carlos who was groaning on the bed, El Cuchillo locked him in the cabin. Followed by the crew, he led me below onto the main deck. One of the men climbed into the power launch that was still suspended between davits. Leaning over he grabbed me by the arms. I was hoisted and goosed aboard by grinning crewmen.

In the boat the crewman forced me to lie on the floor. Sitting in the rear seat of the boat he stared down at me. When I tried to wrap my mink coat more securely around me, he persistently rubbed his foot along my thighs and over my stomach, flipping aside the coat, and pushing up my shirt. I finally gave up, deciding that since he was determined to see me stretched out naked on the floor of the boat, it was better to let him look without the necessity of sandpapering me with his shoe. I was frightened beyond tears. The days of freedom with Carlos had been illusory at best. But then there seemed to be some hope. Now, I knew all too clearly what was going to happen to me. I was no longer in the hands of a benevolent dictator. I had a cruel, vindictive master who simply viewed me as desirable female flesh.

The sky grew darker while we waited in the boat. I guessed that we must be coming into the harbor. Overhead, gulls were circling and swooping down on the ship. The weather seemed warmer. I could hear the noise of engines of other ships we were passing. Finally, the vibration of our engines stopped. I heard the rumble of the anchor and the huge splash as it hit the water.

133

Five minutes later El Cuchillo and four of the crew-men scrambled into the boat with us. I was yanked to the seat between El Cuchillo and one of the crew. As the boat was lowered into the water, I could see the crescent shore of Valparaiso, a sickle of trembling lights with the shadow of a mountain range behind it. Valparaiso . . . Vale of Paradise . . . what kind of place was it? For me it might just as well be the entrance to Hell. El Cuchillo was ferrying me across the River Styx. Purgatory would come into view, momentarily.

I wondered what had happened to Carlos. By this time the Chinese would have found him. How would he account for his missing passengers and the missing money? Maybe by this time the accounting was over, and Carlos was "making the feesh" happy in place of El Cuchillo. I shuddered. What about Craig? Had he ever reached Panama City? Maybe he was dead, or starving, or being eaten by some jungle cannibals. I was beginning to believe the Bible . . . maybe the old boys were right. Men had a peaceable existence until they were led astray by some Eve with a golden apple. But my own peril quickly distracted me from worries about Carlos or Craig. As we came into the dock areas, I could see El Cuchillo was looking for a lonely landing place. They circled several quays, decided against them because there seemed to be too much activity, and finally located a moldy pier at the far end of the harbor. The crew tied up the launch. There was no ladder, I was once again hoisted and shoved in the air. They dropped me on rough wooden planking at the top of the pier. The crew spoke quickly to El Cuchillo in Spanish, and then walked hastily toward the streets.

When they had gone, El Cuchillo yanked me to my feet. Standing in the shadows cast by a lonely night light at the end of the dock, El Cuchillo took his revolver from his pea jacket and pressed it against my head. Slowly he put it back and then showed me a knife. He spoke

134

rapidly in Spanish. While I didn't understand his words the meaning was clear enough. If I tried to escape from him, I was going to get a bullet through my head or a knife in my ribs or both.

He took my arm. Walking faster than was really possible in high heels, me tripping and panting, we emerged into a broad avenue, and a few minutes later walking north we were standing in a busy Plaza which I learned later was the Plaza Sotomayor. Before I could make up my mind whether I dared to scream and try to attract some rescuers, El Cuchillo hailed a taxi, shoved me into it and told the driver "Ascensore. Cerro des los Lecheros."

I quickly discovered that ascensore meant the elevators or cable cars that haul the citizens of Valparaiso from the lower to the upper levels of the the city. The taxi driver pulled up near to the entrance, El Cuchillo pushed me along with the crowd, jamming us into a decrepit cage hung on wires. The rest of the passengers, Chileans, Negroes, Spaniards, paid no attention to us. Finally when there seemed to be scarcely an inch left in the car, the whole apparatus, creaking and groaning, leaped into the air. In a few minutes we were high on a hill overlooking the bay of Valparaiso. El Cuchillo with his hand firm on my arm, stared at the harbor a moment. He chuckled and pointed. I could see the silhouette of the freighter, a tiny toy ship, anchored far out in the harbor below us.

I wondered if the Chinese had arrived. What had happened to Carlos? There was no doubt in my mind what El Cuchillo hoped had happened. With his hand biting through the arm of my coat, he forced my dragging feet through a maze of alleys finally stopping at the door of a shack with tin sides. He kicked the door open and shoved me inside. Puttering with matches, he finally lighted a wheezy gasoline lantern. I shuddered. The garbage odor that permeated the room evidently came from

135

an open toilet in one corner. The dancing shadows of the lantern revealed a wooden table with two chairs, and a stained mattress on the floor in the corner.

Was this El Cuchillo's home? Were there any neighbors who could save me if I screamed? El Cuchillo grabbed my coat by the collar. He forced me to pull my arms out of the sleeves. I screamed, and he slashed me across the face with his fist half closed. The blow stunned me. Crumbled on the floor, I begged him to let me go. I was sobbing hysterically. Grabbing me by the hair, he pulled me erect and forced me to sit in one of the chairs. Dazed, I watched him rummage in a cupboard. Finally he found a bottle of whiskey and two dirty tumblers. He poured both the glasses full and shoved one at me. Lighting a cigarette, he sat down opposite me, his face a wide evil sneer. With the gasoline lantern sputtering on the table, I watched the smoke curling out of his nostrils. I was shivering both from the cold dampness of the room on my bare thighs, and from sheer terror. With his tiny brown eyes buried in a forest of dirty whiskers, and the livid scar slash on his cheek, El Cuchillo looked like a filthy water rat about to pounce. He spoke slowly to me in Spanish. Here and there words related to French or English. I guessed that he was insisting that I drink with him. If I didn't he would pour the whiskey down my throat. I better get used to it, I was his woman now. He would have me conscious or unconscious. I might as well drink with him before we finally got down to business.

Slowly, my head aching from his blow, I sipped the raw whiskey. It tasted like straight alcohol. I gagged but I didn't dare stop drinking. I wondered if I kept him drinking long enough would he pass out? Maybe in the process I would go into an alcoholic trance, too. Anything, just so long as I didn't consciously have to embrace this monster. My hope faded when he tossed off two glasses in a row and seemed not the least bit inebriated. I had drunk half a glass, and thought any moment I would have to throw up.

I continued to sip very slowly. Halfway through his third glass, still speaking incomprehensibly to me in Spanish, he wiped his moist eyes, and staggered around the table. Bending over me, he snatched Carlos' shirt, ripped it apart at the buttons and tore it off me. Kneeling on the floor he slobbered his face against my breasts.

Screaming, desperate with fear, I shoved him away. Swearing at me, off balance, he fell against the table. The gasoline lantern crashed to the floor. The flame ignited the straw mat and leaped and crackled onto the mattress. On his hands and knees, cursing furiously, El Cuchillo whacked at the flames with my shirt and his bare palms. Crazy with fear, I snatched the nearly empty whiskey bottle off the table. Before he could move to protect himself I smashed it down on El Cuchillo's head. The blow was so hard that it vibrated through my hand to my elbow. Holding the shattered end of the bottle, I stared at El Cuchillo slumped to the floor, face down, his head bleeding profusely. The mattress was a smoking inferno. Any minute the whole shack would go up in flames. I saw my mink coat and rescued it just in time from the flames. What should I do about the unconscious El Cuchillo? If I hadn't already killed him, he would surely burn to death. Then I remembered the money. Trembling for fear that he would revive, I searched his pockets. I found the huge wad of bills and crammed them in the pocket of my coat. Choking from the smoke, I grabbed El Cuchillo by the arm pits and dragged him to the door of the shack. The flames were now jumping through the roof. Outside the alley was filling up with people screaming "Fuego! Fuego!" More were pouring into the street. I didn't wait to answer questions. Brushing off some men who were yelling and trying to hold me, I ran.

137

Through alleys, into dead ends, back into narrow streets, panting . . . my heart pounding so furiously I thought it would jump out of my chest, I ran until I finally found the ascensore that had carried me to El Cuchillo's heaven. I was the last passenger aboard. Groping for breath, trying to ignore the curious expressions of the other passengers, I leaned against the side of the descending cage. I tried to erase the horrible business from my mind. Why had I pulled that monster out of the shack? I should have let him burn to death.

When the elevator finally stopped at the lower city, I clutched my mink around me. Still trying to catch my breath, I wandered into the night. I knew I had to keep moving. I had a vision of El Cuchillo staggering down the street after me, a bloody raging demon.

Half running, fighting the temptation to look back, I noticed a taxi slowly following me. The driver was obviously curious about me. He leaned out the window and spoke in Spanish. It was insane. I had no idea of where I was or where I was going. I couldn't understand the language, but I was certain of one thing, I had to go somewhere . . . anywhere!

I got in the cab and slumped on the back seat. "I don't speak Spanish," I sobbed. "That is not necessary, senorita," the driver beamed. "I speak English. I was very efficient, an honor student at the University."

I was so relieved that I had found a human being, that I started to laugh hysterically. Perhaps at last I might control my life again. I was safe!

No one would ever "own" Marge Wentworth again!

"Drive . . . drive anywhere," I said. "I have to think."

"It is ten-thirty p.m., senorita. Would you like to drive to Vina del Mar? To the Casino?"

What was Vina del Mar? It meant nothing to me. I

138

might just as well have dropped into Valparaiso from outer space for all I knew about it. As we drove, the vague thought was occurring to me that if I could trust this pleasant looking young man, he could help me become a normal, average female again. I needed clothes . . . baggage. I needed identity. How could I explain to anyone how I had ever got here? It I could only transform myself into a tourist, I would be able to fly home. I had money enough. I fished in my pocket. The wad of hundred dollar bills was still there. Then, I remembered Manya Zolotov's passport. It was still in the lining of my coat. I nearly shouted with joy at my inspiration. Could I become Manya Zolotov?

I looked at the back of the taxi driver's head. His hair was red, neatly trimmed. He looked naïvely honest, and trustworthy. Whoever he was, I had no choice. I had to take a chance.

"Could you stop somewhere?" I asked. "I want to talk with you."

Obligingly, he pulled off the road into a narrow circular turn-off. All around us were flowers with the heady odor of natural perfume. He turned off the ignition and waited for me to speak.

"In the day time, senorita, this is a sight to see. All over the hills between Valparaiso and Vina del Mar are flowers, millions of them. It is very beautiful. A few miles from here are lovely beaches. From all over the world, the rich people come here. Just the other day a man from Italy told me, this is the most beautiful place in the world. Better than the Riviera."

"What's your name?" I asked, trying not to wonder what he was thinking about me.

"I am Rojo O'Harris," he said, proudly pointing at his hair. "In Spanish Rojo means red. My father was Irish, my mother Chilean."

"Rojo," I crossed my fingers and prayed. "I need a friend. A friend who will help me. A friend who will

139

ask no questions. Who will tell no one what he is doing . . . or how he found me. I need this friend every day to escort me around. Maybe for a week. I will pay him a hundred dollars every day. Do you know someone like this?"

Rojo chuckled. "Senorita . . . such a friend you now have! Whom do we have to murder?"

"No one. I will cause you no trouble with the law. Right now, all I want is a room in the finest hotel. I have no baggage. All I have are the clothes that I am wearing." I didn't attempt to explain to Rojo that I was naked under my coat.

Rojo turned the back seat light on. He started at me for a second. "I have a friend who is a room clerk at the Hotel Miramar. Very expensive hotel. You have money to pay?"

I handed Rojo a hundred dollar bill. "I have American money."

"Ah, senorita . . . very good money. That is a very nice coat you wear. But your hair, your face . . ." Rojo sighed. "They are not good. You need a comb . . . cosmetics. I will get them for you."

He turned back on the highway and drove rapidly toward Vina del Mar. "I need to know your name, senorita. At the Hotel Miramar, I will see that you are registered. This is a very busy season. My friend may need . . . how do you Americans say it . . . payoff." Rojo smiled in his mirror at me. "There is always room at the inn, if one has a friend and escudos."

I took a deep breath. This was the beginning. Would my new name bring me as much trouble as my old one? "My name is Manya Zolotov. I am from Miami, Florida." I gave him another hundred dollar bill.

In the parking lot of the Hotel Miramar, he told me to wait. I looked out of the taxi window at the hotel. It was built on the edge of the ocean, spectacularly new; concrete and glass modern. It looked quite luxurious, the perfect place to assume a new personality to match my passport. Just as I was beginning to get nervous and wonder if Rojo had disappeared forever with my two hundred dollars, he returned grinning happily. "Here is everything . . . powder, lipstick, facial make-up, eye-shadow, tissues, a brush and comb." Rojo was obviously familiar with females. He held a vanity mirror while I worked on myself. Trembling I dabbed at my tear-ravaged face, praying that my swollen eyes, and hair that desperately needed a hairdresser, would pass muster. Even though I wasn't satisfied, Rojo was pleased with the results.

"Ah, very good, very sophisticated, senorita. You look chic enough to go to the Casino and make our fortune." I ignored his emphasis on our. Rojo's manner was becoming proprietary beyond the call of duty.

"Your room is reserved," he told me as we walked toward the hotel. "No need to stop at the desk. A boy is waiting to take you directly to the elevator. Your baggage is at the docks. You arrived via Grace Line. Tomorrow I will get your baggage." He chuckled. "Or should I say we will find it together? You will need a passport, stamped with your arrival information and inoculations." Rojo shook his head. "For this I do not have the answer."

"I have a passport," I whispered to him as he led me into the lobby. "Tomorrow, I will need you at ten o'clock. Can you take the day off?" I looked at his seedy jacket and worn pants. "I want you to buy a very handsome outfit. You must look like a wealthy playboy. Do you understand? You can rent a car. An expensive one. I will pay for everything. Can you do this?"

Rojo smiled, happily. "Senorita Zolotov, tomorrow your companion will look better than the richest man in Vina del Mar."

It occurred to me that my new friend was too eager, but the bell boy was waiting to take me to my room.

It was too late to restrain Rojo. Still what did it matter? I would only need him for the few days that it would take to transform myself into Manya Zolotov. Then I would purchase airline reservations to Brussels and leave Rojo and Chile forever.

Eighteen

In the room, finally, I thanked the bell boy. Promising him that I would tip him tomorrow, I locked the door, kicked off my shoes, tossed my mink on the bed and danced around the room. I had done it! I was free! My own person again, and from now on, Marge Wentworth . . . oops, Manya Zolotov . . . was not going to be a slave to anyone.

What's more I had money, and I was, by sheer luck, registered in one of the finest hotels in a plush resort . . . Vina del Mar! I had never heard of it before, but it had obviously been created by the idle rich of South America as their own private playground.

How much money did I have? Hastily, I flattened out the wad of hundred dollar bills and counted them. There were eighty-three. Eighty-three hundred dollars, and I had earned every damned cent of it!

I took a shower, scrubbed myself, and that not being sufficient I drew a tub of deliciously warm water and started all over again. As I washed for the second time, the grim thought occurred to me that I was definitely pregnant. I examined my breasts and belly but could see no discernible difference. It crossed my mind that I had enough money to try and find a doctor who would abort me. I had heard that abortions were easily obtainable in Chile. But damn it . . . no! No one was going to fiddle with me again unless it was under circumstances where I was anxiously, hungrily willing. And that wasn't going to be flat on my back with some strange

142

doctor poking around. I'd have my baby! But before that crucial day I had nine months. For at least three months . . . twelve weeks, I could continue to look virginal.

Having completely lost track of time I tried to calculate the date. It must be approximately December 10th I had five weeks to get to Brussels. How I was going to do it was still problematical. But before I could even think about that I had to become Manya Zolotov. Was there danger in assuming her identity? What if Horace Zolotov had already released his secret to the world? But that wasn't likely. He had told Manya he would meet her in Brussels on January 12th. If he was still alive, he would wait to make his next move when Manya had joined him. My real danger was that, in the subterranean channels of international intelligence, the name Zolotov was already too well known. I could be picked up again by any assortment of desperate characters, including the Chinese, who might right now be searching Valparaiso for me.

But there was no alternative, I had to have a passport. I ripped the lining of my coat and studied Manya's photograph. She was plumper than me. But I could have lost weight. She was blonde, probably natural . . . but I could easily dye my hair. My story would be that I, Manya Zolotov, had simply learned the hard way. My husband left me for another womnn. I had awakened to the facts of life, lost weight, come to Vina del Mar, and become a new, vibrant woman; out to scalp a new man. Manya's blue eyes were another problem. Mine were brown. Could I wear sunglasses and get away with it? I finally fell asleep, determined to find a solution.

I awoke with the telephone jangling in my ear. In response to my cautious hello, Rojo answered. "Good morning, Senorita Zolotov. It is ten o'clock in the morning."

I told him to come right up. One thing was sure, I didn't have to worry about dressing. Wrapped in my mink, I greeted a transformed, handsome Rojo O'Harris. He was sparkling in a white linen suit, high collared shirt, and a burnt orange tie.

"It is warm today. You do not need your mink," he said. "For evening yes, but not for the day."

"Today, I need it!" I said firmly. "I know it will look silly. But remember what I told you. No questions. Are you married?"

Rojo grinned. "Senorita asks questions. Does not answer them. I am not married. No money to get married. Do you want me to marry you?"

"No!" I yelled. "Don't even entertain the thought! . . . and don't get any ideas. I'm allergic to men. Just keep in mind that I am paying you handsomely . . . That's all there is to it. Right now I want you to take me to a store that sells women's clothing. A very fancy one . . ."

Rojo led me through the lobby into a bright blue Pacific day. He had rented a Ferrari. As we drove, I looked at the ocean spread out below us. I was in a paradise of golden sand beaches nestled at the base of flower covered hills. We drove through streets lined with flowers. At last, it had happened! The eighty-five dollars a week secretary to the president of the Midhaven National Bank didn't have to read about it anymore. She was here!

"Up there is the summer palace of the President of Chile," Rojo said. He grinned in my direction. "Senorita, I am not asking questions, but you are so busy looking at the scenery, it becomes obvious why you must wear that mink coat." He pointed at my legs. It was impossible to sit down and keep the coat wrapped around me in all directions. "Perhaps you are as allergic to clothes as you say you are to men?"

I froze him with a nasty glance. We didn't speak again until we were in a very expensive store dedicated to clothing wealthy South American women. Using Rojo as a translator, I bought a brassiere, a summer cotton, and a pocketbook. I knew I couldn't get down to serious shopping until I was no longer being stared at in my mink. Did those eagle eyed women know the truth? I was stark naked under my coat. Back in the car, telling Rojo to look the other way, I hooked on the bra, wiggled into the dress, and tucked my money into the pocketbook. Elated, I flung my coat into the back seat. "Now, Rojo, I will prove to you that I am not allergic to clothes." In fact, I thought, for the next few days I may not undress again. I may even go to bed fully dressed. One thing I was absolutely certain of . . . as long as I lived, no one would ever convince me to join a nudist camp.

It is always a source of amazement to me not only how much good clothes cost, but even more surprising, the number of women in the world who can afford to buy them. It took less than three hours. I was famished, but hunger had to wait. With a cheerful Chilean woman guiding me, even language was no barrier. I spent eighteen hundred dollars on a new wardrobe before I got cold feet at how much money I was spending. The white matching luggage to carry my new wealth only cost one hundred and fifty dollars. The grinning thought occurred to me that it was too bad I didn't have Craig's American Express card. I could have hoarded all my dollars and let the bill collectors worry.

With time out for lunch (wine and an exotic Chilean dish which Rojo called "cazuela de ave") before I was due at the hairdressers, I nervously showed Rojo Manya's passport. I tried to gauge his reaction, but he was noncommittal.

"You have lost weight, I see." He grinned. "I think I

145

will like you better blonde. This passport needs an arrival stamp, and certain other documents." Rojo sighed. "It will cost at least a hundred dollars."

It was apparent that Rojo felt no necessity to deal in lesser sums. He looked in my eyes. "Ah, such a deep brown. This, also will be difficult, but perhaps not impossible with sufficient money."

I gave Rojo five hundred dollars and told him to start making the impossible possible. At five o'clock when I emerged from the hairdressers, a sleek silver blonde, Rojo was waiting with Manya's passport. I had now officially arrived in Chile.

"I have also solved the color of your eyes, I think." Rojo beamed.

We drove to a modern office building, and Rojo introduced me to a Doctor von Hagen, an optometrist, who carefully studied my eyes. "Ah, you women," he sighed. "In Japan, I understand the women are not satisfied with their cupcake breasts. They have a liquid latex inserted under them to give them sex appeal. They even bounce and feel good, I hear." Doctor von Hagen stared at me. "But I can see that you do not have this problem."

Doctor von Hagen finally got to the point. He told me it would take several days of fittings and fiddling with contact lenses. Finally, four days later, although the world looked slightly dyspeptic when I inserted them, the brown-eyed Marge Wentworth was gone forever, and blonde, blue-eyed Manya Zolotov emerged, speaking with a definite French accent, which I had gradually perfected while Rojo listened with happy approval as we spent the days sunning on the beaches or drinking cocktails around the hotel pool.

While Rojo asked no questions, and converted to millionairism as easily as I had, he continued to work on the assumption that I had unlimited sources of funds. When I finally sang him the words of that old

146

song "I'll be switched, the hay ain't pitched . . . Giddap, Napoleon it looks like rain!" he was puzzled, but slowly got the point. Not all of it. I hadn't told him that in truth I no longer needed him. Through the hotel, I had made open airline reservations for a flight to Hong Kong.

I had an uneasy feeling that getting rid of Rojo was going to be even more difficult than acquiring him had been. While he had made no overtures, leaving me at the door of my hotel room every evening, I recognized in the way he was beginning to look at me either an acquisitive pecuniary interest or a budding sexual possessiveness. I couldn't determine which. In either case one was as bad as the other.

I have to admit that my first taste of luxury in the world, with a distinguished looking escort who seemed to know the best places to dine and dance in Vina del Mar, had a charm that I was reluctant to leave. There really was no great hurry. I had nearly four weeks to get to Brussels, but the unhappy recollection of a Chaucerian character who had an old devil climb on his back that he couldn't shake off gradually became an obsession.

"If your problems are financial, senorita Zolotov," Rojo told me, "It's time we visited the famous Casino."

Feeling quite naïve (I had never been in a gambling casino in my life) I nervously climbed the marble steps of the Casino with Rojo. While I was trying to appear knowledgeable and sophisticated, but in truth was trying to hide my amazement at the obvious wealth of our betting companions, Rojo introduced me to roulette. He coolly bet away five hundred dollars before I could even understand what was going on.

When he asked me for more money, and brought more chips to finance his "system" which he insisted would double our money, I tried to convince him that I was a very poor gambler.

"But senorita," he insisted. "My system never fails. In the long run it will work in our favor."

"But you are losing now." I argued in whispers. Then I had an inspiration. Roulette looked easy enough to play. All you had to do was choose the right number! Thirty-five. For me it had to win. Gold was thirty-five dollars an ounce, and I needed gold!

I watched the wheel spin. The little ivory ball fell in eighteen . . . Then twenty-seven. Then six. NOW! I grabbed all the chips from Rojo, and bet it straight.

"House limit, senorita," the croupier said.

"What does that mean?" I asked.

"You have five hundred dollars on that number," Rojo grinned. "The limit is fifty dollars."

I noticed an elderly man, evidently a manager, nod at the croupier. "They accept your bet," Rojo said glumly. "But it is quite mad, senorita."

The ivory ball circled endlessly. But I wasn't worried. I was absolutely certain that it would fall into the tiny 35 fret and stay there. Gold—35, Gold—35, I kept saying to myself. It Doctor Pao-lin could hypnotize me, why couldn't I determine, parapsychologically, where the whirling ball was going to stop? And then, as the wheel slowed down, the nice little ball obeyed my commands, popping a complete circuit of the wheel, it finally nestled permanently in 35. While I knew it was going to happen I squealed my joy and hugged Rojo. I had doubled my money!

To Rojo's amazement I did it four more times in the evening. I just waited, and watched, and whenever I got that 35 feeling I told Rojo now was the time to bet. In about an hour and a half I was three thousand dollars richer.

After a few drinks in the lounge, I was ready for my fifth try. On the way back to the roulette tables, we passed a baccarat table. I noticed one of the players. My heart did a flip flop. It was impossible! It couldn't be!

148

But it was. Carlos Fernanda! Impeccably dressed in summer evening clothes, he was obviously winning. After a momentary glance in my direction, he returned to an amused contemplation of his cards. I breathed again. My new blonde hair and blue eyes had passed the test. Carlos hadn't recognized me! At least not this time. Really, when I stopped to think about it rationally, it wasn't so astonishing. The only way he had ever known me was as a naked brunette with stringy hair. But, I had noticed a glint in his eyes. Knowing Carlos if I hung around, it wasn't too unlikely that he would go out of his way to strike up an acquaintance with Manya Zolotov! It was time to leave the Casino and Vina del Mar.

I quickly told Rojo that all the concentration was giving me a headache. I was afraid that for tonight my inspiration had deserted me. He reluctantly cashed in my chips. After a somewhat heated discussion as to whose money it really was, he surrendered the winnings from his bill fold, keeping three hundred dollars for expenses. Rojo was getting difficult to handle. For every one hundred dollars I gave him per our agreement, he was managing to filch an additional hundred. If I didn't leave soon, I was going to have to borrow my airplane fare to Brussels.

Nineteen

On the way back to the hotel I made up my mind. I would drive to Santiago immediately and take the first plane anywhere out of Chile. If I couldn't arrange a fast departure to Hong Kong, I would fly to Buenos Aires. My mad Portugese lover was too close for comfort! How had he escaped from the Chinese? Where had he gotten the money to transform himself into a

149

gentleman gambler? Was it the money that he had claimed was due him from the Chinese for kidnapping Marge Wentworth and Craig Barnett? That seemed unlikely. Why would the Chinese have paid him when he couldn't produce either of us? They would have fed him to the fishes fast. Maybe he had joined forces with them. Maybe he convinced them that he had been tricked by El Cuchillo, or told them in any event that, naked in a mink coat, I couldn't have escaped from Valparaiso. All they needed was a careful search to find me cowering and abandoned somewhere in the city.

While I was deep in thought Rojo had followed me into the hotel elevator. He was obviously planning to come up to my room.

"It's early, Manya," he said, pressing my arm. "We will have some Chilean champagne sent up and relax on your balcony for awhile."

I was about to tell him that my name wasn't Manya. It was the first time he had addressed me by any name other than senorita. His glistening eyes warned me that champagne was simply a preparation for a longer evening with further surprises to come! He probably didn't even intend to go home.

At the door I tried to dissuade him. We could drink champagne tomorrow. I was really getting a very bad headache.

"It's the tension of the betting, Manya," he soothed me. He took the key out of my hand, and guided me into the room. "Once you get into something comfortable, you will feel better."

Before I could protest further he telephoned for room service. When the waiter arrived Rojo told him not to open the bottles. Grinning at me seductively, he twisted the champagne in a bucket of ice. I knew that somehow I would have to ease him out of the room with promises. Before morning I would silently fold my tent and sneak away. But then he took off his jacket and tie, smiling at me as if he were already in possession of the fortress. I knew it wasn't going to be easy. I watched him twist the wire off one of the bottles. He poured the champagne, and touched his glass to mine. "We have done it. Manya Zolotov. With the help of Rojo, you have become a beautiful woman. Add to that your gambling ability, and the world is ours."

"I've appreciated your help," I told him. "You have been a very good friend."

Rojo smiled. "Not have been, Manya . . . but *will be*. Even more than a friend. I think it is time that we became partners. We will be rich together."

"That would be nice, Rojo," I said, "But the truth is that I have other plans. In a few days I must leave Chile. Perhaps, someday, I will come back. But I will be honest with you. I am in love with a man whom I intend to marry very soon."

Rojo extracted a newspaper clipping from his breast pocket. He sat on the bed grinning at me. "As you must realize, Manya, if I may call you by the name you have assumed, I am a very efficient man. How you arrived in Valparaiso wearing only a mink coat might not have bothered a less curious person. But it became an obsession with me. Since you preferred not to answer any questions, I took the long chance that somewhere in the newspapers there might be a clue to your odd behavior. It was tedious, but I searched back through newspapers for the past three weeks. And then . . . there it was!" Rojo waved the clipping happily. "It is in Spanish . . . but I will summarize it for you. Approximately two weeks ago, your United States Navy picked up a woman and a boy abandoned in a rowboat between Cuba and Key West. The woman had been badly beaten. Both the woman and the child were suffering from exposure. Before the woman died she regained consciousness for a few minutes and told her rescuers that her name was Manya Zolotov. She believed that she had been kidnapped by Cubans, because her husband Horace Zolotov had made a discovery that secret agents all over the world were after. The boy whose name is Zoltan is recovering, but he did not know the whereabouts of his father. All he told the reporters was that his father was a great man who was going to fix the world." Rojo coolly put the clipping back in his pocket. "So . . . it is obvious that you, senorita, *are not* Manya Zolotov!"

I listened to Rojo, my thoughts awhirl. Manya was dead! The Zolotov business was getting rougher. What horrors had she been subjected to? Had she revealed where she had been planning to meet Horace Zolotov? If she had, by going to Brussels I was most certainly taking my life in my hands. On the other hand, if Horace didn't know she was dead, he was going to discover it very unpleasantly on January 12th. What about Manya's passport? Did I dare to use it? Would some other efficient character, another Rojo, make the connection? But all these questions popping through my mind, vanished before the present reality. Rojo was obviously planning to blackmail me into becoming his mistress.

"So what are you suggesting?" I demanded. "You knew by the picture on the passport that I wasn't Manya Zolotov."

Rojo put his arm around me. "Of course, I realized this, senorita. But at the time I knew that you probably wouldn't tell me who you were, or what you were up to." I felt his arm grip me tighter. "Now, of course, I know you will wish to tell me everything. We will go into business together. No matter what the business may be, there will be other enjoyments. Tonight, in bed, we will talk about it."

"You can forget it," I said angrily. "I've paid you well, and it doesn't include delights of the bed." I fumbled in my pocketbook. "Here's five hundred dollars. Take it and get out of here. I don't need you anymore!" I knew that it wasn't going to work. Rojo held the trump card. But I needed time to think.

Rojo chuckled. He poured another glass of champagne. "Senorita, you know my answer. Let's not make it unpleasant. The Chilean police would not be very happy with someone who arrives here without proper papers." He lifted his glass in a mock toast. "Tonight, I think we shall become very happy partners."

Feeling sick to my stomach, I stared at Rojo with tears in my eyes. It couldn't end this way! Marge Wentworth, the mistress of a red-headed taxi driver. A woman without a country! There had to be some way out of this trap. I just wouldn't go to bed with him! What I had done with Carlos was bad enough, but then it had seemed to be inevitable.

I was reasonably sure that Rojo wouldn't try to rape me. I guessed that he was planning on a trembling acquiescence. If I could convince him that eventually I would become his mistress, that I would go along with his plans . . . but not tonight. If I could keep him at bay until I packed my clothes, checked out of the hotel, and hired a driver to take me to Santiago, I would take the first airline reservation to the moon if necessary. The problem was how to convince Rojo that tomorrow was another day.

I picked up my glass of champagne. With a warm smile, I tried to shift gears without being too apparent. All right, I would tell him the whole story, from the beginning, but if we were going to really and truly be partners, he shouldn't force me into bed. A young man should woo a woman, not command her. I agreed with him. It really was quite early, we had a long wonderful night ahead of us. While I was talking, my thoughts were seizing and rejecting one method of escape after another.

153

"Ah, Manya . . ." Rojo smiled. "I can't think of you by any other name. But I do agree with you. I shall be the most romantic lover you have ever known. You will be entranced. We will be wonderful both in bed and in business!" He took me in his arms and kissed me enthusiastically.

And then a dangerous idea sprang full blown in my brain. Psychologists might call it brainstorming, or evidence of high creativity, but to me, at the moment, it was an act of sheer desperation.

"Rojo," I said demurely, lowering my lashes. "If you really want to sleep with me tonight, will you do it my way?"

Rojo was ecstatic. "Ah, Manya," he sighed, kissing me and feeling me with an enthusiasm that made it clear the only way should be his way. "Anything . . . anything you wish. The moon is coming up. Soon it will peak into this room from the balcony and bathe our bodies in its pale yellow sheen. You will be my golden lover."

I tried not to shudder. Fighting fire with fire is a tricky business. I crossed my fingers and prayed. "Rojo," I murmured, "Later when it happens . . . are you prepared? We could not be in business together long if I were pregnant."

I was in luck. Rojo jumped up and looked at me approvingly. "But, of course. How stupid of me! You are a gem of a woman." He embraced me. "Never mind, it is a problem easily solved." He put on his jacket and tie. "Get yourself ready, Manya. I will be back in fifteen minutes."

"Wait," I said softly. "Please, Rojo, you will humor me, won't you? When you return I will be in the bathroom. I will wait in there until you turn the lights off in the room. You will bring the champagne out on the balcony. Then you will take off your clothes, leave them in the room, and wait for me on the balcony. You will lie naked on the chaise." As I spoke I tried to appraise Rojo's reaction. He was grinning enthusiastically. I continued with a husky voice: "When I know you are waiting I will join you. The evening air is warm. We will lie together in the moonlight, drink champagne, and . . ." I paused and stared at him suggestively. "Hurry back, I will leave the room door open."

I hoped that I hadn't overdone it. Rojo left in such a state of anticipation that I was terrified. I wouldn't have the full fifteen minutes that he said his search for the artifacts of love would require.

It actually took me less than eight minutes. I literally threw my dresses and underclothing into my suitcases. Then I checked the bolt on the door leading onto the balcony. My flash of genius was correct so far. Even if Rojo were angry enough to put his bare fist through the glass, the frames that held them were too small for him to squeeze through. Naked, with no weapons, he was going to have a difficult time to knock that door down. If I were lucky, the bolt and the door should hold him a prisoner until morning.

Waiting with my two suitcases (I decided it would be impossible to carry the hat box and travelling case) I sat on the edge of the bathtub, fully dressed, wearing my mink. I tried to stop trembling. Anything could go wrong. If it did, I knew that I would be in trouble up to my ears. I would never be able to cajole Rojo into trusting me again. On the other hand, if I were successful I would be rid of Rojo. Already, I was joyfully anticipating what would happen when morning came, and Rojo was discovered naked and raging on the balcony.

Finally (it seemed hours, but it really was only a few minutes) I heard the door open. "I am back . . . well prepared," I heard Rojo chuckle.

"Good," I said from the bathroom. "I am nearly ready. Remember what I told you." Peeking through a sliver of the open bathroom door, ready to jam it shut, if

Rojo started in this direction, I watched him undress. Very methodically he folded his suit and placed it on one of the chairs. Finally, naked, he examined himself in the mirror over the dresser. His face showed his self-approval. To my surprise he ruffled the crushed red hairs around his penis, fluffing them out in a glorious setting for his manhood. Evidently deciding that he would pass the inspection of an ardent female, he gathered up the champagne bottles and glasses, put out the room lights and disappeared on the balcony.

The time had come! Trembling, feeling like a commando about to trap the enemy in his own gun emplacement, I quietly opened the bathroom door and tip-toed toward the balcony. If he came back to the room now . . . I was dead!

"Close your eyes, Rojo," I said huskily, "I am coming."

"Ah, my sweet, I am waiting" he croaked. "With my eyes closed, ready to open them and be overwhelmed by your loveliness."

With my heart pounding, I slammed the door on the balcony and bolted it. Rojo sprang to life, pounding furiously on the glass.

"Be quiet, Rojo," I waved at him through the glass, amazed that I had imprisoned him so easily. "You'll wake the whole hotel!"

While he wailed through the door that it was a nice little joke, and he was laughing, too . . . but now, please the fun was over, let him out, I ran in the bathroom and grabbed my suitcases. "Goodby Rojo," I chuckled. "You were a very good friend for awhile. Don't get a moon-burn!"

I quickly scooped up all his clothing in a ball. Juggling the mess together with my suitcases, I ran out of the room to freedom once again.

Twenty

The next day, after driving the Ferrari to Santiago, I passed through customs at ten in the morning, as Manya Zolotov. Without a hitch, I boarded the Panagra flight to Hong Kong.

In the airplane at last, alone, finally in complete control of myself, I ordered a scotch and settled down to the luxury of a trans-Pacific flight. When I remembered Rojo, I couldn't help grinning. If only I could have seen what actually happened to him! Before I left the hotel, in a maid's closet, I hurriedly searched through his suitcoat and trousers, found the clipping describing Manya Zolotov and discovered in his billfold ten of my hundred dollar bills. Rojo had been more economical with my money than I had thought. After tossing his clothing into the maid's disposal basket, I quickly took the elevator to the lobby.

"I am leaving rather suddenly," I told the manager. "I haven't time to wait for an itemized bill. I have been here nine days. Do you think a thousand dollars will cover everything?"

"Oh, I am sure it will." The manager smiled, accustomed evidently to the eccentricities of American tourists. "If you will leave us your forwarding address, we will send the overage to you."

I gave him the money from Rojo's billfold. "This billfold belongs to a friend of mine, Rojo O'Harris. You can give the difference to him. I am sure that he will turn up one of these days!"

The drive to Santiago, about one hundred and sixty miles over cliffs, and through tunnels burrowed through the mountains was a little terrifying. I kept praying that I wouldn't lose my way, or worse, have tire trouble. Visions of myself stranded on a highway, unable to speak Spanish, or even more frightening, the possibility that the headlights of automobiles which seemed to be tailing me might turn out to be Rojo, in hot pursuit, kept me in a state of nervous jitters.

But my naked, hopeful, redheaded lover must have had to sweat it out on the balcony, cursing me and waiting for a chambermaid to rescue him. I hope when she finally came that she was not too young. Just old enough to appreciate a helpless, naked male, who probably, cursing Manya Zolotov, dashed into the room, grabbed a sheet off the bed, and departed through the lobby to his broken down taxi, in high disdain . . . nevermore to mess around with female American tourists.

At the airport, I had parked the Ferrari. It was three in the morning. Afraid to check into another hotel I waited through the long night in the terminal. While I had open reservations for a flight to Hong Kong, scheduled for eleven a.m. I was determined to leave Chile fast. Potentially, I had Carlos Fernanda, El Cuchillo, some unknown Chinese, and Rojo O'Harris searching for me. If the first confirmed reservation that I could make had been for Alaska, or Buenos Aires, or United States, I would have taken it. My original idea of flying to Brussels via Hong Kong had no particular logic to it; except the logic of whatever makes Marge Wentworth tick.

When you stop to consider it how many of us really know what motivates us? What makes a person happy, or sometimes bewildered and ashamed when the hidden depths of his personality creep into the sunlight and move him in directions and to deeds that he thought impossible for him? Was it Shakespeare who said something like "Be true to thyself, and thou cannot be false to any man . . ."? But the rub is, what is really "thyself"?

Relaxed in an airplane bound for Hong Kong, I knew that the real Marge Wentworth was both a frightened

158

little girl ready to jump into the protection of marriage and family with Craig, and something else besides. Something that boded no good for the kind of marriage that Craig, or for that matter Carlos, imagined with me. I was no longer content to live on the fringes of existence. As I drank champagne, and indulged myself in the seemingly endless courses of the in-flight dinner, with no occupant in the seat next to me to disturb me, I knew that I had temporarily moved one step toward the center of what I visualized as a series of concentric circles, representing life, with a bull's eye in the middle. On the outer perimeter of the first circle the poorest people in the world simply existed for their three score and ten years. Actually, their existence was so marginal they rarely achieved this longevity. Living their fecund, short lives, they perpetuated themselves in a frightening progression, and then vanished without a personal trace. As you moved toward the center of the circles, you found the stolid middle class citizens of the world whose lives revolved in the illusion (probably influenced by radiation from the center) that they were achieving something. But they were no less slaves in the whirling circles of life. They worked and saved, tried to educate their children, thanked God that they had, at least, escaped the fate of living on the outer fringes and finally, some of them middle aged and worn from their toils, managed the one big event of their lives—a magnificent vacation where they obtained fleeting glimpses of the people who lived at the center of the wheel of life, the hub of the mechanism that kept the whole business in motion.

Some, who had forced their way to the center circle, were not rich; they had arrived there by sheer perseverance dependent on the skills of their chosen metier. Some arrived at the center by manipulation of power, and in the process achieved the manners and the look of power. Some, the aristocracy of wealth, were born

159

there. But no matter how they got to the center, the power they wielded was the power of money.

Whether it was a western society, or a communist dominated eastern society, the measure of what a man could command ultimately came down to his power over the productive slave people of the world, and the economic wealth that they produced for him as a by product of their own desperate struggle for survival.

I suppose it was a cynical philosophy. Through college and graduate school, I had listened to the sour grape attacks on the "bitch goddess, success" and I had once almost believed that the life of the spirit, the enjoyment of the finer things in the world, was something that escaped the Philistines. But now I realized that it was a con game invented by the people who lived at the center of things to keep those on the outer circles happy with their existence. While I might not be lucky enough to get to the center of my imaginary circles and stay there permanently, I had by some weird chance fallen into a centripetal machinery that was whirling me toward the vital center. I had jumped on the merry-go-round, grabbed the brass ring, and lo and behold . . . the ring was gold!

So why not Hong Kong? I had three weeks to get to Brussels. If it all ended in a fool's chase, at least I would have gone around the world in luxury. To Marge Wentworth of less than three months ago that was as unlikely as marrying a rich man!

I stayed in Hong Kong for three days enjoying the luxury of the Hilton Hotel and the amazing contrasts of wealth and poverty which served to confirm my theories. Every morning after fighting nausea, and returning to my room to heave up an expensive breakfast (there was no damned doubt that I was pregnant) I gathered up my strength and toured the city, adding exotic custom made clothing and perfumes to my wardrobe. Each night I modeled my loot in an expensive cocktail lounge or dining room. While I discovered that I was the cynosure of male eyes, I was also aware that I was the target for propositions that began with a dinner and would end in the sack, if I had been willing. I suppose if I hadn't had bigger fish I hoped to fry in Brussels, it would have been one way to accomplish my objectives. I had the merchandise. More than one woman in history has sold her body and retained her mind. But I was safe. My middle class virtues triumphed. Even with Carlos, I had made love first because I couldn't help myself, and then because I couldn't help liking the big grizzly bear. Maybe I could have convinced myself I liked the pot-bellied, middle-aged exporter of Chinese objects d'art (he was obviously quite rich) or the four-times divorced actor who was in Hong Kong to make a moving picture (he assured me I was the answer to Marilyn Monroe and Jean Harlow) . . . but it wasn't possible. I fled to my room, and put in an oversea telephone call to Midhaven, Connecticut.

When I finally reached Vin Hadley, managing editor of the *Midhaven Herald,* he was more intent on discovering my whereabouts than admitting he didn't know where Craig was.

"Is this call really from Hong Kong?" he demanded. "Is Craig there with you? What the hell is going on?"

"It's a big joke," I yelled into the phone. "If Craig shows up, tell him I love him." And I did, in a sort of mixed up way.

Twenty-one

I left Hong Kong with a nagging worry that something serious had happened to Craig. I counted the days. Eighteen days ago Carlos had put him overboard in the

Gulf of Panama. Craig should be back home by this time. What if he were dead? I tried not to think about it. More likely, he had arrived in Panama City and decided to enjoy life. He had nearly eight hundred dollars and an American Express credit card. I couldn't help chuckling. If Zolotov didn't come through with at least one bar of gold, Craig and I were going to be working to pay for this escapade well into our middle age.

To give my world tour an exotic flavor, I flew to Bangkok, stayed there two days, and then flew to India via Rangoon. From New Delhi, I flew to Cairo, and then to Athens where I spent Christmas. By the time I arrived in Paris, I was a sophisticated world traveller, moving through customs with Manya's passport with the greatest of savoir faire, renting automobiles and taking my own tours, and moving in and out of the finest hotels with no problems that a smile and a pretty, flustered look couldn't solve.

I arrived in Paris on December 30th. With time out for New Year's Eve, when I had to use forthright English to get out of the clutches of an American playboy, I spent every waking hour perfecting my French.

While I had thoroughly assumed the identity of a *bon vivant,* a sophisticated Manya Zolotov, I had given little thought as to how I could establish an immediate rapport with Horace Zolotov. He certainly wouldn't recognize the former secretary to the president of the Midhaven National Bank, either as a blonde or a brunette for that matter. I was certain that the one time that Zolotov had seen me he was definitely not interested in my nubile femininity. One other thing was certain. I couldn't rush up to him and tell him that I was his wife Manya Zolotov! Nor would introducing myself as a fluttering Marge Wentworth, anxious to split the golden melon with him, be an adequate approach. I would have to play it by ear, omitting the fact

162

that I had been travelling half way around the world using his wife's name and passport. The awful thought occurred to me that if he already knew that his wife was dead, he wouldn't show up in Brussels at all, and my wild goose chase would come to an abrupt end. On the other hand, if I had to tell him the sad news about Manya it wasn't going to be an auspicious beginning.

By this time I had more or less convinced myself that probably nothing would come of my meeting with Zolotov. I had approximately two thousand dollars left and twelve days to go. If Horace didn't appear, or if he did and there were no room in his plans for Marge Wentworth, I would fly to London, finish my world tour, and then go meekly home to live into quiet middle age, sustained by the memories of my youthful follies. I took the train from Paris to Brussels and arrived at the Hotel Westbury on January 9th. With the feeling that I was courting trouble again, and afraid that Manya had been forced to reveal the plans of her meeting with Horace, I decided that it would be quite insane to register under the name of Manya Zolotov. Since I had no other identity except Manya's passport, I immediately faced the problem headlong. I asked the room clerk if I might speak with the manager before I registered. In a small office, behind the registration desk, I explained my problem (cooked up on the spur of the moment) to a kindly gentleman who listened with obvious sympathy.

"My name is really Manya Zolotov," I told him in French and showed him Manya's passport. "My father was a former citizen of the Soviet Union. He escaped and became an American citizen. Working with him, I am travelling abroad on a very special diplomatic business. Because my father's name is well known in certain circles, it is essential that my real name not be listed on the hotel register."

"I understand perfectly, mademoiselle. What name would you like to use?"

I had anticipated that.

"Jeanne D'Arcy," I said quickly. Well, I was no virginal Jeanne d'Arc, but in the last month I had certainly gained a thorough knowledge of the methods of the inquisition.

The following day, with nothing else to do, I explored Brussels, from the Grand Place to the Palace Royale, up and down hills into cathedrals and museums, until my feet ached, and I finally hired a taxi and drove through the Bois de Cambre and the Forêt de Soignes and ate a late lunch in the Villa Lorraine.

Weary from sightseeing, I showered, dressed in a black woolen sheath and took the elevator to the Penthouse Cocktail Lounge. As the waiter served me with a martini I glanced toward the bar. Several men were sitting with their backs to me. Was I seeing things? The haircut and the shape of the head of one of the men was all too familiar! I thought for a moment I was having hallucinations. But then I saw his profile. There was no doubt about it! It was Craig Barnett! He was alive and here in Brussels!

Without thinking I half rose from my chair about to run over to him and throw my arms around him. Thank God, somehow, he had made it back to civilization. I was bubbling with questions to ask him. But then I had a second thought. For every question I asked him, I was sure that he would have three or more to ask me. I had an uneasy feeling that now was not the time to attempt to answer questions such as: How I had managed to escape Carlos? Where I had acquired the sudden affluence? Why I was a blonde? etc. etc. I knew myself. In my happiness at finding Craig I would inevitably confess the whole lurid business. In ten minutes we would end up hating each other. Worse, even though he was here in Brussels, I had a premonition that it wasn't to help me find Zolotov. More likely Craig was bent on dissuading me from what he would call my mad folly.

Frozen with fear that he might turn around and surely recognize me, I sipped my martini and stared out the window to the roofs and towers of Brussels below the hotel. Afraid that if I left the lounge before him, I might attract his attention, I continued to order martinis. Finally, I didn't dare drink one more. Craig, talking to the bartender, was apparently settled in for the night. Deciding that I would have to leave before I was actually staggering I paid the waiter and was about to totter toward the elevators when I received the knock-out blow that turned me cold sober!

Walking toward the bar was Carlos Fernanda! Handsomely dressed in an Italian silk suit, wearing his tie in a broad windsor knot, huge cuff links on his white shirt, his moustache clipped and precise, he took me in with the smile of an international diplomat relaxing for a moment or two from the cares of State. I gasped involuntarily. But it wasn't a smile of recognition. Thank God for that! It was just the confident leer of a handsome predatory male about to test his virility, and powers of conquest on a hopefully fawning female.

From his occasional glances in my direction I was sure that it was just a matter of time before Carlos arrived at my table, and made his opening manoeuvres toward the conquest of the fascinating blonde whom he was already savoring as a late evening bed companion. But luck was with me.

Craig was staring at Carlos with slowly dawning recognition. I could almost hear the words churning in Craig's brain. Was it? No it couldn't be? But Craig kept looking at Carlos with a puzzled expression on his face. Finally, he must have become determined to find the truth. He slipped off his bar stool and moved toward an empty spot next to Carlos. It was my golden

165

opportunity. Quite casually I walked out of the lounge, catching for a second the look of utter surprise on Carlos' face as he remembered Craig.

Hurrying back to my room I couldn't stop laughing. Craig finding Carlos was like a crash of meteorites hurling through space. I expected to hear a terrifying explosion. Would my lovers murder each other on the spot? . . . or would Craig demand pistols at twenty paces? I decided that it would really be best if they immediately started slugging each other, asking no questions, until the Brussels police arrived, and threw them in separate cells. God forbid that they should sit down like gentlemen and over a few drinks, compare notes on Marge Wentworth!

I ordered dinner sent to my room and spent the night worrying. By now Craig knew that I had become intimate enough with Carlos to tell him in some detail about the Zolotov business. Was Carlos insisting to Craig that I was "hees moca"? . . . that he had the notches on his gun barrel to prove it? To keep myself from such phallic thoughts I tried to convince myself that I had succeeded. They were not really interested in me. I had simply convinced them that Zolotov would share his secret, and somehow all of us would end up richer. But it wasn't likely. More realistically Carlos had come to "find hees woman" and take her to Lisbon, while Craig was planning to drag his mad girlfriend back to surburbia and pound some sense into her. How in the world did I ever get involved with such obsessive marrying males?

Undressing for bed I stood naked on the bathroom scales. My belly still seemed quite flat. But it might be wishful thinking. I had gained a pound. Maybe it was the exotic living of the past three weeks. But if it were junior, like coming events casting his shadow before him was it Craig Junior or Carlos Junior? One of these days if my ardent suitors succeeded in putting me

166

in captivity, they were going to have to toss a coin, or draw cards, to see who won the prize. Winner take mama and her mewling brat!

In the meantime, somehow, before the day of reckoning, I was going to talk with Zolotov. I had two things going for me. Neither Carlos nor Craig knew what Horace Zolotov looked like. Thus far neither one of them had recognized me. I had one day to go to January 12th. All I had to do was to keep a good distance away from both of them. If I should get too close, I must keep reminding myself that I was Jeanne d'Arc . . . damn it, no! Jeanne D'Arcy!

Twenty-two

On the morning of the eleventh after examining my face in the mirror I began to lose confidence. I still looked like Marge Wentworth to me. If I were going to sally up to Horace Zolotov tomorrow in the lobby of the hotel right under the eyes of Carlos and Craig, simply a new name, blonde hair and blue eyes wouldn't do. I must become quite a different person. Tomorrow at noon, I didn't have to pass customs inspection as Manya Zolotov. I didn't have to be Jeanne d'Arcy. All that was essential was that I be completely unrecognizable to Carlos and Craig. If I were lucky, and the lobby was reasonably busy with people, once I found Horace Zolotov, I would whisper to him that I had a message from Manya. Somehow, I would whisk him out of the hotel into a taxi.

Using the telephone, I finally located a cosmetician and makeup expert who agreed that he thoroughly understood my problem. I wished to transform myself into an unspectacular, middle-aged dowager about fifty-five years old. It would be costly but he would be delighted to try.

I left the hotel at ten o'clock. Luck was with me. Neither Carlos nor Craig were in sight. The aging of Marge Wentworth, Manya Zolotov, Jeanne D'Arcy took until late afternoon but the results were worth the time and money. Dressed in a tweed suit, my hips broadened with padding, wearing a grey haired wig (done in a French twist) supported by combs, I looked for all the world like an ancient Lady Chatterley who had long since forgotten the follies of her youthful dalliance with the gardener.

With gold rimmed glasses on a chain around my neck, I sat in the lobby and waited to test my disguise. If Craig hadn't had Carlos arrested for kidnapping or Carlos hadn't felt compelled to shanghai Craig again, one or the other was bound to appear soon.

To my amazement they both emerged from a cocktail lounge off the lobby, talking quite seriously to each other. They were obviously alcoholic buddies. On their way to the dining room they passed Lady Chatterley with no apparent interest in that faded lady.

"I agree," I heard Carlos say, as they passed. "Eeef she ees come, we argue, then. Now we be frans."

"She'll be here. You can bet on it." Craig replied sarcastically, "I know Marge Wentworth!"

Deciding that he who listens learns, I followed them into the dining room and waited until they were seated. I told the headwaiter, who smiled at the foibles of an elderly woman, that I preferred a table next to those distinguished-looking men.

The back of my chair a few inches from the back of Craig's chair, I found that I could follow their conversation quite easily. Out of curiosity, not knowing what it was, and trying to improve my vocabulary I nearly ordered *Les Grives a la liegeois*. When the waiter courteously informed that it was thrushes cooked in a casserole, I hastily switched to *Fricadelles bruxelloises*. I heard Carlos finally convince Craig to order *Anguilles au vert* without telling him that it was eel. Then he proceeded into a cool discussion of the fact that Marga really loved him and not Craig.

"Maybee not at the beginning, you understand. Meeting thees way was not good. But later . . . ah, later, Carlos know women. Marga ees vairy happy. Everay night she wait. That smile on her leeps. Her eyes saying, Carlos . . . hurry, hurry, I cannot wait longer."

Craig's voice was sour. "Carlos, you were 'had.' Marge can't help it. When she wants something she doesn't ask for it, or try to convince with reasons. With a little tear in the corner of her eye she just automatically gives you the 'treatment.' "

I nearly choked on a warm roll I had just buttered. I never used feminine wiles on any man! Craig Barnett was a blithering idiot!

"Ha . . . such a treetment," Carlos was saying. "I would be 'had' by Marga, twice a day and three times on Sunday. She ees a woman who should go barefoot and wear only dress. Ready on an eenstant to make love. Ah, such beautiful teets."

"You are talking about my future wife!" Craig said angrily.

"Carlos does not theeenk so, my fran. Have you ever geeve her bath?"

"Have you ever played 'Ride in Central Park with her'?"

"What ees that?" Carlos demanded.

This conversation was too damned much like something out of Noel Coward.

Why didn't one of them punch the other in the nose? But not Craig. The rat. Blushing, I listened to him describe our zany bed business in lurid detail. Was nothing sacred? I was sorely tempted to shove my fork in Craig's back and stomp out of the dining room in a maidenly huff. Then I remembered I was Lady Chatterley.

169

"Thees story do not make me jealous, my fran. Marga ees a woman . . . not a leetle girl. She have to learn somewhere. Carlos ees glad you teach her so well."

So there, Craig Barnett, what's your answer to that?

"I can't return the compliment," Craig chuckled. "Until tomorrow night . . ."

"Tomorrow she sleep weeth Carlos, I theenk . . ."

With that I had heard enough. I lost my appetite and I hurriedly left the dining room. Both of them were going to get a surprise. Tomorrow night Carlos and Craig could sleep together, or alone . . . but they weren't individually or doubly going to sleep with Marge Wentworth. I couldn't help smiling. What if I had to marry them both? I had learned that such a menage à trois was not uncommon on the Continent. Two males torturing themselves as to who was getting the best half of their better half, or would I, in that case, be a better third instead of better half? Oh well, it was really too insane to dwell on.

I went to bed happy in the knowledge that while my suitors continued to argue with whom Marge Wentworth was the most provocative in the sack, the lady in question planned to sail right out the hotel with Horace Zolotov.

But I was too over confident. After carefully considering every detail, and with the certainty that Lady Chatterley had the tiller of her life well in hand, at nine the next morning, I packed my bags. Then in my excitement damned if I didn't jibe the ship!

The weather had been chilly. Even old ladies wear mink. Without thinking I put my lovely coat on. Not until I was in the elevator, two hours early, but too impatient to pace the room any longer, did the horrible thought occur to me that my mink was a dead giveaway. Craig or Carlos would most certainly recognize it. Probably they had a fixed image of me in it . . . naked! There was nothing to do but go back. When the

170

elevator reached the lobby, I hastily pushed the button to return to my floor. But you don't hurry automatic circuits. Failing to respond to my impatient button pushing, the door opened on the lobby and I found myself staring into the impassive faces of Doctor Pao-lin and Chang Yu!

Shrinking frantically against the wall I pushed the button again and again. I was certain that Chang Yu had looked directly at me. Had he recognized me? I didn't think so, but if he had managed a good look at my mink, I had no doubt of the outcome. Did I dare to go down to the lobby again without my coat? My knees were knocking so badly I was about to resort to that old adage and kneel on them. I had to go back! After all that I had been through, I had to see Horace Zolotov. I had to warn him! If they came near me or him, I would scream loud and clear. Doctor Pao-lin wasn't going to get a chance to look into my eyes again, and say "you are growing sleepy . . . Miss Wentworth!" But I never got back to the lobby. My lovely mink finally betrayed me. As I got off the elevator on my floor, I saw Craig walking down the hall toward me. It was too late to run. I tried to pass him with the haughty look of an elderly lady who was no longer interested in young men. I saw his eyes widen in surprised recognition. I tried to walk slowly, fighting every instinct to run.

"Wait a minute!" I heard him explode behind me. "It's a neat get-up, Marge Wentworth. But I know it's you!" He grabbed my arm and whirled me to him.

I tried to bluff it. In a reedy old lady's voice, I jabbered at him in French. "Prenez, votre main de moi, monsieur. Vous etes trompé. Je suis Contessa D'Arcy D'Orleans." I saw a flicker of doubt in his eyes. He let go of my arm but he continued to follow me toward my room. "Come on, Marge. I know it is you. What in hell are you up to?"

171

Praying that a bell boy or a janitor might appear and rescue me, I continued to rave hysterically in French. He was utterly mistaken, I would report him to the gendarmes. But though he seemed doubtful, he forced his way into my room with me."

"I'd know that damned mink anywhere, Marge Wentworth," he said staring at me, still not sure.

"Je ne suis pas votre amie." I said indignantly. I ran for the room telephone determined to yell for help, but Craig tackled me. We fell across the bed. While I pounded him, screaming furiously, clawing, biting and kicking him, my wig fatally askew, he yanked my dress up to my crotch.

"No old lady has a pussy like that," he yelled triumphantly, poking me in the groin. "And only Marge Wentworth has too little moles, right here." Grinning, he kissed me.

"You've got a nerve," I sobbed, trying to catch my breath. "I wish I really were an old lady. I'd have you arrested for attempted rape! What are you doing in Brussels, anyway?"

"That's a hell of a greeting," Craig released me. His smile turned sour. "You get me damned near murdered by Russians and Chinese, you convince that Portuguese wind bag to toss me overboard in the Pacific, and then you run off with his money . . ."

"His money!" I yelled. "It strikes me that you are pretty chummy with a man who got paid for kidnapping you."

Craig looked at me bitterly. "Not so damned chummy as you were, my fair whoring wench. I am under the impression that you would stop at nothing to get Zolotov's gold."

"Zolotov! . . ." I suddenly remembered. I had to get back to the lobby. "Craig, we've got to save Zolotov. I just saw them in the lobby. Doctor Pao-lin and Chang

172

Yu. They must have found out that Manya would meet him here."

Craig didn't answer me. He bolted the room door.

"Undress!" he said grimly.

"Undress? Have you gone crazy? I'm going downstairs!"

"I'm not crazy, and you are not going downstairs." Craig said grimly. "I'm sane for the first time since I heard about Zolotov. Strip yourself. Right down to the buff, before I do it for you!"

"Don't you dare touch me," I yelled as Craig grabbed my arms and pinned me on the bed. Cursing him, I struggled helplessly while he unzipped Lady Chatterley's dress. Slowly but surely, while I occasionally got loose and fought back savagely, he stripped me. When I was completely naked, ignoring my fingernails and fists, he rolled up my clothes in a ball, swept the sheets, blankets and pillowcases off the bed, ripped down the drapes and curtains in the room, searched the dresser drawers, gathered up the towels in the bathroom and tossed the whole mess into the closet along with my suitcases and mink coat. Triumphantly, he locked the closet door and put the key in his pocket.

"There," he said puffing. "Unless you want to wear the broadloom rug, I don't think you are going anywhere."

"What the hell is this all about?" Shaking with anger I flung a lamp at him. He ducked and it crashed against the wall. "You can't get away with this. I'll have you put in jail. You don't own me!"

Craig just grinned. "I've decided that you need a guardian. I've elected myself to save you from yourself. I'm going down to the lobby alone. I don't trust you with Zolotov. Unless you feel like making the trip in your birthday suit, I am now reasonably sure that you will be here when I get back." Craig started for the

173

door. "Wash that old lady's mask off your face, it doesn't match your titties sticking up in the air so angrily!"

"Craig," I wailed. "You don't know what Zolotov looks like! Doctor Pao-lin and Chang Yu will recognize you. Craig!" I pounded his back, following him down the hall, heedless of the fact that I was naked. "You can't do this to me!"

"You'll catch cold running around like that!" He coolly punched the button for the down elevator. "The next thing you know Carlos will be getting off the elevator looking for me. He promised to meet me in the lobby. You just go back to your room like a good girl. If Carlos *is* in the lobby, there is either going to be one dead sea captain or two dead Chinamen . . . in which case I'll take what is left over which will be Zolotov." Craig patted my behind. "Go back to your room like a good little girl and wait. I'll bring Zolotov up to inspect you!"

Twenty-three

Suddenly aware that I was in no condition to pursue Craig I ran back to my room. Did I dare telephone for room service? What would I say? Send Jeanne d'Arc up an empty floor sack? I searched the room looking for a scrap of anything to cover me. Craig had been thorough. All I could find was my pocketbook and a few face towels.

In the bathroom I looked at the miserable tearstained face of Lady Chatterley. My pursuit of El Dorado just couldn't end this way! I was certain that Craig would never find Zolotov, or if he did, would most certainly never introduce him to me. I considered wrapping myself in pink toilet paper, and marching angrily through the lobby in search of Craig. Giggling, I pictured his embarrassment. Before I could do anything I decided that the old dowager face that I was wearing simply didn't match the Lady Godiva impression I intended to convey.

Just as I had thoroughly soaped my face and was scrubbing away the aged wrinkles, I heard the squeak of the room door being opened. I was sure that it was Craig coming back to apologize. He was sorry that he had been so wretched to me. I ran out of the bathroom to greet him and squealed in horror!

It wasn't Craig! It was a grinning devil with a black pointed beard! Fleeing back to the bathroom, I retained an impression that it was a fairly young devil with flashing white teeth and the distinctive look of a Frenchman. I tried to jam the bathroom door shut but he managed to insert his cloven hoof between the door and the lintel.

"Armand Delacroix, at your service, mademoiselle," he chuckled, inexorably pushing the door and me into the bathroom.

"Get the hell out of here," I screamed. "Can't you see that I am naked?" The thought occurred to me that I should be getting used to entertaining men in a state of pristine splendour.

"There is no better way for a female to be, mademoiselle. I am delighted with the sight. Rinse that soap off your face. I am taking you to Zolotov!"

I suddenly forgot that I was naked. What was happening wasn't real. I had passed from a pleasant dream of wealth into some kind of mad nightmare. Zolotov didn't even know I existed! With no vantage point whatsoever, crouching with one arm over my breasts and one hand across my delta, a modest maiden of high virtue, I retreated against the bathroom wall. I knew that

175

eventually I had to wake up, screaming my way back to reality.

"I don't know any one named Zolotov," I pleaded. At the moment I fervently wished that I didn't. "Please have the decency to get out of my room."

"We are wasting time," the devil said grimly. "If you have never heard of Zolotov, Mademoiselle D'Arcy, then please explain why you informed the manager that you *really* are Manya Zolotov?" He transfixed me, his small brown eyes boring into my brain.

My bluff had been called. Trembling, trying to close my mouth and breathe normally, I said: "I am really Marge Wentworth."

I might just as well have told him that I was Alice in Wonderland, or a chocolate ice cream cone. The way he was staring at me I was afraid that he would start lapping before I melted.

"I am not interested in the story of your life. You can save that for Zolotov. Just wash that soap and slop off your face before I do it for you!"

The tone of his voice brooked no delays. Hopelessly, I turned on the faucet in the sink. While Armand Delacroix sat behind me surveying my rear end, I desperately tried to restore some semblance of Marge Wentworth.

My thoughts raced through a maze, backing hastily away from dead ends. Why hadn't Zolotov just come to the lobby of the hotel as he told Manya that he would? There was only one answer. Zolotov knew that Manya was dead! It was so obvious that I wondered why I had overlooked it. Zolotov would know that whoever turned up in the lobby of the hotel on January 12th, looking for him, was involved in Manya's death. Had he come for vengeance? How could I ever convince him that I wasn't responsible?

Then I made another fatal mistake. Fumbling in my pocketbook for my lipstick I noticed Manya's passport

176

and Zolotov's letter. Armand caught the look of consternation on my face and snatched the pocketbook from me. Grinning, he opened Manya's passport, looked quickly at Zolotov's letter and shoved them both in his pocket.

"Come my chickadee!" He grabbed my arm and pulled me yelling into the bed room. "We've got to get out of here before your friend Jack the Ripper returns."

"Give me that passport and letter. They are mine!"

Armand chuckled. "If you really are Manya Zolotov, Horace is going to be pleased with the re-incarnation. From what Horace has told me I would guess that you must have lost about fifty pounds in the spirit world. But right now you scarcely seem ectoplasmic. What did your boyfriend do with your clothes?"

"They are locked in the closet," I sobbed. "You'll have to bring my corpse to Zolotov. I'm not going anywhere like this."

"No problem," Armand opened the door into the corridor. A heavily built, dark skinned man with Arabic features stared past Armand at me. He turned his head quickly away.

"This is Zolotov's bodyguard, Ali Hassan," Armand said, pulling him into the room. "Ali is a Mohammedan. For him you are worse than the temptation of St. Anthony. Arab females never show more than their bellies." Armand closed the door. "You do not have to look, Ali. We need your strength to break open this closet. We must make this female presentable to Allah and Sahib Zolotov."

With eyes averted Ali hurled himself against the closet door. It burst open with the protesting snap of metal and splintering wood.

Armand looked at the mess inside. "We haven't time to wait while you dress." He flung my mink coat at me. "Put this on. We will go now!"

"Not on your life," I shouted. "I am not leaving here

177

until I am fully dressed." No matter what happened I wasn't starting on another world tour dressed just in mink. "If Zolotov wants to see me, he can come here to my room." By this time I was quite certain it would be better if I never met Zolotov. I had a premonition that he wasn't going to be very happy with the new Manya Zolotov.

Armand held my coat out for me. "Young lady," he said coldly, "I'll give you one second to get into this coat. We will leave the hotel by the service elevator. Ali Hassan will bring your suitcases. If you insist upon an unseemly commotion we will leave without you."

I suddenly noticed that Ali Hassan, no longer concerned about my nudity, was pointing a pistol at me. Deciding that it would be better to accept the tide of events and try to control them later, I put on the mink and my shoes. At least this time my clothes were going with me. But then my bad dream took an abrupt turn for the worse.

Ali Hassan, leading the way out of the room with my two suitcases in his hands, peered warily into the hall, then backed quickly into the room.

"Three men . . . come," he whispered hoarsely and closed the door tight. "One her friend. Two more . . . not know!"

I was sure that it was Craig and the two Chinamen. "It's Doctor Pao-lin and Chang Yu. They are the ones who murdered Manya Zolotov!"

Cursing, Armand bolted the door. "Damn, I told Zolotov to keep the hell out of this mess." He ran to the window, and leaned far out. "There's a room directly below us." He looked at me disgustedly, poked around the closet, found the sheets that Craig had torn off the bed, and started to knot them together. "You can come with me or stay with your friends. I don't intend to get mixed up any further in this."

"Only one of them is my friend," I said thoroughly

frightened. "Please, you've got to help me. God knows what they will do. They are determined to find Zolotov."

"That's what I am afraid of," Armand said grimly. "My instructions were only to bring you to Zolotov . . . not the whole United Nations." He tied one end of the sheets around the leg of the bed and dragged the bed to the window. "Ali Hassan will stay with you. He can take care of himself." He lowered the sheets out the window.

Grinning, Ali was aiming his pistol at the door.

"Marge," I heard Craig say as someone pounded on the door. "Don't open the door! Use the room telephone, call for help!" I heard a grunt of pain and the oily voice of Doctor Pao-lin. "It's all right, Miss Wentworth . . . your friend is not hurt. He simply didn't understand. We must talk with you!"

Frantically, I looked at Armand. He had crawled out on the window sill. "The window below us is open," he whispered. "Make up your mind. I'll wait for two minutes. No more!" He slithered his legs out the window, and hung suspended by his arms. "If she comes, Ali . . . you stay. Let them in. Tell them where the gold is, just as Zolotov told you." He disappeared.

Hopelessly, I listened to Doctor Pao-lin insist that I open the door. I snapped the lock leaving the night latch in place. Through the crack I could see Craig staring at me dully. Behind him Doctor Pao-lin gestured impatiently for me to open the door.

"I'm naked. You can't come in until I'm dressed. Craig has the key to the closet where my clothes are."

Doctor Pao-lin smiled nastily. "Unhook that bolt, Miss Wentworth. We are quite familiar with you in a state of undress."

Then, to my amazement, a broad grin on his face, I saw Carlos coming up behind Chang Yu and Doctor Pao-lin. He had the butt end of a heavy revolver in his hand. Slamming it down with a sickening crunch on Chang

Yu's head, almost in the same gesture he threw his arm around Doctor Pao-lin's neck and started to squeeze. I jammed the door shut.

"Marge, it's okay," I heard Craig yell excitedly. "Carlos did it! Two Chinks in one blow! Let us in!"

I was petrified. If I let Armand get away I might never find Zolotov. If I opened the door, Craig and Carlos were going to try and straighten out my love life without further ado. It was insane, but then I was getting accustomed to living my life with a touch of madness. I opened the door again still leaving the night latch on.

Carlos grinned at me. "Don't worry, Marga, Carlos feex them. Let us in."

I could see the crestfallen faces of Doctor Pao-lin and Chang Yu. Carlos still had his arm around Doctor Pao-lin's neck. Craig was pointing a gun at Chang Yu.

"Give me the key to the closet, Craig," I insisted. "I am not entertaining four men in my birthday suit."

"For God's sake," Craig whispered hoarsely. "Cut out the modesty crap, and let us in. We are going to attract attention out here." Grimly, he handed me the key.

I slammed the door shut and ran to the window.

Armand stared up at me from the room below. "It's a cinch," he chuckled. "Just back out the window. Lower yourself two feet, and I'll grab you."

I tried not to see the street and the tiny automobiles that seemed miles below. I was committed. Shivering, I backed out the window. If the sheet tore, or the knot parted, someone was going to pick up a naked lump of unidentified flesh off a Brussels sidewalk. My mother had always told me that all that glittered was not gold. Why hadn't I listened to her? Slowly, I inched my way down the sheet. My knees scraped the side of the building. I wondered if my arms had strength to hold me. My hands were frozen on the sheet. They refused to open and let me down one more foot. I hung paralyzed until I felt Armand's fingers slide under my mink. With my coat hunched up around my shoulders,

Armand pulled me limply through the open window. Darned if he didn't start kissing me enthusiastically from head to belly.

"Good girl!" He sighed ecstatically, "I never thought you would have the nerve!"

"Cut it out," I told him as I tried to catch my breath. I wriggled away from his osculations. "I didn't risk my life to play postoffice with a stranger."

Armand grinned. "All right. Maybe later. We are lucky. Whoever occupies this room is not here, now." He peered into the hallway. "No one is about. Come, my chickadee, you look quite devastating. No one would suspect that you are not fully dressed. When the smoke clears away upstairs, Ali Hassan will rescue your clothing."

Coolly, we took the elevator to the lobby. Quite unnoticed we walked out the hotel to Armand's automobile, a Rover, which was parked a block away.

As I watched him start the car I was beginning to have second thoughts. If I had stayed with Craig and Carlos at least I would be safe. What was I letting myself in for, now?

"What is this business about Ali telling them where the gold is?" I demanded. "Are they going to follow us?" Armand was driving rapidly up one street and down another as if he were being pursued by demons. I knew that I could never find my way back. What was more I didn't have one cent of money. My traveller's checks and about four hundred dollars in cash were still in the hotel. Probably by this time all my worldly wealth was securely in Craig's pocket. Even if I got back to the hotel I would be destitute and dependent again either on Carlos or Craig. The cold truth was that I was trapped by Armand and Zolotov. I couldn't go back. Armand having escaped the downtown congestion was driving on a boulevard leading out of the city. He still hadn't answered me. I repeated the question.

"This whole thing is Zolotov's idea," he said. "Zolotov

expects your friends will be lured into a web he has spun for greedy pursuers."

I noticed that Armand was driving more slowly. "You don't have to meet Zolotov," he said looking directly at me with an expression that wasn't difficult to interpret. "If it's money you want, I am a very rich man."

I tried to react coolly but my spine tingled unpleasantly. I was sure that Armand was going to offer me a tat for tit arrangement. It might be difficult to convince him that I wasn't interested. At least, I didn't think I was!

"Zolotov is quite insane, you know," Armand chuckled. "If he were convinced that you were responsible for Manya's death he would be quite capable of tossing you into one of his smelters. The process for transmutation is quite hot! What remained of you would spend eternity inside a gold bar." Armand smiled grimly. "Maybe buried in Fort Knox!"

I hoped he was joking but I wasn't sure. "I have an idea what Zolotov is planning to do. What I am really interested in is whether he can really make gold, or if the whole business is an elaborate hoax."

Armand shrugged. "If your interest is simply reportorial, then I presume that you are not interested in gold per se. But, assuming that your interest tends toward the monetary, what makes you believe that Zolotov is going to share his wealth with you? What have you to offer him? Zolotov and I have been watching you for the past several days. He claims that he never saw you before in his life. I hope that you have a good story to tell him!"

My hands felt suddenly clammy. "Maybe you'd better take me back to the hotel," I said, shivering.

"It is too late for that! Right now you have two choices. You can convince Zolotov that you are a lily white angel and are simply interested in his welfare, or . . ."

"Or what?"

"Or forget Zolotov, and enjoy a fling with me, before the bubble bursts. You see, chickadee, three months ago I was a simple man. I owned a lead refinery. I

182

wasn't rich, I wasn't poor. Then Zolotov found me. He wanted someone with courage to finance the purchase of three hundred thousand pounds of lead; and investment of about ninety thousand dollars." Armand sighed. "I don't know where I found the nerve to do it, but I did. The rest is a long story that adds up to twenty-five million dollars that I now have in a Swiss bank."

"Then it is true that Zolotov can make gold!"

Armand laughed. "Not only can he make something that is to all intents and purposes gold, he developed a shrewd method of selling it. But I am no longer interested in Zolotov. I do not care about saving the world from its delusions. Zolotov's plans are quite insane, but that is his business." Armand put his arm around me. "We are poor people who could learn to be rich together. Not married, you understand! I am thirty-eight. I intend to share my wealth with at least thirty-eight women before I die. You can be the first!"

"Thanks just the same," I said, grinning at him. "I think I'll take my chances with Zolotov. He is at least forty-eight. May be he would prefer quality to quantity. Why don't you just settle for twenty-five women? Then, after you have worn them out you could give each one a million dollars. Of course, when you got to number twenty-five, you might have to pick her for permanency!"

"If it is only a million dollars you want," Armand said glumly, "I'll consider the expense justified. Before I can properly assume the mantle of my new wealth, I need polishing. I need to acquire savoir faire."

So there I was with practically a million dollars in my pocket. And at last a man who didn't want to marry me! I should have been elated. Wasn't this what I had told myself were my true goals in life? But I couldn't escape my New England heritage. If Armand had offered marriage, would I have capitulated? After all that was the dream package of every American girl. The handsome millionaire who loves her and will give her a wedding with a thousand other millionaires in attendance. Was that what I wanted? If I took over the job of "polishing" Armand seriously, maybe I could have convinced him that one thirty-eighth of the pie tasted like all the rest. I might have even persuaded him (if I acted fast enough) that the baby in my belly was our own love child.

But I guess the hard truth is that any one truly obsessed by Eldorado doesn't leave the main road for glittery side paths. Had I guessed what meeting Zolotov finally entailed, would I have settled for Armand? I guess not, because this time opportunity knocked twice, and I rejected it again . . . this time to save Craig and Carlos.

Twenty-four

Armand turned off the boulevard we had been following into a narrow tarvia driveway. On one of the stone posts at the entrance I noticed, written in small neon lettering, the words, "Le Labyrinthe." A quarter of a mile or so the tree-lined drive came to an end in front of a slate roofed chateau with impressive towers and ivy covered walls.

Scarcely prepared for my meeting with Zolotov I let Armand guide me up the steps.

"You are looking at a historic monument that a quite mad Flemish adventurer built in the seventeenth century," Armand told me. "It has forty or more rooms built without rhyme or reason. Some rooms do not even have doors or windows. You enter them through fireplaces or trap doors. I am not sure that, even now, I have discovered them all. But it doesn't matter . . . for now history has caught up with it. Temporarily, it is a club dedicated to your great American invention rock and roll!"

When Armand opened the front door it was obvious that he was telling the truth. The foyer and a large living room off it was literally jumping with a hundred or more bearded characters and girls in tight dresses, twisting, frugging, swimming to the music of a combo composed of three electric guitar players and a boy about twelve or thirteen years old who was enthusiastically whacking drums, cymbals, chairs and even beating rhythms on the floor when the mood seized him. The three men and the boy were all wearing blonde mop wigs!

Wondering if I should stick my fingers in my ears so that I could hear myself think, I let Armand lead me toward the tables that ringed the room. But before we reached them an enthusiastic twister swung me onto the dance floor.

"I can't dance this stuff," I yelled. But he whirled me into the confusion of the dancers.

"Just let your body express itself," he murmured in French, and shook his pelvis at me. "This number is called Penetration." His eyes had a far away glazed look. "Very sexy . . ."

The way he and the others were dancing I wondered how long before they would suit the action to the title. There was no escape. Clutching my coat around me I shook and wiggled and answered my partner's grimaces with the same vacant, I'm-not-really-here-look that I noticed on the faces of the other dancers. The music finally stopped. Perspiring, I groped my way to the table.

Armand grinned at me. "You weren't with it, chickadee! You should have taken your coat off. A twisting nudie would have brought Zolotov and the house down."

"Big joke," I puffed. Using the handkerchief he handed me I mopped my face. "I thought you were taking me to Zolotov. If this is your idea of polishing, you can polish yourself!"

"You just had the pleasure of dancing to Zolotov's

Gold Bugs. Zolotov plays the rhythm guitar. His son Zoltan plays the drums. Zolotov hates beat music. But feels that he owes his motherless son some form of companionship. I told you that he was quite mad!"

"Nobody calls Zolotov mad!" One of the guitar players, a tall man still wearing his blonde wig grabbed Armand by the hair and yanked him out of his chair.

"Sorry," Armand mumbled, tears of pain in his eyes.

"Meet the man with the golden pick!"

Without a smile, he let go of Armand's hair. His pale blue eyes staring at me seemed almost to protrude from his emaciated face. Even though his head had a massive bone structure, his cheeks were sunken. He was either way very ill or had dieted too quickly. Was it Zolotov? I wasn't sure. My Zolotov had plumper cheeks, wore thick lens glasses and had a very high forehead. This mop-wigged man who had been playing a hot guitar was not my memory of an absent-minted, puttering Zolotov who needed a loving female hand to guide him!

"Meet Manya Zolotov," Armand said warily patting his hair in place. "Here is her identification!" He gave Zolotov, or whoever he was, Manya's passport.

"I am not Manya Zolotov," I said trembling, I tried to look into those intense bulbous eyes but I finally had to look away. Frighteningly, his eyes never seemed to blink. My name is Marge Wentworth."

"I don't know you!" His voice was a flat monotone. I had a feeling that he was looking inside my brain and was not very happy with what he saw.

He looked quickly at Manya's passport, and put it in his pocket. "Tell Pierre to take over," he said to Armand. "I will take this woman upstairs. Where are her friends?"

Armand shrugged. "Gone to seek their fortune, no doubt. Shall I join you?"

Nodding, Zolotov led me back into the foyer down a narrow passageway and into a small electric elevator with an open cage of wrought iron. He pushed the

186

button. We rose slowly up two flights. When the elevator stopped Zolotov opened a small fuse box on the inside, took out what seemed to be a fuse, and put his finger into the hole. While he replaced the fuse the elevator inched upward another ten or twelve feet. We seemed to be facing a solid brick wall-shaft with no opening. But then the wall facing the door of the elevator rose slowly about five feet vertically. Zolotov pushed me toward the opening. Ducking under the wall we were in a large attic room with no windows. The only light in the room was from a skylight about eighteen feet above us. Zolotov lighted a candelabra, the wall slowly merged with the floor again.

"This is an ancient room where political prisoners were once kept. When Armand discovered it, it hadn't been opened for at least a century. There were four skeletons crumpled on the floor. Evidently they died here and their flesh disintegrated." Zolotov looked at me coldly. "Perhaps they, too, were grasping for gold."

I shivered. Was this room going to be my final resting place? I was beginning to believe that Armand was right. Zolotov's almost forced detachment and disinterest had a Hamlet-like overtone to it. I didn't know whether to start pleading that I was really innocent or wait and pray.

The room was filled with ancient furniture . . . dusty and decaying. The faded canopy and original damask counterpane on a huge bed was nothing but rotted cloth hanging dismally in the dancing shadows created by Zolotov's candle. I felt as if I were breathing the fetid air of centuries long passed. Time was trapped in this horrible attic. Zolotov opened an iron studded, cathedral type door that led into the adjoining room.

"You came after gold. Here it is." Zolotov pushed me into the room. I gasped. In the flickering light I could see bars of gold—hundreds of them—spread around the room.

"If you are counting, do not bother." His voice was

flat, emotionless. "There are fifteen hundred bars of pure gold here. They are worth approximately twenty million dollars. Since they weigh nearly forty thousand pounds the weight has been distributed. In one pile, the load on the floor would be too much, even for a house as well constructed as this. Zolotov sounded as impersonal as a guide taking me on a tour of a museum. Leading me out of the room he closed the door on the gold. I noticed that Armand had arrived. Sitting in a Queen Anne style chair he looked at me quizzically.

"Sit over there," Zolotov said. "Take off your coat. It is warm here in the daytime, even in January. The afternoon sun slants on this side of the house."

"I can't take off my coat," I said nervously. "I am naked underneath it."

I might just as well have said it looks like rain. There was not the slightest flicker of surprise on Zolotov's face.

"Flagrant nudity is not appealing to me," Zolotov said finally.

"You can be sure that it is not appealing to me. I am the victim of circumstance."

"I would say that you are about to be the victim of your greed, young lady." Zolotov stared at me for as long as a minute. I was on the edge of terror. There was not a sound in the room. The candles burned straight up. I felt stifled. Perspiration was trickling uncomfortably down my back.

"Why are you here in Brussels?" he asked finally. "Why are you registered under the name Jeanne D'Arcy? Where did you get Manya Zolotov's passport? What country are your friends working for?"

Bewildered, I tried to suppress a sob of despair. Even though he had shown me the gold in the next room I wasn't at all sure that he was Horace Zolotov. Wearing a wig! Playing a guitar! It *was* insane! He certainly didn't resemble the Zolotov I had met that fatal day in

Harold Nichols' office. What could I say to him? How could I make my story plausible? Whatever I said was going to reveal the true Marge Wentworth with her hair down. If he were actually Zolotov, I'd be nothing more to him than an adventuress who would stop at nothing to obtain money.

The disconcerting fact was that I was beginning to believe that it was true. Else why was I here? Could I ever explain to Zolotov what had motivated me if I couldn't justify myself?

"I don't even know if you are really Zolotov," I sobbed. My tears had no effect. His look was harsh. "Just how did you find out that Zolotov would be in Brussels?"

"I read a letter that he wrote to his wife."

"Manya Zolotov is dead," he said flatly. "You know it. I know it. How did you get this letter? You and your accomplices murdered her. Isn't that the truth?"

"Listen to me," I said, thoroughly frightened. "You've got it all wrong! Manya's murderers are here in Brussels all right, but I had nothing to do with it. Neither did Craig or Carlos. Please, I beg you . . . let me tell you the whole story." Hopelessly I plunged in. As I tried to make some sense out of my insane pursuit of Zolotov, I tried to see his face in the slowly darkening room. All I could detect was disbelief. I was quite obviously not Zolotov's dream of a fair and innocent maiden.

"I know that I am not a nice person!" I couldn't hold back the tears flooding into my eyes. "But it's true . . . every damned word of it . . . and what I've told you is only the surface. I started chasing a rainbow and ended up in a tunnel of horrors."

Zolotov was silent for a long time. Armand, now little more than an outline of a man in a shadowy room, had lighted a cigarette. He smoked it reflectively.

"You are not out of the tunnel yet, young lady," Zolotov said. "I find your story quite fantastic. It is true that I made the unfortunate mistake of contacting a Mr.

Harold Nichols in Midhaven, Connecticut, but I have no memory of a Marge Wentworth, or even that his secretary was present!"

"I was a brunette then," I said desperately. I was still not convinced that this man wearing a blonde wig was Zolotov.

He shrugged. "It doesn't matter. In the past few months I have come to accept the fact that I am one of the few sane persons left in this world. Your story appalls me. It is unbelievable that an attractive young woman would jeopardize her life in the wild hope that a man completely unknown to her would make her rich." He smiled grimly. "You have been parading around the world as my wife. For all I know, despite your mad excuses, you and your accomplices may have murdered her. Just how avaricious are you, young lady?"

"I have always been poor," I tried to control my almost hysterical sobs. "I am just like most people in the world. I wanted to be rich. You should understand that. When you first brought your bar of gold to the bank you wanted money. You told Manya that in your letter."

"You are an idiotic young woman," Zolotov said. "I will prove it to you. You have just looked at twenty million dollars worth of gold bullion. You can have it! Tomorrow, I am leaving Brussels. This house has served its purpose. Armand is planning to vacate it and eventually put it up for sale. I will leave you locked in this room tonight. Food will be brought to you. There is a commode in that old wardrobe. Before Armand and I leave, the wall opening will be set on a time switch. When the wall is open the house and grounds will be deserted. You may then leave with your gold!"

Zolotov moved toward the wall which had risen again. The room was grotesque, dancing with shadows from the candelabra he had left on a huge oak table. "Come Armand, we will let this ridiculous woman enjoy her wealth . . . alone!"

190

"Wait," I screamed. "Please . . . I'm frightened. I can't stay in this ghastly place alone!"

"You want gold. It is a small price to pay. There is nothing to fear in this room but the dust of centuries . . . What is left is only the decomposed flesh of men who died here seeking temporal power."

"Please! My God, have pity on me! I'm terrified. What happens when the candles have burnt? It will be pitch black in here. Don't leave me here!" I moaned. "I don't know what I want!"

"It's time you decided," Zolotov said coldly.

Armand, who had listened to the entire conversation without saying a word, finally spoke. "Maybe the young lady has lost her zest for gold. Maybe she would prefer to be the first of thirty-eight!"

Zolotov asked what he meant. Coolly Armand explained the proposition that he had made me. "You see, Horace, you have made me rich, but I am not adjusted to my new wealth. With the assistance of this young woman who so desperately wants a fortune, I could commence my career as an international playboy."

Zolotov shuddered. "You both disgust me. But if that is her choice, she still can have this night to think it over. You and I have some final details to settle. This is a good place for contemplation." He stopped at the elevator and looked at me frigidly. "Perhaps, I may give you a third alternative, young lady." For the first time a fleeting smile crossed his lips. "I won't, however, promise you gold."

Armand ducked under the wall with him. Slowly the wall merged with the floor. Far above me the remains of a winter day—January 12th—was a cold grey spot in the skylight. I had my wish! I was entombed with Zolotov's gold. I fell sobbing to the floor. But I wasn't completely alone! When I finally managed to control my sobs I looked into the corner of the room into the beady eyes of a rat, and I screamed and screamed!

Twenty-five

When Zolotov and Armand left, the three candles in the candelabra were shivering rapidly through the last half of their length. With a feeling of panic, knowing that I couldn't survive a night in that room with no lights, with rats scurrying busily around the edges, I rushed to the wall. Screaming, pushing, shoving I tried to make it rise again. But it wouldn't move. Sobbing hysterically, knowing for the first time the narrow gap that separates anyone from absolute terrified madness, I hopelessly searched the room for another exit. There was none.

Trembling, I took the candelabra into the next room where Zolotov had shown me the gold. As I opened the door and slowly inched my way into the room catching the glitter of the gold bars spread at my feet I must have created a draft. The candle flickered. Desperately, I tried to sustain its dancing life but it was too late. I was in complete total darkness. I stood stock still. Someone else was in the room! My body crawled, a cold chill paralyzing me. I listened to shallow breathing coming from the corner of the room.

I tried to stop the scream rising in my throat. "Oh, dear God . . . please, please don't touch me!" I moaned.

"I don't go around touching dames," the voice in the darkness said disgustedly, "I'm not old enough yet."

I was suddenly focused by the ribbon of a flashlight piercing the blackness of the room. Behind it, in the aura of its glow, I could see the shadow of a young boy staring at me. Laughing hysterically I ran to him and hugged him.

"Please, stay with me," I pleaded. "You've saved my life!" Tears pouring down my cheeks, I couldn't stop kissing him.

"Hey, what's going on?" he demanded, pulling away from me. "I don't go for this mushy girl stuff." He

192

looked at me disdainfully. "What's my old man got you up here for? Are you a spy? Is he going to kill you?"

I knew the boy was Zoltan Zolotov. Could I convince him to help me?

"Where did you come from? Can you take me out of this room?"

Zoltan chuckled. "Whoever built this house had a ball. There's secret stairways and rooms everywhere. My room is just below this one. My old man doesn't know that there's a secret stairway that connects them. He thinks his kooky elevator is the only way up here." He held the flashlight on my face. "You're kind of pretty for a girl. Is my old man going to make you go to bed with him?"

Zoltan was obviously a product of the television age. "Would you take me down to your room?" I begged him. "I'm very frightened up here."

Zoltan was dubious. "You can't sleep with me. You can't get out of my room without going through my pop's room. Besides, I don't think he wants you to escape. He's downstairs now discussing it with Armand."

"Please," I cajoled him. "I'll be your prisoner. We can talk. I'll sleep on the floor."

"Can you play a guitar?"

"No . . ." I said desperately. "But you can teach me. I'll be a very good pupil." I hugged him fervently.

"No damned mush." He pulled away from me angrily. "I don't like mush."

He led me to the corner of the room, pushed against a panelled wall and slid it back. Leading the way, he guided me down a curving dusty staircase into his room.

"I don't like to clean up," he said proudly, displaying chairs littered with unwashed clothing. His bed was piled high with magazines and books. Pictures extolling famous guitar players and drummers were tacked on the walls. I tried to walk without stepping on phonograph records, or drums mixed up with shoes and dirty stockings and pieces of electronic equipment. Zoltan explained that he was building a new amplifier. "My old man is kind of crummy. He could buy what I wanted. Instead he buys me a kit. 'If you insist on playing that god-awful music at least you can know why the sound comes out,' he says." Zoltan shrugged at the insanity of adults.

"If he doesn't like the music, why does he play with you?"

Zoltan chuckled. "He thinks it makes togetherness. He's lousy. He's got no rhythm." Zoltan picked up a pair of drumsticks and beat them rapidly on the floor. "What's my old man up to anyhow? Are you trying to steal his gold?"

"No." I shuddered. "I don't have to steal it. He gave it to me."

Zoltan laughed. "It's no good. It isn't real. He made it."

"Everybody thinks it's real."

Zoltan shrugged. "I think my old man is cracked." He handed me a Spanish guitar. "I'll show you how to play chords. It's easy. Take off your coat. You can't play with your coat on."

"I can't take it off."

"Why?"

"I haven't any clothes on under it."

Zoltan looked at me surprised. "I never saw a real girl naked. Go ahead, I don't mind."

"But I do."

"Why?"

I was stumped. "Because it's not nice. Didn't your mother ever tell you?" The words were out before I remembered that Manya was dead.

"My mother never told me anything. She didn't have to tell me. I read it in a book. Big deal. A man puts his dingus in a girl's dingus and makes babies." Zoltan looked at me speculatively. I wondered if I were going to have to tell him that he wasn't old enough, yet. "My old man is worse than you. He said not to talk about it. If you don't talk about it how do you ever get to try it? Did a boy ever put his dingus in your . . ."

"Zoltan," I said nervously. "Can't you lead me downstairs and out of this house without your father knowing it. I have to go home."

"No dice," Zoltan grinned. "My old man will be mad enough if he finds out that I brought you down here." He turned on a small radio. "There's a good combo on pretty soon. Want to listen to it?"

I sat on Zoltan's bed trying to figure out what to do. If I ran out of his room the chances were that I would never find my way to the front door without alerting Zolotov and Armand. If I did succeed in getting out of the house, what then? With no clothes and no money how would I get back to the hotel? Worse, without Manya's passport I had no identity. It suddenly dawned on me why Zolotov had so casually offered me the gold. For me the gold was valueless! Naked in a mink coat, in a foreign country with no way of proving who I was or why I had come here in the first place, what could I do with gold? If I left the house carrying even two bars of it, more than fifty pounds, I would be staggering. To move forty thousand pounds of gold, nearly twenty tons —for that was what the fifteen hundred bars weighed —I would need a truck, laborers and God knew what else. And if I succeeded in moving it what would I do then? I could see myself, the naked vanguard of my truck fleet, driving up to the national treasury of Belgium demanding fourteen million dollars in exchange for my gold. I would rapidly be given a room in an asylum with reincarnations of Napoleon for my roommates.

Zoltan was drumming to the music of the radio. "Would you do something for me?" I asked him, daring to interrupt the holy beat of rock and roll.

Annoyed, he didn't answer for a minute. "What?" he asked finally.

"Find your father. I want to talk with him."

"Why?" He kept staring at the radio. I had a momentary impulse to strangle him and run from the room but I repressed it. I made some comments about how good the music was. "I want to ask your father to help me go home to the United States."

"He won't do that," Zoltan said, still engrossed in the radio.

"Why not?"

Zoltan grinned. "Because he is flying to Marrakesh tomorrow. He bought a castle in the Atlas Mountains. Maybe he's going to sell you to the Sultan Ben Youssef for his harem. You might as well come with us. I'll teach you to play the electric guitar and we'll form a new group."

I was about to assure Zoltan that my travelling days were over. Come hell or high water I wasn't going to Morocco. Being a placid housewife in Midhaven, Connecticut was beginning to have merits I had overlooked. But then the music on the radio stopped for a news broadcast in French. Just as Zoltan switched stations I caught the first words. I persuaded him to turn back. I listened to the radio stunned. It was scarcely possible to believe the extent of Zolotov's carefully planned madness. "An hour ago," the announcer said, "the police arrested four men in a storage warehouse located on the Rue d'Alembert, a few miles from the center of Brussels. The four men were loading gold bullion into a rented truck. Five hundred bars of gold with a value of nearly three hundred and fifty million were seized. Police believe that this hoard of gold may be traced back to a cartel of international gold smugglers supposedly operating in Brussels in the past few months. Two of the men, who are Chinese, are said to be citizens of the People's Republic of China. They have been identified with espionage activities in Europe and the United States. One of the men, an American, told the police the incredible story that the gold was not really gold (at this point the announcer was unable to repress a chuckle) but had been made from lead. The fourth man, a Portuguese, insisted that a young woman named Marge Wentworth was involved. If the police could locate her she would clear them all. Preliminary tests have revealed that the bullion assayed 100% pure gold. All four men are being held in indefinite custody."

Zoltan, not understanding the French, had listened impatiently to the broadcast. I was too shocked to even pay any attention to the guitar record that he had put on his phonograph. He was banging his drums in a frenzied accompaniment that made my head spin. All I could think was how I had underestimated Zolotov. There was no doubt that he had planted the gold in that warehouse. He had been certain that eventually a situation would arise where he could use it to trap unwary pursuers. And now, until, *and if* Zolotov confessed, Craig and Carlos were going to find it impossible to prove that they weren't involved in a gold theft of international proportions. Why had they ever attempted to steal the gold anyway? I knew the answer in advance. Craig would proudly have said that he had made a deal with Chang Yu and Doctor Pao-lin. Here, Marge Wentworth, was the damned gold you wanted! So, now, let's go back to the United States and forget Zolotov forever. Even if I escaped and went to the police, all I would do now was tie a noose in a rope that could hang us all. Our only hope was that I could make Zolotov admit the truth. I had to save Craig and Carlos. Even if they hated me, I owed them that much. Wrapped in a blanket which Zoltan finally offered me on the condition that I permit him to look at me (he stared for a minute without comment, shaking his head, evidently convinced that the nude female body was greatly over-rated) I finally fell asleep on the floor. Early in the morning, insisting that he wasn't taking any more chances for a "dame," he escorted me back to my attic prison. He tried to convince me that I should

197

persuade his father to let me fly to Marrakesh with them.

"I know it would be kind of boring to be stuck with my old man all the time," he said wistfully, "but I could teach you how to play the guitar." He grinned. "Besides, after thinking it over last night I might want to take another look at you. You aren't so bad for a girl."

In the cold grey light of morning, the attic room was more dismal than scary. I waited with an uneasy feeling. What was Zolotov's third alternative? Could I convince him? I no longer wanted his gold. All I really wanted was to free Craig and Carlos and then go home, there to wait patiently until I discovered who had fertilized my eager ovum. I wondered whether "Daddy" in either case would want to acknowledge the blossom of his joy. I had finally convinced myself that I would gladly trade the "feminine mystique" for a frying pan.

Twenty-six

Zolotov finally appeared carrying my breakfast on a tray. Stunned by his alternative, I quickly discovered that he had eliminated all possibility of choice. Perhaps, subconsciously, from the first moment the mad idea of sharing Zolotov's wealth had occurred to me, I had cast the die. Craig would believe that. But the decision to accept the inevitable was somewhat more complicated.

Zolotov was not wearing his blonde wig. His creeping baldness had been disguised by a hair piece that blended into his receding grey black hair. His eyes, which I suddenly realized were seeing me through contact lenses, were no longer so glaring. He was "my Zolotov" all right, thinner but distinguished by the emaciation of his cheeks. He had the appearance of a man who had suffered the fire of his own convictions and still survived.

"I discovered you last night asleep on the floor of my son's room," he said coolly. "I see that Zoltan put his playmate back in her cage."

"Zoltan saved my life," I told him bitterly. "If I had stayed here all night, you would have had to put me in a strait jacket this morning."

Zolotov smiled. "Perhaps I was unnecessarily cruel. But you must realize that I had to check out your story." He handed me a Brussels newspaper. The story of Craig and Carlos was on the front page. "Unbelievably, Miss Wentworth, you seem to have been telling the truth. Of course, you must realize that despite the unfortunate predicament your friends are in, there is little that you can personally do to help them."

"You could tell the police that the gold isn't real . . . that you made it."

Zolotov looked at me amused. "This modern age seems to have an odd conception of reality. I am sure that the police will find it 'real' enough. At the moment I can't oblige you by revealing how the reality came to be. It will be much more effective for my purposes if the truth dawns slowly. In this way . . . how do the television gangsters say it? . . . your friends' theft will become the convincer."

Drinking the orange juice and trying to swallow the oatmeal (which I detest) I should have detected the proprietary interest Zolotov was suddenly showing toward me. But even if I had, I doubt if I would have been fully prepared for this "third alternative."

"I trust," he said, "that you have had time to weigh the choices offered by Armand and myself. I presume you have come to the conclusion that neither of them are tenable."

"It didn't take me all night to figure that your gold would do me no good," I said disagreeably. Zolotov had a pontifical manner that was extremely irritating.

"But I haven't discarded Armand's offer to become the first lady in his harem."

Zolotov chuckled. "I have discarded it for you. Last night I purchased you from Armand for the fifteen hundred bars of gold in the next room. This in effect wipes out both alternatives." He sighed, and looked at me with moist eyes. "Three months ago Armand was a relatively poor man. I made him a millionaire many times over . . . but, such is human nature, enough never seems to be sufficient. Never mind, you have had a small loss, you can't carry the gold. If Armand leaves it here I can scarcely guarantee its ultimate value." Zolotov stared at me silently and then guffawed. "Perhaps if I had autographed it, the collectors of art objects would pay handsomely for it."

The oatmeal stuck in my esophagus. What in the world was coming next?

"I could give you back Manya's passport," Zolotov continued. "But in view of the suffering my poor wife must have experienced such an action scarcely seems appropriate." He paused while I digested that fact. Then he underlined it. "Of course, without a passport, a vagrant . . . naked in a mink coat, on the streets of Brussels, I imagine that you would experience some difficulties. On the other hand . . ."

I waited.

Zolotov cleared his throat. "On the other hand you can marry me!" He paid no attention to the fact that I choked on the oatmeal. He simply patted my back. "It is really not such an extraordinary idea. In fact, since I can only presume that your basic greed has not been extinguished, it seems that your best hope would be to attach yourself to me. While I don't feel the necessity to make any more gold, I do have at the moment some ninety million dollars in quite liquid assets."

I had lost the power of speech. All I could do was to gawk at him. "Why do you want to marry me?"

Zolotov was silent. "There is the obvious reason that as

a man some twenty years your senior, I might find my lost youth in your desirable body."

"But I don't love you."

"My dear young woman, your morality of love scarcely seems in accord with your ethics of fortune hunting. I don't love you either . . . in fact I am not sure that I even like you." Zolotov paused. He looked at me grimly. "But, despite that, I presume you could still fulfill whatever sexual requirements there might be. As a matter of fact, there are other reasons. I believe that Zoltan has told you I am leaving for Marrakesh today. In pursuit of my plans, a month ago, I purchased a 'casbah,' an ancient Sultan's fortress, deep in the Atlas Mountains in South Morocco. This is now being equipped as my command post in what you might call my coming war with the world. Since my army is composed largely of Berber tribesmen recruited from the Arab world, I would find it valuable to have you as a sounding board."

I was about to tell him that what little I had gleaned of his ideas convinced me he was having delusions of grandeur, but I remembered in time that no one questioned Zolotov's sanity.

"You see, Miss Wentworth, I am a very thorough man. Last night by trans-Atlantic telephone, I unearthed a bit of your background. You have a master's degree in economics. I believe that you will find it interesting to be an observer at the center of things. While I doubt if either of us will be able to predict the full outcome of the events I will soon set in motion, nevertheless not everyone has the opportunity to be at the center of history."

I'm afraid my mind was not on economics or history. I kept trying to picture myself in bed with Zolotov. While it probably wouldn't be a fate worse than death, I couldn't convince myself that it would be inspirational.

"I'm afraid that I wouldn't make you a good wife," I said, trying to hide the distaste that I was positive was showing on my face. I was about to tell him that I was pregnant. That should convince him. But Zolotov broke the silence.

"Understand . . . I don't expect miracles," Zolotov smiled beguilingly. "Actually, Miss Wentworth, you have little choice. Since you are a woman without a country, since I believe that you are interested in one, if not both, of those men whose greed may well keep them imprisoned for life, I can obviously count on your temporary faithfulness to me."

"If I marry you, would you help get them out of jail?" I was beginning to feel like the heroine in an old time melodrama. Take my quaking white body, you monster, but don't harm a hair on my loved one's head.

"Really, I can promise you nothing," Zolotov said. "As for your friends, if they keep insisting that the gold they appropriated is really lead, they may end up in a mental institution. All I can tell you is that ultimately events may work in their favor, but I cannot promise it." Zolotov picked up my breakfast tray. "I must have your decision now. If you are agreeable, you may come down to my room with me. Ali Hassan has rescued your clothing from the hotel. You may bathe and dress. We will leave here by noon time."

I watched the wall slowly rise, wondering how Zolotov controlled it without any overt movement. Zolotov walked toward it. "The stairway my son discovered leading to the other room has been sealed off. There is no other way out."

Stunned, I watched him get into the elevator. "Wait," I pleaded and ran after him. "There's one thing you don't know about me. I am pregnant!"

"My dear woman," Zolotov said good naturedly, "I am pleased that, despite appearances, you must actually have maternal instincts. You will have endless opportunities to develop them further before your child is born. One of my reasons for making this unusual proposal to you is that I am convinced that Zoltan needs the benign influence of a mother nearer to his own age level."

If I hadn't been safely in the elevator, I might have dashed back to my prison. How could I be a mother to a boy of thirteen . . . especially when he had a "dingus" complex about me?

Twenty-seven

I married Zolotov in Marrakesh. Did I really have to marry him? Once I retrieved my clothes, I suppose I could have easily escaped from him. Even without a passport, I could have gone to the American Embassy and eventually convinced someone that I was really an "innocent abroad."

The truth lies somewhere between. Actually, when I agreed to go to Marrakesh, I never really believed that Zolotov would insist on marrying me, or that he would act so rapidly that I would scarcely have time to consider what I was doing. I was certain there was little I could do to help Craig and Carlos. Furthermore, when the chips were down, even Craig and Carlos were corruptible. Else why did they go into partnership with Doctor Pao-lin and Chang Yu and attempt to steal Zolotov's gold?

Ali Hassan drove Zolotov, Zoltan, me and two other Arabs who were evidently Zolotov's private guards, to a private hangar at the Brussels airport. To my amazement, Armand Delacroix greeted us from the open hatch of a Beechcraft *King Air*. "I see Zolotov won," he said cheerfully. He helped me board the richly appointed executive airplane.

"What choice did I have?" I asked him grimly. "You sold me for fifteen hundred bars of gold. You got such a bargain maybe you could spare me a few."

Armand grinned. "Tell me how to convert it into cash

203

and not end up in the pokey like your friends and you've got yourself a deal."

"How did Zolotov do it?"

Zolotov, who was listening to the conversation, smiled. "I learned how to be a wholesaler, not a retailer. The world is full of hungry middlemen."

I was still wondering why Armand was going to Marrakesh with us. Zolotov explained that the airplane was registered in Armand's name.

"It's mine, of course. Despite my warnings, Armand continues to hoard his ill-gotten wealth. Naturally, I avoid using my name in all these transactions. Armand is a licensed pilot. He flew with the French airforce in Viet Nam before the French debacle."

"Zolotov brought me along to be his best man." Armand stared at me thoughtfully. "Despite my own actions, the acquisitiveness of others is always a source of surprise to me. How much did Zolotov pay for you?" His voice was sour.

I looked at Zolotov who just shrugged, and fastened his seat belt. "He didn't buy me," I said nastily. "I just decided that Zoltan needed a mother."

"Big deal," Zoltan said. "I don't need an old lady. I need a bass guitar player."

With Armand in the cockpit, the wedding party of three Arabs, Zoltan, Zolotov, and his pregnant bride-to-be finally received airport clearance and took off. Zolotov ignored me completely. He opened up a folding table. After an extended discussion with Ali Hassan, in what I guessed was German, he proceeded to make what seemed like a listing of supplies. Zoltan plunked on a guitar to the evident annoyance of his father, but Zolotov said nothing.

"If you don't mind," I said finally, growing bored with a view of clouds and occasional open spaces of ocean below us, "even though I have agreed to be your captive spouse, I think I'm entitled to know a few wifely details."

204

Zolotov put down his pen. "The wheels are in motion."
He looked at his watch. "Within the hour, a gift from
Zolotov weighing some twenty-seven pounds will be on
its way to the President of the United States and the
leader of every government of the non-communist world.
With it is this letter." He handed me a two-page letter
with a heading engraved in black: Horace Zolotov,
High Atlas Mountains, Morocco.

I read it, scarcely believing the cool high-handedness
that was apparent in every sentence.

"Four months ago, I, Horace Zolotov, former chemistry
teacher in a small high school on the Eastern seaboard
of the United States, perfected a process for transmuting lead into gold. Accompanying this letter is a bar of
100 percent pure gold bullion given to your country
with my compliments. A similar bar of gold has been
dispatched to the leader of every non-communist government in the world. As a Citizen of the World, with
no petty nationalistic leanings toward any country, I
am now deliberating whether I will reveal the secret of
this relatively simple process for making gold to the
people of the world. If I should do this, the sudden
impact of this forced devaluation of gold, making it
useless as a medium of exchange between nations, will
raise havoc with the internal economies of all nations. I
believe that it is possible for men and women of all
nations, all races, all colors and creeds to work together
toward a true Golden Age for all men. Because of greed,
hate and jealousy, man is relentlessly approaching his
ultimate destruction. At this moment in history, God
has granted me the means to jar the world into a re-
appraisal of this insanity. I, now, issue the following
ultimatum to the heads of all governments. Working
through the United Nations, you must immediately
proceed to set up a Sovereign World Government to
which all nations must eventually cede their narrow
nationalistic pride; taking responsible places in a world
of community states; pursuing common objectives of

205

peace and love and humanity to all men. Once such a Sovereign World Government has been established, it will be possible through the already existing International Monetary Fund to quickly avert the danger of economic crisis and anarchy resulting from my discovery. For the first time in the history of man, a sovereign authority will have the power to issue currency under world control laws that will prevent inflation and deflation; thus, money will be used for its prime purpose; an equitable distribution of the world's wealth.

"Realizing that with this revelation, my life is in imminent danger, I have taken steps to protect myself. The method of transmuting lead into gold, fully described, is now well protected. If I should die at the hands of foreign agents, the secret will be immediately released to the news services of the world.

"By means of this letter, I give the world leaders fair warning. My discovery will, in any event, be kept secret only until March 15th of this year. The nations of the world have two months to take the initial steps toward a brotherhood of world co-operation. I shall follow the course of your decision by radio from my fortress retreat. Do not attempt to reach me with emissaries from your government. The time is short. I will remain inaccessible, but well protected against the follies of those who may seek my life. Very sincerely yours, Horace Zolotov."

"They will never believe you," I gasped. "They will think you are . . ."

"Mad." Zolotov supplied the word I didn't dare say. "Perhaps . . . but the large events in the tides of men have usually occurred from what might be considered the madness of the few. My letter may leave doubts. But they will believe the gold. To further convince them, every week, for the next month, they will receive an additional bar of gold with my compliments. By the third week, I am sure that any initial doubts will be fully dispelled." Zolotov spoke with a calm infallibility that made me want to puncture his day dream. "Even if they believe you, so what?" I asked heatedly. "Gold doesn't circulate in the world. If everyone could make it, what good would it do them? Like me . . . who could they sell it to? Anyway, the governments of the world will simply prohibit their citizens from making it."

Zolotov chuckled. "My dear girl, you are naive. The gold myth is too imbedded in the human psyche. No government could enforce such a prohibition. They might try, but it would be ineffectual. Please understand, I do not envision the average man attempting to make gold. But there are numerous governments in the world who would be unable to escape the temptation. Just imagine all the African countries proudly hoarding gold in their own Fort Knoxes!"

"But your dream is quixotic. The nations of the world could never agree to a one world government or a one world currency, not in two months . . or twenty years!"

"In an emergency of this kind," Zolotov said coolly, "they have only one hope . . . to achieve the impossible tomorrow."

Before we landed in Marrakesh, Zolotov gave me a thorough indoctrination in what he termed the psychology of the gold myth. "You see," he explained, ignoring Zoltan, who was improvising flamenco music and occasionally yelling "Ole!" "At this moment in history, there is insufficient sound money in the world to facilitate the movement of goods and trading between nations. Many of the countries of the world are relying on the United States dollar to substitute for the world shortage of gold. Thus, in a very real sense, their own local currencies are based on the ability of the United States to withstand any inflationary attack on the dollar. Actually, the dollar could function as a world currency. Because the United States is willing to buy gold from all nations at thirty-five dollars an ounce, the United

States is, in effect, making up for the shortage of gold by substituting the dollar for it. But the sad fact is that the monetary leaders of the United States are far from geniuses . . . the key to everything is faith and trust, and no country in the world really trusts the United States."

"If you have really discovered how to make gold from lead," I asked him, "isn't it possible that, right now, someone else has made the same discovery? The history of all invention seems to proceed by nearly simultaneous discovery in various parts of the world."

"Gold has been made from silver," Zolotov smiled. "But not in any appreciable quantities. While it is quite conceivable that others may discover my secret, the truth is they will be too late."

I looked at him puzzled.

"You see, my dear, *I* have been chosen. Some men have an inevitable destiny. It is my duty to precipitate the crisis." He chuckled. "Ten years from now, if a man named Zolotov walked into your bank and said he had invented a process of making gold from lead, and my secret had been lost forever, it still wouldn't be possible for you to achieve your dream of sudden wealth through him. No matter what should become of me, I can promise you I will end the gold myth forever." Zolotov stared into the fuselage of the airplane. "Three thousand years ago, it was an achievement for Hannibal to cross the Alps. Now there is a tunnel through them. I am the catalyst of the inevitable. Do you have any idea what will happen in the money markets of the world when my discovery becomes known?"

"Panic," I said softly, realizing suddenly that Zolotov had not said "if." He knew there would be no need for him to tell the world of his discovery. The damage would be done whether the method of producing gold from lead were revealed or not. Again, I wondered if he actually had discovered how to do it. What was the true secret? Would it die with him? Whom else had he told? What if he died or was murdered? I was sure that Armand had only been a pawn in Zolotov's game. Then, it suddenly dawned on me. I, Marge Wentworth, was going to become Zolotov's wife for a purpose. Someone had to assume the mantle of his monomania. In a carefully prepared campaign, Zolotov was preparing me for succession to the throne.

I walked forward in the plane and sat next to Armand. "We will land in Marrakesh in time for lunch, Mrs. Zolotov," he smirked at me. "Your wedding night is ahead of you. Bride of the man with the golden. . . ."

"Forget it," I told him quickly. "Zolotov doesn't think of such things. Maybe, you ought to grit your jaw . . . be a hero . . . and crash this plane into the sea, now, while there is still time."

"What would happen to my millions?"

"If they are millions of dollars, you may end up burning them to keep you and your mistresses warm," I told him. But Armand's economic education was only rudimentary. He just grinned at me.

Twenty-eight

I suppose someday if they ever build a monument to Horace Zolotov, it belongs in Marrakesh. I soon discovered that during the months I had been searching for him, he had been very active in the muddy financial waters of Tangier, Casablanca and Marrakesh. Using the devious ways of high finance he had also sold gold in the "free-gold" markets of Hongkong, Bangkok, and Zurich. There were a great many wealthy men in the world who had so little trust in the currencies of their countries, that an investment of a portion of their wealth, even in non-interest bearing gold, was an eminently practical maneuver. In a remarkably short time, Zolotov had not only shifted his gold to cash and securities, but he had acquired a good speaking knowledge of Arabic. He had found a path of communication with key people in the Mohammedan world that was beyond the ability of most Westerners.

Si Ben Youssef, round and laughing, in full regalia, wearing a turban and silk *djellabah* flowing in the wind, came to the airport in a ten-passenger black Cadillac within seconds of our arrival. Zolotov introduced me, explaining that he had telephoned the Pasha from Brussels early this morning.

"This is Miss Wentworth, who will become my wife."

Ben Youssef, grinning, felt my arms, looked at my teeth, turned me around twice, and patted my behind. "An excellent choice, Zolotov. Should she prove too expensive, I will be pleased to buy her from you and marry her myself."

Armand, who was following us, grinned nastily at me. "You couldn't afford her and all your other wives."

Ben Youssef ushered me into his Cadillac as if I were fragile China. "An amusing thought, young man, but I might even consent to monogamy. In truth, Miss Wentworth, one wife is very lonely. In my wives' compound, you would have pleasant companionship every day, plus the joy of anticipating all day whether this night was *your* night. In any event, you will soon meet my wives. Zoloto has leased my kasbah indefinitely."

"Why do you call him Zoloto?" I asked, looking at Horace who was squeezed in on my left.

"Because, my child, that is his name. Zoloto means gold in Russian, and my friend Zoloto certainly measures up to his name." He smiled at Zolotov affectionately. "For the magnificent sum of twenty million francs, he has leased my humble fortress. Ah, the preparations he is making! . . . An army, he has hired, with machine guns, ammunition, and vast supplies of food. Such plans, and now, Zoloto, in the name of Allah, may I at last know? With whom are we at war?"

"With the world," Zolotov snapped. "Did you locate a minister?"

Ben Youssef nodded without enthusiasm. "He waits now in the suite I reserved for you at the Hotel de la Mamounia. One of your good citizens from the Peace Corps, a Doctor Harry Teeter, who is dedicating his life to converting the infidels to the even crueller ways of Christianity."

I listened to this conversation bewildered. I couldn't believe that Zolotov wasn't going to discuss the idea of our marriage further. I needed time to marshall arguments as to why I couldn't marry him. What would he do if I simply refused? I decided that I didn't dare to be that blunt. Zolotov might immediately betroth me to Ben Youssef!

"I didn't know that Zolotov meant gold," I said, trying desperately to think of a diplomatic way out. "Really, Horace, I think we should get better acquainted. Can't we wait a few days before we are married?"

"Zoloto is an English approximation for the Russian word meaning gold," Zolotov said, ignoring my question. "What does it matter who I am or how well you know me? Jesus was a Jew. If a Russian saves the world, the coincidence will simply be ironic, not golden."

"Jesus was nothing," Ben Youssef shrugged. "Mohammed is the Prophet. I am sorry, Zoloto, that I couldn't convince you to have a proper marriage."

Zolotov smiled. "While it might not matter to Miss Wentworth, I doubt if the conversion to your beliefs would please her. Besides," he said as we drove through the gardens and past the olive and tangerine trees that surrounded the Mamounia, "it would take too long. I am in a hurry!"

As we were brought to our suite in the hotel, I couldn't escape the feeling that I was dreaming. Was this really Marge Wentworth casually noting the luxuries of what was obviously a very expensive hotel? How had I managed to come so far from the eighty-five dollar a week world of a proper secretary to a bank president? How could I so calmly shake hands with the greying Doctor Teeter who looked at me worriedly through his unrimmed spectacles?

"It is somewhat surprising to find American citizens coming all the way to Marrakesh to be united in a Christian ceremony." He stared at Zoltan and then me. "I presume, Mr. Zolotov, that you have been married before. This young woman looks a little young to be the mother of such a husky youngster." Unspoken was the question on his face. Why was I marrying a man so much older than me? I wanted to tell Doctor Teeter that we were all dreaming, and, of course, the truth was that any minute now, Zolotov would change his mind. It just couldn't be happening. Even though I had accepted Zolotov's offer, the truth was I never believed he was serious. The worst I had expected was to be Zolotov's somewhat reluctant mistress, certainly not his wife.

Numbly, I watched Ben Youssef hand Zolotov a huge diamond ring (I learned later it was ten carats). "This is a marriage of convenience, Doctor Teeter," Zolotov said. "Not love. I am sure you agree that most marriages are not made in heaven."

I tried not to see the sardonic expression on Armand's face. What was I doing? If I had ever loved Craig, I was making a travesty of that love. A female Faust selling her soul for the Devil's gold which would probably turn to ashes as just recompense. But come what may, I had to follow my Pied Piper. It was more than money. Zolotov had hypnotized me with the mad tune he piped. Willy nilly, I had to follow, knowing in my heart that the excuse I had married Zolotov to save Craig or Carlos would never survive Craig's wrath. Even if Craig knew that I had been practically a virgin when I first went to the couch with him, there was no denying that in two months my Cinderella dream was leading me rapidly away from my charming Prince.

"There will be no gold band," Zolotov was telling Doctor Teeter. "I do not believe in the binding efficacy of gold."

As Doctor Teeter started the ceremony, I crossed my fingers. I could always divorce Zolotov. Even if, from Craig's standpoint, my morality had suffered an irreparable blow, maybe someday I could persuade him that I really hadn't strayed too far from the paths of virtue.

Somehow, I managed to hold back my tears long enough to make the correct answers in response to Doctor Teeter's short ceremony, but I am afraid the "I, Marge Wentworth, take Horace Zolotov" was uttered with a suppressed sob. Zolotov quickly kissed my cheek. Armand insisted on a full kiss on the lips of Margery Zolotov, and whispered with a grin. "Like gold, you can't take it with you. If Zolotov can't use it . . ."

I wanted to slug him, but at least managed to grind my pointed high heel into his toe. I smiled at him as he grimaced in pain.

Zolotov paid the much confused Doctor Teeter and dismissed him. "I have reserved the room next to us for Zoltan. Armand is well acquainted with Marrakash. He will take you and Zoltan sightseeing. Ben Youssef and I will be very busy making final preparation for our departure the day after tomorrow." He pointed out the window to the snowcapped peaks of the Atlas Mountains. "Ben Youssef's casbah is a two day truck journey from here. It is a rugged trip. I suggest you pass your time leisurely. Purchase any clothing you may wish."

Was Zolotov telling me that there would be no nuptial night? I hoped so. When he handed me a huge roll of Moroccan dirhams for my expenses, and told me they were worth five for one dollar, I tried to smile my gratitude at him. I wanted to hug him and tell him that even if I couldn't be a good wife, I would be a fine sister to him.

Zoltan wasn't so obtuse. "Why did my old man have to

marry you? Do you have to get married to sleep together? Are you going to make a baby?"

"I'm your mother now," I told him, "and boys don't ask their mothers questions like that."

When Zolotov left, Armand took us to lunch in the Mamounia. We sampled mint tea and Kous Kous. Armand gave me instructions on how to roll the rice into golf balls and get them into my mouth before they exploded enroute.

As we ate lunch, I noticed that Armand had adopted a new attitude toward me. His pointed barbs and sarcastic remarks were replaced by a conspiratorial, hand touching manner. He seemed to be suggesting that since Zolotov was taking such a cavalier attitude toward his new bride he would be more than willing to fill the gap. "Marrakesh does not come alive until midnight," he said. "While you rest in your room for an hour or so, I will make arrangements for this evening." He ruffled Zoltan's hair and winked at me. "This is a city of music. Zoltan will come with me while we find some new and different drummers for him."

While I suspected that an evening in Marrakesh with Armand could lead me into further trouble, I certainly didn't anticipate the denouement. He returned to the room about five o'clock. To my amazement, he was dressed in a turban and *djellabah*. He handed me a package, ignoring for the moment my question as to what he had done with Zoltan.

"This is a Moorish woman's dress, a caftan. These are babooches for your feet. Put them on please, we are going to a special party with friends of mine."

"What have you done with Zoltan?" I demanded, as I examined the flowing silk saffron gown and gold girdle that was evidently worn over it. Weakly, I protested that this was ridiculous. I felt like some high school kid about to appear in a class play. But Armand insisted on helping me put the dress on.

214

"Ah, when you drop your veil, you will look more exotic than any Eastern woman." He chuckled. "Zoltan will scarely recognize his mother!"

Feeling somewhat trembly, as if I were Armand's new bride instead of Zolotov's, I let him lead me through the hotel. We took a taxi to the great central square, the Djemaa El Fnaa. "It means the Market-place of the Dead," Armand explained. "Many years ago, a Sultan laid out his dead prisoners of war in this square. Over there is the Koutoubia, the famous mosque of Marrakesh. The minaret was topped once with three balls of pure gold." Armand smiled. "Now they are copper. If your husband is right, the copper balls may someday be more valuable than gold."

"Right now, I'm not worried about gold. What have you done with Zoltan?"

"In a moment. Do not worry. He is with friends. First, as good Moslems, we must pray." As he finished the words, I felt as if the world had suddenly gone silent. From the minaret on the Koutoubia, the quavering wail of a muezzin intoned, "Allah Akbar! Allah Akbar! La ilah, ilallah." A hush spread over the square. Armand had spread a prayer rug. He pushed me down, with our backs to the sunset. While I tried to stop giggling, we prostrated ourselves toward Mecca.

Finally, he pulled me to my feet. "Now, the night commences. Since the bride of Zolotov may be spending her life in this exotic land, it is fitting that she make some concession to its customs." Armand grinned happily at me. "I must say, you look ravishingly Oriental."

Feeling like a Princess out of the Arabian Nights, I followed him into the Djemaa. The square was rapidly coming to life. "Here all Morocco blends," Armand said. He identified dark skinned Arabs from the coastal cities, blue-eyed Berbers from the mountains, Algerians from the desert, fuzzy-haired Soudanese, and swarthy

Jews slowly emerging into the night. Jostling through the crowds, I listened momentarily to a blind man pounding a tambourine and singing some story or song through rotten teeth. Further on, a snake charmer was playing a high pitched cadence on a wooden pipe while two black coils with wedge shaped heads swayed to the music. As Armand led me away, I saw the snake charmer pick up one of his snakes and thrust its head into his mouth.

"It won't bite him," Armand said as I shuddered. "They are very nice playthings."

The place was now so congested it was nearly impossible to move from one bit of entertainment to another. Pushing through the crowd, we were on the edge of a group of musicians. In the middle, dressed in a white burnouse, sitting on a straw mat, pounding away on a pottery type vase covered with sheepskin, was Zoltan. Sitting with him were three other Arab boys, one playing a drum similar to his and the other two playing African lutes with two strings.

Zoltan recognized Armand. He grinned as he discovered me. "Hi," he waved enthusiastically, and kept pounding. "This is neat."

We watched while an older man, evidently the leader, introduced a wild, high pitched melody on an instrument shaped like a viol but with only one string. He played it with increasing frenzy and sang a love song while three young boys with shaved heads, wearing girls' clothes, earrings, bracelets, and beaded necklaces, their eyes and cheeks streaked with kohl, danced and undulated and underlined the words with obviously sexual movements.

"My God," I whispered to Armand. "Those kids are queer. You'll ruin Zoltan."

"Don't worry," Armand chuckled. "The man playing the lute is Ahmet, he will take care of Zoltan and get him back to the hotel. The boys dancing are Shelluhs. This is their profession."

216

"What are they singing?"

" 'Oh, my fair mistress, cry aloud with joy,' " Armand translated happily. " 'For, by Allah, the only God, at the sound of thy voice, the sick man will throw away his mat, the old man will throw away his cane.' " Armand chuckled, "It grows better. Shall I continue?"

"No," I said weakly, and followed him into the crowd. The square was alive now with the dancing light of lanterns and acetylene torches. Armand led me into a maze of alleys between low mud walls. He pointed out the five-fingered hand of Fatima, a good luck sign, adorning many of the doors.

The remainder of the evening is a kaleidoscopic mirage. We passed through a dimly lighted courtyard into an inner court. I remember candles flickering in Moorish Lanterns, I remember thick mattresses piled everywhere and silk pillows and cushions in profusion. I remember Armand telling me to take off my babooches. I remember dancing girls arriving, taking off their veils; their bangles of gold and silver jewelry tinkling as they warmed their tambourines before a charcoal brazier. I remember someone passing me a small pipe and my happy laughter as I inhaled a few puffs of what I thought was tobacco. Then, suddenly, I was floating in a dream world. Nothing was important or real any more. When Armand asked me how I liked hashish, I remember smiling vacuously and kissing him. I remember dancing, feeling certain that as I weaved to the strange music, I was obeying ancient rules imbedded in some part of my primitive brain.

Did I actually make love to Armand while we lay buried deep in those luxurious pillows? Did I think, since only this morning I had gone through the formalities of a wedding ceremony, that I held my only true lover in my arms? I'm sure I didn't. Not then, in that place, floating and erotic with the heady odor from the kief pipes, but I probably would have later when Armand brought me back to the hotel.

217

I remember trying to thank Armand for a lovely evening, but the words coming out of my mouth seemed actually tangible; like butterflies, they swooped around my head. Nor were Armand's eyes, as he followed me into the room, just ordinary eyes. They filled his entire face and then detaching themselves from his body, they flew after my butterflies which fluttered helplessly and finally merged with Armand's glaring eyes. Giggling, I felt my caftan take on a life of its own. It disappeared in a soft purple cloud over my head. I noticed that the chairs in the room were all nodding and smiling at me in delightful acquiescence. They liked my naked body. I agreed with them that it was beautiful. I held my breasts in my hands so that they could see how lovely they were.

Then the dream shifted and suddenly I realized that Zolotov, standing at the door with two Arabs and Ali Hassan, was watching me. Zolotov didn't seem pleased. Yet he didn't seem angry. But his face was terribly rigid. He was pointing a gun at Armand! I couldn't help it, I was laughing happily. Naked, I prostrated myself on the floor and paid my respects to Allah. Allah seemed quite angry now, but his gun floated out of his hand and joined Armand's eyes. Why was Allah so furious with Armand? Why were Ali Hassan and the other men leading Armand out of the room? Allah wouldn't answer me. He picked me up and dropped me on a soft, white cloud. Slowly, I sank into it and went to sleep.

I awoke shivering. Lying on the bed naked, I was focused in the cruel glare of a standing lamp aimed at my body. The rest of the room was pitch black. Zolotov, in his underwear, was sitting in the shadows at the edge of the bed, staring at me.

"I'm freezing," I moaned. "Why did you undress me?"

"I didn't undress you. Armand did," Zolotov said coldly. "You smoked a pipeful of dreams . . . hash-hish."

"I thought it was just a cute pipeful of tobacco," I said feebly. My head was aching and I felt quite miserable. "Please, what have you done with the bedcovers? I am freezing."

"Moroccan nights are cold," Zolotov said grimly. "The winds are blowing off the Atlas Mountains. You need to be chilled back to reality."

"Horace, please," I begged him. My teeth were chattering. "I'll catch pneumonia. Why are you staring at me like that?"

"I am wondering how such a marvellous creation as your face, your breasts, your legs, the breathing, living, beautiful femininity of you can exist and not somehow reflect the corruption of your mind!"

I sat up on the bed and moved nearer to him. His face looked very worn and emaciated. I wondered if he were sick. Suddenly, I felt very sorry for him, and for me, and for the world, and all the helplessly groping and striving men and women trying to find each other. With tears in my eyes, I told him to please come to bed. "I didn't make love to Armand," I said softly.

"If I hadn't arrived, you would have." Zolotov wiped his brow. I noticed for the first time that despite the chill of the room, he was perspiring. He rose from his chair. "You will have to excuse me. I feel quite nauseous."

I heard him retching in the bathroom and ran to him. "How could I make you so unhappy?" I asked him, holding his head over the sink. "You can't love me."

"I am not sick from jealousy." Zolotov wiped his face. He struggled to regain his dignity. "I have occasional bouts of this kind. I am somewhat anaemic. I have difficulty with my digestion."

He let me lead him back to the bed. "I really hadn't planned to sleep with you," he murmured.

I found the blankets and covered him, put the lights out, and climbed in beside him. "I did marry you, Horace," I said quietly.

I felt him skinny and naked beside me. "For the worse, Margery," he muttered. "For the worse. That I can assure you."

I felt a surge of pity for this strange man. I put my arms around him. He lay with his face against by breast. "Are you all right?"

"I will live, thank you!"

"What did you do with Armand?"

"I gave him what he wanted. Ali Hassan took him to a brothel," Zolotov said with an unpleasant chuckle. "For the next twenty-four hours, Armand will get the treatment." He gave the word treatment a nasty inflexion.

I shuddered. "What's the treatment?"

"They will lash him to a bed and leave him for the girls. When the whores in the Djemaa finish with Armand, he won't have a sexual thought for several months." Zolotov was silent for a moment. "In this world of excess, I am the last believer in moderation. Goodnight, my wife."

I don't know why. I cried.

Twenty-nine

We left Marrakesh a day later. Zolotov's caravan of three trucks led by a Land Rover driven by Ali Hassan was waiting for us at the gates of the city. Worn, his beard uncombed and shaggy, his eyes bloodshot, looking as if he should fall into a bed and sleep for a week, Armand saw us off.

"I am only a little angry at you," he said to Zolotov, who listened to him impatiently from the front seat of the Rover. "I suppose I deserved it."

Zolotov shrugged. "Gold and women are equal temptations. At least, you have the gold. Enjoy it in good health."

220

"I am certainly not a man to poach on another man's territory. I didn't really think you gave a damn." Armand looked grimly at me. "The prize seemed available for the taking."

If I hadn't been in the back seat sitting beside Ben Youssef, I would have punched him. "You played a dirty trick on me," I said indignantly. "I was drugged. I didn't even know what was happening." My curiosity got the better of me. "You certainly look terrible. Who have you been sleeping with, a nymphomaniac?"

Armand sighed. "The unwilling erotic capacity of the male subjugated by an army of enthusiastic females is an area of life I never plan to explore again. Good luck to you, Marge Zolotov. Be careful that your daydreams don't get the better of you, too!"

Zolotov waved goodbye. "The Beechcraft is yours, Armand. I signed the papers over to you this morning. Enjoy yourself. Monetarily, it may be later than you think."

While our caravan bumped and twisted along parched Moroccan roads toward Ben Youssef's casbah in the Atlas Mountains, with dust behind us occasionally so thick that we lost sight of the following trucks, Ben Youssef regaled us with a long history of the wars between the local caliphs. We passed the remnants of walled cities with crenelated towers and minarets.

"Prior to the first World War, this country was very similar to your land in the Middle Ages. The caliphs had local power on their lands. They fought continuously to extend their domains. The casbahs then were very similar to your European castles. The serfs were protected by the lord of the manor, and in exchange for this protection, produced the wealth that made the caliph powerful." Ben Youssef sighed. "Now the state takes care of such things. But the people are not any better off. Most men live and die and leave no mark on the shifting sands of the world."

Ben Youssef explained that his hereditary casbah had

survived the years in much better condition than the
ruins we passed. "It is in the foothills of Tizi Ouiched-
dan." He pointed out to a snow capped mountain in the
distance. "On the edge of a mountain cliff, it is nearly
impregnable. Not today, of course, with airplanes . . .
but who would seek us out in this poor, unwanted
land?"

"If Zolotov has his way," I said, "The world is going
to beat a path to your door."

For the first time, Zolotov, who seemed quite preoccupied with his thoughts, spoke: "The world will be
caught in Zolotov's mousetrap. It will be too late to
seek out the inventor. Like Greek Gods on Olympus,
we will enjoy the struggle, but not participate."

I looked at him surprised. I realized suddenly that
Zolotov was entertaining the idea of never returning to
the civilized world. "I don't plan to spend the remainder of my life in the wilds of Morocco," I told him.
Zolotov smiled. "As a woman who tied herself to the
wheel of fortune, I would think you have remarkably
little choice. When the bubble bursts, Zolotov and
anyone identified with him, such as his greedy wife,
will inherit the stigma. We will be hated before we
will be loved."

I couldn't help it, I started to cry. "All that idealistic
garbage that you wrote in your letter isn't true at all, is
it?" I demanded bitterly. "You know that the nations
of the world can't unite quickly enough to avert financial
disaster."

Zolotov shrugged. "You knew it, too, Margery. France
has an outstanding economist, Jacques Rueff . . .
poor man, for some thirty years, he has been trying
to convince the world to place their faith in gold.
'Money will decide the fate of mankind,' he said. And
he is right. If a thorough going inflation is unleashed on
the world, men will wake up to find their freedom is
closely related to the value of money in their pockets.
Such is the greed of men to have things and not work

222

for them, that it is inevitable within two weeks the world will plunge into a depression that will make 1929 seem like a pleasant 'rolling adjustment' as the economists say."

I knew Zolotov was right. For several days, I had tried to anticipate the sequence of events that his letter would set in motion. That a process had been discovered for making gold from such an inexpensive and fairly abundant raw material as lead was not likely to be kept secret. Ministers of Finance in foreign countries would move fast to unload their gold. Who would buy it? The United States, of course! The United States had a fixed price on gold of thirty-five dollars an ounce! Before the official price of gold could be changed, the United States would be deluged with it.

"The known world reserves of gold are about fifty billion dollars," Zolotov said. "Russia has an unknown quantity, let's guess about fifteen billion dollars. The United States, of the world total, has about seventeen billion dollars' worth. When the rest of the world starts selling to the United States, there isn't going to be room enough in Fort Knox to hold it all."

Slowly, the horrible picture was beginning to dawn on me. "When the United States buys gold, it prints paper money to pay for it," I said softly, feeling a sinking sensation in my stomach as I realized the enormity of Zolotov's madness. "With so much paper money available, interest rates will decline, borrowers will go on a spending spree."

"I think it will be somewhat different," Zolotov said happily. "When the foreign countries who hold gold sell it for dollars, they won't want dollars either. They won't trust the value of the dollar. Where can they turn? What values will be left in the world? Real estate and stocks. The stock market will react first because stock in industry at least represents something tangible; stocks at least give an ownership in something that can produce wealth. But, of course, everyone will be chasing rainbows. My guess is that within the next two or three weeks, there will be such a boom on the stock markets of the world as governments and citizens unload their paper currency that the value of shares in any company will have no relation whatsoever to its productive capacity; let alone its profit-making potential. Profits will be academic anyway, since they can only be measured and paid in paper money that will have no purchasing capacity."

Listening to Zolotov, I was slowly realizing that he had a deity complex. Fate had at last given the world a little man with deep hidden hatreds against the established order of wealth; a little man with the power to do something about it.

"It is amusing to me, Margery," Zolotov smiled, but there was no laughter in his words, "that a woman like you, so typically a prototype of the vast majority who want wealth without labor, who believe it quite moral to live on the sweat of another man's toil, should question my motives. It should be apparent to you that God has given me the power to produce the deluge. When the flood waters recede, a new world may emerge. Rational men would be able to cope with my discovery, but irrational man must be tried by fire. Reason and good sense emerge only with adversity. When trading between nations has finally stopped because there is no medium of exchange in which men have faith and trust, when savings have been wiped out, and the people of the world have been forced to accept the fact that their arduous lifetime hoardings of paper money will no longer buy the products of their labor, men all over the world will be forced to work together in a harmony of nations. It will be the only way possible to restore trust in paper money. When that happens, the world will no longer revile Zolotov. He will be recognized as an instrument of God."

"And what will we be doing in the meantime?" I demanded.

224

"We will live like Thoreau," Zolotov grinned at me maddeningly. "Rejecting the false values of the world, we will raise Zoltan and your coming child in our mountain retreat. By the sweat of our brows, we will learn what freedom really means."

While I was near tears, Ben Youssef had listened to our conversation with numerous chuckles. He told Zolotov that he was happy to offer his casbah to Noah Zolotov who could use it as his own private ark. Ali Hassan, ignoring the conversation, twisting and turning the wheel of the Rover, drove us through a wild green valley called Oued Nfi's. In second gear, we climbed through barren hills and then emerged into a valley of scorching hot wheat fields irrigated by streams flowing from the snowcapped Atlas.

Ben Youssef tried to cheer me up. "Of course, my casbah is not luxurious by American standards, but Zolotov is coming prepared. In the trucks following us are gasoline generators we will use temporarily. Zolotov says, however, we must not be dependent on money to buy gasoline. Under construction near my casbah is a dam, and with us are turbines. Eventually, we will be electrified by nature's water. There are also short wave radios, refrigerators, and a truck loaded with canned goods." He grinned. "In our mountain retreat, we will be Little America . . . but, alas, there will be no Coca Cola. Zolotov refused to buy Coca Cola!"

Thirty

The shock waves of Zolotov's impending earthquake reached us at Ben Youssef's casbah, the first week in February. I was still somewhat dazed by the realization that I was not only Zolotov's wife, but I was also virtually his prisoner. We were nearly one hundred and fifty miles from Marrakesh and Zolotov, with great amusement, had informed me that if I found Moorish marital life too difficult, I could have a mule and sufficient food for the journey back. Nevertheless a somewhat tentative routine had been established.

Mornings I wandered with Zoltan through the casbah or beyond its walls trying to make smiling acquaintance with the Berber women who threshed the wheat in the valley below us, or we would watch Ali Hassan assemble Zolotov's rag-tag army of about fifty Berber tribesmen each morning before the fountain in the courtyard. Ali Hassan issued instructions to the fierce looking men. He evidently chastised them for leering at me, the infidel woman, who coolly stared at them with her veil lifted. When Ali wasn't looking, I winked at the handsome ones.

The days and nights flowed together. There was little or nothing to do. After his generators were finally operating and his short wave radio was emitting squeaks and groans in the palace room that Ben Youssef had assigned to us, Zolotov developed a ritual that began at sunrise with the nasal morning prayers of the muezzin invoking Allah.

"Good morning, my wife," he would smile at me as I lay beside him on the mattresses and cushions piled high on the floor. Zolotov slept in his shorts. I, with a silk coverlet, slept naked. "It is time to rise and face the facts of life!" Groaning and burying my face in the pillows, aware that he was looking at my belly as he sprang to life and did a few quick arm and knee bends, I muttered that only old men were so enthusiastic about the sunrise. Young women preferred their dreams.

A black Soudanese boy, with head averted, brought us coffee, bowls of vermicelli and a platter of grapes, tangerines, and figs. While Zolotov twisted dials and listened to the news broadcasts from the capitals of the world, I languidly doodled with the food and contemplated my fate.

Zolotov had never attempted to make love to me. At

night, Horace would turn off the garish electric lights, with unshaded bulbs, that Ali Hassan and his men had strung into the room. Lighting the candles in the Moorish lanterns, he would watch me undress.

"Your belly is getting rounder," he said one night. "Your breasts are a little fuller. Whose child is it?"

Surprised that he was even aware of the slight changes, I told him with tears in my eyes that I wasn't sure. "I am not a good woman," I said sadly.

"You are a woman. Morality for the female is a male concept. You are simply fulfilling your function on this earth." He sighed. "I remember Manya when she was carrying Zoltan. A pregnant woman is a delight to watch, sufficient at last unto herself."

"A female always needs a male," I said, lying on the cushions beside him. "Were you a stranger to Manya, too?"

He didn't answer for awhile and then said. "Every human being is ultimately a stranger. Good night, my wife."

I wondered if he expected me to take the initiative and attempt to arouse his passions. But Zolotov passionate about anything except gold seemed ludicrous. While I didn't love him, a growing feeling of pity for this obsessed, skinny wreck of a man (perversely, I suppose) made me want to put my arms around him. I wondered if I could penetrate his remoteness. If I was going to spend a lifetime with him, I couldn't escape forever my desires as a female. I knew that I was hopelessly entangled in middle class concepts of marriage. I wanted a male who needed me a little. I didn't love Zolotov, but the new life growing in my body was slowly puncturing my assumed sophistication. Sometime, soon, I wanted a husband who, at least, actually made love to me!

Finally, the night that Zolotov handed me two pieces of paper closely written in a copperplate script, and demanded that I commit them to memory, I tried to seduce him. The paper was covered with detailed chemical formulas numbered in sequence from one to eighteen.

"What do they mean?" I asked him bewildered. "I can never memorize these. I was a horrible failure in math."

"You don't have to know what they mean," Zolotov said patiently. "I'm sure that you can learn them by rote. One other person in the world will know my secret. Should I die, you can write them down again. With this knowledge, any competent person can transmute lead into gold. In a few days, I will test you to make sure you have learned the procedure."

"Why should I bother? Gold will be no good, anyway."

"It is my legacy to you, Margery," Zolotov smiled. "I have made a will leaving you all my worldly possessions. However, the truth is the assets of the Zoloto Corporation which are largely in stocks and real estate, now residing in a bank in Zurich, may not survive the debacle. Certain countries may feel that since Zolotov came by his wealth illegitimately, it should be impounded by the state. In any event, this formula will have monetary value for you. I assure you, the world will be interested, if only in unhappy retrospect."

I asked him why he kept talking as if he were going to die.

Zolotov shrugged. "I am twenty-two years older than you, Margery. You may decide that the world is right. The woman who destroys Zolotov would be a heroine."

"You will destroy yourself, first," I shuddered. "I'm sorry you believe that I am so corrupt."

Zolotov lay down on the cushion next to me. He held my hand, and stared at the ceiling. The candles on the wall flickered. A cool breeze blew off the mountains. "I am afraid that I have already destroyed myself," he said finally. "You must be aware that I am ill."

I smiled at him. "I am aware that you don't react like a normal man lying beside a naked female who is practically his captive." I pulled his face to mine and kissed him. "Since I am probably going to finish out my life here, you might just as well make love to me."

"I love you as a friend who grows dearer to me every day." Zolotov looked at me with moist eyes. "The truth is, I am not capable of loving you any other way."

I stared at him astonished.

He shrugged. "If I didn't know otherwise, Margery, I would assume that you had never seen a naked man in the presence of a willing female; either that, or you are strangely unobservant. My illness has made me impotent."

I couldn't help it. I started to laugh hysterically, and ended up crying myself to sleep in Zolotov's arms. It wasn't that I actually wanted Zolotov to make love to me. At least, I don't think so. It was just the insanity of it. I was sure that if Craig knew where my obsession had led me, it would make his incarceration in a Brussels jail more tolerable. Marge Zolotov, nee Wentworth, had certainly got her comeuppance!

The next afternoon, after I had returned from a giggling session with Ben Youssef's wives (they didn't speak English and I couldn't understand a word of their happy Berber dialect . . . there were three of them, Aziza, Khira, and Kbira) and I was wondering if ultimately I would have to accept Ben Youssef's proposal, join the harem, and bounce on Ben's enormous belly every fourth night, I found Zolotov happily listening to a clear broadcast from London.

"Reflecting the unusual activity in the United States and in the London gold market," the announcer said, "The United States has today demanded an immediate meeting of the directors of the International Monetary Fund. Former objections of France to a demonetization of gold have been withdrawn. Amazingly, French economists are advocating strenuously a new international exchange medium, and full monetary control of the Western nations by the International Monetary Fund. The French government is selling gold with an amazing abandon. France seems quite eager to substitute dollars and pounds for gold in their national reserves. What this will do to the value of the franc is being openly questioned. While gold prices on the London free market suddenly tumbled to twenty-five dollars an ounce, at this broadcast, the United States is continuing to attempt to stabilize the market, and is purchasing gold in huge quantities at the established rate of thirty-five dollars an ounce. It is estimated that today alone, several billion dollars were purchased by the United States government."

As the news switched to war in Asia, Zolotov turned off the radio. "It is beginning to rain," he grinned. "The floods are coming soon."

The next day practically all the news broadcasts from around the world were devoted to gold. An N.B.C. broadcast with a well known commentator attempted to summarize the developments:

"International Monetary Fund officials have been in almost continuous session since the beginning of the week," the commentator said, "While there are conflicting opinions in financial circles as to the underlying causes, the head of the New York Stock Exchange said today that it is obvious that the world's confidence in the value of gold has been rudely shaken. Rumors persist that a cheap process for the manufacture of gold from lead has been discovered. Gold mining stocks, long accepted as a hedge against inflation of the dollar, have fallen to new lows today. But no one seemed to care what happened to gold stocks. All stocks, both those listed on the New York and American Exchange as well as foreign stock exchanges throughout the world, are being purchased with increasing frenzy. Not only blue chip stocks, but even lowly over the counter stocks of small companies were bid up to new highs. Former yardsticks such as the price-earnings ratios of stocks vanished in smoke as foreign governments and private citizens threw caution to the wind and bid stocks up to a thousand and two thousand times earning potential. While all governments, including Russia, were selling gold, not until yesterday did the United States stop buying at thirty-five dollars an ounce. It is rumored that United States gold reserves have jumped close to forty billion dollars within six days."

I sat in fascinated horror as Zolotov and Ben Youssef sat twiddling dials through the night. We listened to broadcast after broadcast, interspersed with heated discussions as we tried to comprehend what Zolotov happily described as the "destruction of the gold myth." A day later, a news commentator excitedly summed up the "Mad Week of Panic". "It all started ten days ago when rumors that a scientist, now identified as Horace Zolotov, living in the High Atlas Mountains of Morocco, had achieved the dream of the alchemists. He had actually made gold from lead. No one seriously believed it at first. Top physicists and chemists throughout the world generally admitted that while it was possible in small quantities, as a threat to gold mining, transmutation could be discounted as impractical. They insisted the manufacturing costs would exceed the cost of mining and refining gold which was once not far from the world price of thirty-five dollars an ounce. Whether they are correct or not, somewhere in the world, a man named Horace Zolotov may be having grim satisfaction tonight at the destruction he has wrought.

"The first signs of panic started ten days ago with gold being sold in the New York and London markets in quantities that threw all economic theories about ratios of gold to currency in national reserves to the winds. It reached a climax last Friday with stock exchanges all over the world closing their doors and refusing to sell shares of stock at any price. Before the exchanges were shut down stock of any kind was being grabbed up by a world that has lost faith in money.

"The stock exchanges did not open this morning. Congress has been in closed session for the past five days. Finally, yesterday, a very sober President of the United States addressed the world in a belated television broadcast that has done little to ease the fears of the people, who are now transferring their stock buying frenzy to millions of real estate transactions. While the nation is split into hopeful believers who think they will be rich beyond their dreams and disbelievers who would rather have real property than paper money, the President carefully admitted that 'the world had been caught napping.'

"There seems to be no doubt that a cheap process for making gold is available, the President said, but, he pointed out, gold has no relationship to the productive capacity of this country which is at an all time high. Gold never had value in and of itself. Productive labor of free men is the only unit of value in the world. According to the President, the nations of the world are now at work on a world program for a new international medium of exchange. While ultimately this new money may supersede all national currencies, the people of the United States must understand that the dollar has not lost its value. The President announced that effective today, price control regulations have gone into immediate effect. Despite the President's confidence, this week will go down in history as the Week of Doom. A general madness seems to be seizing the people. Rumors are spreading that savings will be wiped out, that the United States will have to surrender its fiscal control to a sovereign authority and that everybody will eventually have to start from scratch. While prices may be held, the general public seems determined to spend every dollar they can get their hands on. Night clubs and the entertainment industry are booming as the philosophy of 'today we live . . . tomorrow we will be broke,' pervades the entire country."

"Too bad you aren't home, Margery," Zolotov said grimly as he turned the radio off. "Everybody has decided to live like millionaires. In a few weeks, the people will probably stop working altogether. Then the rich and poor can lie down together in the same sty."

Thirty-one

As the days went by and we sat in our mountain oasis twiddling the radio dials, the world crisis deepened. On issue after issue, the western nations squabbled. Arguments persisted that it was all a hoax. Gold was still valid as a medium of exchange between nations. Who was Horace Zolotov? Where was he? If he could actually make gold, why didn't he come forward and reveal his formula?

No country, particularly the United States, was agreeable to having its monetary policies dictated by a sovereign world authority. Because a method of settling international payments could not be agreed upon, foreign trade had, within a month, come to an almost complete halt.

While Zolotov and I listened to the vastly conflicting proposals, the fear of world depression deepened. Hundreds of thousands of people in Africa and Canada engaged in gold mining and refining were unemployed as the gold mines shut down completely.

Zolotov delighted in discussing the irrationality of the whole business. "No one knows for certain that gold can actually be made from lead; everyone knows in their heart that gold isn't the key to prosperity, yet all one man has to do is to attack one myth that men live by and the world starts to tumble. Even when the solution is found, men will discover that there are other myths. All it takes is a loud clap of thunder and the sheep panic and run."

"You didn't really expect the leaders to solve the problem, did you?" I asked him bitterly. "All that business about a deadline was just a nasty joke. People reacted just the way you thought they would. And now, the Great God Zolotov chuckles in his beard."

Zolotov, who was eating a spoonful of greasy kous-kous without enthusiasm, looked at me painfully. "I have no beard, Margery. I'm afraid that I should stick to a milk diet; this food does not agree with me." I had noticed that Horace was, if possible, getting even thinner. His gums had turned a mottled blue and red. "Truly," he said, "I do not relish what I have done. I am simply the instrument of fate. If it were not me, it would have been someone else. Perhaps out of this evil and suffering will ultimately come good."

But Horace, the great father administering the spanking that hurt him more than it hurt the child, had misjudged his children and their accumulated wrath at the builder of a better mousetrap. Within three days after the text of Zolotov's letter was released to the public and read and translated into every language of the world, Ben Youssef's casbah was no longer a remote hideaway in the Atlas Mountains. The world had angrily beaten a path to our door.

To get away from the incessant blasting of the radio and Zolotov, who was making copious notes on every broadcast and was evidently planning to write his own version of the Decline and Fall of the Western World, I established a morning routine of leaving the walled city and walking about a mile with Zoltan to the waters of a clear, cold mountain waterfall. Since there was no adequate plumbing in the casbah, Zoltan and I undressed and happily frolicked in our natural cold shower, bathing in the clear basin of rocks beneath it. Although at first Zoltan kept staring at me, he finally grew accustomed to seeing his "mother's dingus" and calmly accepted the flora of the female body as simply an interesting phenomenon. Later, dressed again in my caftan (Ben Youssef had delightedly supplied me with a complete Moorish wardrobe) with my veil lowered so that I would attract less attention from the Berber tribesmen perched on the walls, we usually returned to the casbah before noon.

I persuaded Ben Youssef that while I knew it was against the rules, really a thirteen year old boy could do no harm in his harem. Afternoons, Zoltan and I sipped mint tea with Ben Youssef's wives while they taught Zoltan and me to play the rhab, a two-stringed lute. Zoltan, strangely, was fascinated by the twelve-tone scale and the never ending monotony of their songs. To his wives' and Ben Youssef's amusement, Zoltan improvised rock and roll rhythms to Arabic songs.

Ben Youssef offered me a pipe of kief which I politely declined. "Horace is a strange man," he said, puffing contentedly. "He does not make love to you. Why is this?"

I didn't answer. I wondered how in the devil Ben Youssef could know what went on after we went to bed.

Chuckling, he answered the question I didn't ask. "There is a tiny hole in the wall of your room. When my wife of the evening comes to me, I tell her tonight we will watch and see how Americans make love. It is very nice for a female to watch another couple, it arouses her. But alas . . . night after night . . . nothing happens." Ben Youssef's happy, round face, expectantly waiting for an answer, suddenly turned serious. "Do you hear something strange?"

There was no time to answer. We all heard it together . . . the steady drone of approaching airplanes. We dashed into the courtyard and found Zolotov watching their approach. There were two of them. As they came closer, they pealed out of their lonely formation and zoomed in over the casbah.

"What are they doing?" I screamed at Zolotov. One of them banked and dived at us, not five hundred feet over our heads. The shattering explosions of their engines vibrated and shook the mud walls of our fortress.

"They are invading my privacy," Zolotov shouted angrily, shaking his fist at them. The planes had flown out of sight for a second, but they reappeared, flashing by us in ear splitting dives. Over the roar of the engines, I suddenly realized that Ali Hassan's machine guns were chattering and exploding in the wake of the planes. Tiny bursts of smoke, like mosquitoes chasing eagles, appeared in the sky.

I clutched Horace's arms, yelling at him frantically. "For God's sake, stop them! They can't do that. They might shoot one down!"

Zolotov angrily shoved me away. "This is war! I am defending my sanctuary from the world. If one gets shot down, good! They will learn to leave Zolotov to the Gods and not attempt their own petty conceptions of justice!"

The planes swooped in once more, obviously taking pictures of the casbah, and then disappeared in the West. The pop-pop of the machine guns ceased.

Ali Hassan ran up to Zolotov dejectedly. "Next time, master, we will not miss. The infidels will be destroyed."

"There were no markings on the planes," I told Horace. "They are probably newspapermen. Pictures of Ben Youssef's casbah will be in all the Sunday supplements. What did you expect . . . that the world would sit idly by and let you get away with it?"

"I expected the worst," Zolotov said grimly. "That's why I prepared for it. I am not trying to get away with anything. The only solutions that I can offer the world are readily apparent to sensible men. The world will not listen, to me, anyway. I do not intend to be an object of shoddy publicity. The world can hate me, but it can let me alone."

The next morning, it was apparent that the infidels had no intention of letting Horace Zolotov alone. They arrived, en masse, in a steady parade of dusty jeeps and trucks that had evidently left Marrakesh the day before. With Ali Hassan's troops, leveling machine guns at

236

them, they camped a few hundred yards from the walls of the casbah and shouted at us through battery powered megaphones.

"We have come to interview Horace Zolotov. We intend no harm. There are men here from the press services of the world. We are unarmed. There are famous economists here who wish to have Zolotov's views on the world monetary crisis. There are chemists and metallurgists here who would like to discuss Zolotov's discovery with him. Open your gates and let us in."

All through the afternoon and early evening they exhorted Horace to see them. " 'The earth is the Lord's and the fullness thereof. Lift up your heads, O ye gates,' " Horace shrugged bitterly, ignoring my pleas. "I am afraid that the people outside are not messengers of the King of Glory. I will see no one. I have nothing to say to them."

From the escarpments of the casbah, I watched the trucks still coming through the valley. By late afternoon, there were several hundred men setting up camping equipment. They came as close as they dared to the casbah, photographing the place from every angle with telescopic lens on their cameras. As I watched, the thought slowly occurred to me that I was free at last. All I had to do was to run through the gates and join them. I would be eagerly welcomed. I knew more about Horace Zolotov than any person on earth. I even knew the formula for transmuting lead into gold. My adventure was over. I would be famous . . . or infamous . . . but who cared? At least, I would no longer be a non-entity. I had cut my way through the forest and arrived at last at the inner circle; queen bitch, goddess of success!

But I couldn't do it. Watching the evening stars fill the sky, enjoying the hushed night sounds as men and women inside the casbah pursued their lives oblivious to the strangers at their gates, seeing the peaks of the

Atlas remote and disdainful of the problems of men, I realized that I was no longer Marge Wentworth who wanted fame or fortune. With the right man, I would be willing to merge my existence with the simplicity of this tiny Moroccan world. Was Horace the right man? Perhaps. I liked him. But I scarcely knew what motivated him.

I found Horace in our room. Lying on cushions, the radio no longer blaring, he stared at the ceiling and listened to me without answering.

"Isn't this what you really want?" I demanded. "You asked the world to unite. You have told me over and over again that the keystone to a one world government will be when monetary control is finally relinquished by separate nations to a central authority. You could be a leader. The world will listen to you. They will understand your dream. Maybe you can be instrumental in making it work. Everywhere men are waiting for you. You can tell them what they must do."

Zolotov finally looked at me and shrugged. "No one ever loves the person who destroys illusions. I have been writing my ideas. But the world is not ready for them. Zolotov will only be understood by generations not yet born. Now the name and the man is anathema."

"I could go out and talk to those men if you would let me," I told him. "I could tell them what you really wanted to accomplish."

Zolotov smiled. "I haven't stopped you, Margery." He leaned on a cushion and took my hand. "If I were you, I would walk through those gates, I would tell them it never happened. You never married Zolotov. You were his captive. Twist your story a little. Make them believe that you chased me around the world because you wanted to prevent the debacle that has occurred. You will be a heroine. If you stay with me, you will be tarred with the same brush."

"I married you," I said softly. "I am not the best person in the world. Maybe once I did want something different. But I want you to know, I am not ashamed of the name you have given me."

The evening shadows were lengthening. The world and the night noises inside the casbah seemed remote. I had a strange premonition that this might be the last evening I would spend with Horace Zolotov. I wanted somehow, momentarily, to make our room a temporary womb of escape from the world. I noticed that Zoltan had tiptoed in the room and was sitting beside his father. "I learned a poem written many years ago by an Arab poet. Ben Youssef translated it for me," I said. "If you'll play the rabat, Zoltan, I will tell it to your father." Slowly, I recited the words.

"When the Pleiades shone in the heavens,
 Glorious as a belt sewn with precious stones,
 I came to her.
 With her day garments laid aside
 She was clad only in a light robe,
 She waited for him behind the curtain of her tent.

She is like a pure pearl
The shell of which hath a delicate cloudy whiteness.
A pearl nourished by kindly waters in the deep seas.
She turns aside;
She shows me the profile of a lovely cheek,
She looks in my eyes,
And her eyes show the softness of the antelope of Wadjra
Watching over her fawn.
Her neck has the grace of that of a white gazelle,
But the gazelle's neck is not covered with jewels like hers.
Her long black glossy hair falls gracefully over her
    shoulders,
Thick as a palm branch laden with dates.

In the morning her bed is perfumed with musk
She sleeps long after the rising of the sun,
For she does not need to wear the dress and girdle
Of those who labor.
The radiance of her brow scatters the shadows of night
Even as a torch lighted by a hermit in his cave.
Time calms the wild desires of most lovers,
But nothing, O my Love, shall make my heart forget
The passion it feels for thee!"

When I finished, the room was silent. Zolotov brushed a tear from his eye. "We have both learned something, Margery. I am sorry I couldn't have been that lover."

"Never mind," I grinned. "I don't have the eyes of an antelope or the neck of a gazelle."

"She's prettier than that dame in the poem," Zoltan told his father as he snuggled between us. "I know. I take a bath with her every day."

The next morning, dressed in a pale blue caftan with my veil lowered, Zoltan and I, accompanied by Ali Hassan and two of his men carrying machine guns, walked through the gates of the casbah and down the road to the camp of the reporters. I was immediately surrounded by fifty or more men.

"What's the story? Why won't Zolotov see us?"

"Has he really transmuted lead into gold?"

"Where did he get the musical comedy army?"

"He won't get away with it. Zolotov has got to talk!" While Ali Hassan and his men held them at bay, I listened bewildered at the hundreds of questions being flung at me. Without lifting my veil, I finally said, "I am sorry. You will have to go back. My husband will not see you. He has nothing to say to you. I beg you. Go away. Leave us in peace!"

Shocked, I heard someone yell my name. "Marge! Marge Wentworth. It's you!" A man elbowed his way into the center of the crowd. It was Craig! Terrified, I was about to run back to the casbah. Before I could escape, he snatched the veil from my face.

"So you did it . . . you bitch," he said angrily. "You finally married the bastard."

I looked at him dumbly, tears in my eyes. "Craig," I sobbed, "It's not what you think," I wanted to hug him, to tell him how sorry I was for all the trouble I had caused him. "Oh, Craig, I am so glad that you are free."

"No damn thanks to you! You can thank your balmy

240

husband. They finally realized that the gold they thought we were stealing wasn't really gold at all!"

The crowd of men listening to us laughed. "It was real enough to burst the world apart," one of them yelled. "Come on, Marge Zolotov, you are hot news! Tell your sugar daddy we won't hurt him. We only want to talk with him."

"Craig," I said, shaking off the man's hand. "Horace is sick. He won't see anyone. How did you ever get here? What happened to Carlos?" I was happy that Craig couldn't see my round belly under the voluminous caftan.

"Oh, I'm quite famous," Craig said sarcastically. "I am the *Midhaven Herald's* star reporter . . . on a special UPI assignment." I suddenly realized that flashbulbs were popping as photographers took pictures of Craig and me. "Shoot away, fellows," Craig yelled coolly. "I can see the headlines now. Zolotov's Wife's Lover Reunites with the Woman Who Helped Destroy the World! Ex-lovers in the romantic Moroccan Mountains! Come on, Marge, dry those crocodile tears. We want to see Zolotov!"

Shivering, I told Ali Hassan to take me back to the casbah. His men shoved the reporters aside. I couldn't stop crying. What had I expected, anyway? I couldn't blame Craig. Somehow, I just wanted to talk with him without all those gawking faces grinning at us, waiting to hear my sordid confessions. I wondered vaguely where Carlos was. Would he understand? Probably not! Despite Ali Hassan's men who looked as if any moment they would fire point blank into the crowd, the reporters hung on my footsteps. As I ran, I heard the distant rumble of a high-powered airplane engine. Etched black in the clear blue Western sky, like an avenging deity, and ancient World War II bomber flew toward the casbah.

"It's those damned fools connected with the Eldorado

Gold Mining Company," I heard someone yell. "They've been threatening to wipe out Zolotov!"

Screaming, I hitched my caftan over my knees and raced for the casbah. The roar of the engines as the plane dropped altitude burst in my ears.

"My God," I heard Craig yell. "The bomb bays are opening . . . the damned fools are going to bomb the place!"

I saw the bomb for an instant as it hurtled through the sky. It exploded in a burst of flames near the center of the casbah, hurling mud and plaster and debris into the air. I reached the gate a few seconds later. Choking with dust, terrified, I groped through the crowds of screaming natives. The walls of Ben Youssef's palace were shattered. Dead and mangled bodies littered the courtyard. Searching frantically, I finally found Horace, half buried beneath the collapsed roof of the palace.

Screaming hysterically, I brushed dirt away from his face and shoulders, Frantically, I kissed his cheeks. "Horace . . . you can't die! Please!" I sobbed, hugging his poor bruised face while Craig and Ali Hassan attempted to dig him out. "Please . . . please . . . live! You must live!"

He opened his eyes and managed a grim smile. "Don't cry, Margery," he said faintly. "The poor damned fools. All they had to do was wait a few weeks more. I was doomed anyway. I have incurable lead poisoning." He pulled my face down to his lips and whispered softly, "I really would have liked to make love to you, Margery . . . Anyway, you still can have the last laugh . . . Have it for me, please." He babbled almost incoherently into my ear, and then stared blankly into the sky. Horace Zolotov was dead!

I flew back to Midhaven, Connecticut, with Zoltan. As I sit here listening to my thirteen year old son play rock and roll music on an electric guitar, I can't help smiling. Some of the kids from his school have finally been given permission to visit the home of the nefarious woman who married Zolotov. Zoltan has given up trying to teach me the guitar (I haven't got the beat). Yesterday, I heard him tell his friends that I'm really a "good egg." Occasionally, he even accepts a little mush and lets me give him a hug before he goes to bed.

Nine months ago when I persuaded Craig to take up the mad search for Eldorado, I scarcely expected to return to Midhaven a mother twice blest. My baby, keeping time to Zoltan's music with an occasional joyous shove in my belly as he does the "Swim" in my womb, must be a boy. I'm sure that a girl would just relax and enjoy its golden uterine life.

Despite what the world thinks about me, I am unworried. My reputation as the woman who caused the economic collopse of the United States is really quite silly. What could I have done to stop Zolotov? I simply happened by, the unsuspecting recording angel.

Living here in my farmhouse, behind a chain link fence with several nasty police dogs to help Bill Jensen patrol the place, I know that I may not exactly deserve the sobriquet of angel. But, if you are a female, and have read my story, and think you would have done things differently, I would like to know at what point you would have got off the merry-go-round. Maybe you would have been more placid than I. Maybe right from the beginning you would have ignored the interesting possibilities of Zolotov's gold. All I can tell you is that I still don't believe that it is strictly a male's world. I don't think you feel differently, either. A girl can be quite practical and still be enjoyably female in the sack!

The truth is, despite Zolotov, the world hasn't changed much. Gold may have disappeared as a matter of monetary interest, but the inner circle of wealth and power is forming again. Some will be poor and some will be rich. Writers will continue to delude you with the Cinderella story. So, if you are female . . . while you scrape your dishes and load them into the dishwasher, while you lug your dirty clothes to the laundromat, while you scrub your kids and get them off to school so that you can spend the day planning what you'll take out of the freezer for supper tonight; while you generally try to live the life expected of a good mother and scintillating wife, and, finally, before bedtime, while you even watch the old television daydreams with your husband, who is too pooped for active romance, if your fairy god mother just happened to pop out of that box of soap powder, wave her magic wand, and offer you an interesting proposition, wouldn't you listen . . . just a little?

I told Martha, Bill Jensen's wife who has come to live with me and assures me that she is an excellent midwife, the reason a lot of women don't like me is that I simply dared to take things into my own hands. I suppose I'm a bit pragmatic, but honestly, until the soap powder manufacturers offer fairy god mothers as premiums, I believe that a practical female will wave her own magic wand. Come what may, even if my jeweled coach has turned into a pumpkin shell, I'm not going to marry a pumpkin eater!

Even though Martha and Bill aren't angry with me, personally, I am sure they believe that eventually I am going to reveal the happy ending. Somehow, we will all be rich again! I've told Martha that even if I should legally inherit the Zoloto Corporation and become a millionairess, living off my portfolio of stocks, together with the two hotels that Zolotov purchased on the Riviera with his homemade gold, it doesn't change the present fact. Like everyone else, I am just plain broke.

Not only haven't I any money to pay their wages, but I told Doctor Brightman (he is still quite peeved that I insist on having my baby here in what little privacy I have left) I have no idea how I will pay him for his prenatal advice and care.

The truth is, when the final secret of Zolotov's donnybrook against the world leaks out (I estimate about the first of next year), the question as to whether the wealth of the Zoloto Corporation is stolen wealth or not will be academic. Week after week, the newspapers and magazines debate the problem of whether Zolotov's fortune belongs to the nation (which nation is a good question) or his widow. I hope somewhere Zolotov is watching and having a good chuckle.

Thank God the newspapers have always believed that Zolotov was the father of my child. So, I still have some moral standing left in the world. I suppose ultimately, the problem of who the papa really is will solve itself. At least, I am reasonably sure that Daddy isn't Doctor Pao-lin. As for Craig or Carlos, neither of them have rushed here to admit paternity. Maybe Armand Delacroix would like to share his poverty with me? Poor Armand, I doubt that he will recover from the blow. Neither his paper nor his gold will buy thirty-eight women anymore.

I received a letter from Carlos in May. He had read about me in the newspapers. Carlos is once again Captain of a nitrate freighter. He threatens to fly up from Miami one of these days and visit "hees bad moca." I haven't encouraged him, but I did write and ask if on his next trip to Valparaiso he would look up a taxi driver named Rojo O'Harris and give him my best wishes. Darn it, I hate to leave things unfinished. Maybe some day I'll find how Rojo escaped from his bower of love. No doubt, he chooses females, with whom he plans naked evenings on balconies overlooking the Pacific, more carefully.

Since I have to think of Zoltan, too, I suppose I should

forget Craig. At least Carlos can play a guitar! Craig hasn't bothered to come see me, anyway. I presume that he has found a more likely companion to share his suburban flower garden. I listen to him every day on his new afternoon telephone radio program. He answers telephone calls from his listeners, but gets quite tongue tied when some of them ask him to explain why the United States is in such an economic muddle. What did a certain woman named Margery Zolotov have to do with it? Since Craig's knowledge of economics is somewhat shaky, I have been tempted more than once to telephone him and straighten him out over the airwaves both on monetary problems and the vagaries of females.

But that would only bring another avalanche of reporters and curiosity seekers down here. Eventually, I suppose the International Monetary Fund and the United Nations will straighten out the mess. Trading between nations will start again. While a great many fortunes have been lost, the world will finally come to its senses. People will realize that poor Marge Zolotov had nothing to do with it.

"I can't really understand why you are not rich," Martha keeps saying to me. "Of course, sugar, Bill and I aren't blaming you. I heard today that regulations on bank savings will be relaxed soon. Everyone is going to receive Federals in place of the dollars they had on deposit. They say that the Federals will be like the old dollars. Everyone in the world, except Russia and China, is going to use them." Martha sighed. "It's about time. Nobody wants dollars anymore. I've been trying to buy a new electric toaster for the past week. They've got them again in the stores. But everyone is waiting for the Federals. Did you know that they are going to be engraved in gold color? People will know they are worth something then!"

"My only hope is to sell the story of my life," I told her. I couldn't help chuckling. A month ago, the Cousins

Syndicate had offered me a hundred thousand dollars or their equivalent for the inside story of That Zolotov Woman. It was appropriate that I should be paid in paper printed the color of gold. Somewhere, Zolotov must be grimly shaking his head.

"You still have that diamond," Martha pointed out. "If that's real, a rock that size would be worth a fortune."

With tears in my eyes, I looked at the ring on my finger. "I'd starve before I sold Zolotov's ring. Anyway, I've been reading that it is only a matter of time before they can make synthetic diamonds just as big and just as glittery as this. So you see, Martha, I'm just like everybody else. Why don't people look on the bright side of things? Since the government has been forced to repudiate the dollar, we won't have to pay such big taxes. We are all starting from scratch. At least Zolotov solved the problem of our four hundred billion dollar debt. At the rate we were going, it would have made slaves out of our grandchildren."

While Zolotov didn't live to see his dream realized (in truth, the agreement of the Western nations to surrender their monetary and fiscal control to a new World Currency Reserve System is scarcely any assurance that the Golden Age of Peace and Brotherhood to Man has at last arrived), perhaps the world has taken one step up the ladder.

To be honest, I can't worry about it anymore. I started to write the end of this story a few days ago. Then as Zolotov might have put it, my privacy was rudely invaded. Carlos arrived! After he had patted my belly, approved of my fertility, played the electric guitar raucously with Zoltan most of one evening, I finally discovered the big ape could count!

"Ees thees baby een a hurry?" he demanded.

"Right now, it's five days overdue," I told him, "If it doesn't get here soon, I'm going to burst." I no sooner got the words out than I realized my mistake.

"Ha . . . you not find thees Zolotov until January." Happily, he hugged Zoltan. "Thees baby belong to Carlos."

I finally admitted that it was a toss-up between him and Craig. "What difference does it make? Why don't you leave me alone? I'm not going to marry you or Craig!"

Carlos insisted on calling Craig. "Thees Marga, a beeg bag of weend," he told Craig on the telephone. "She got two keeds, she have to marry someone! I theenk she bettair marry Carlos."

When Craig arrived, and somewhat sheepishly admitted that he would have come long before if he had known that it wasn't Zolotov's baby, the arguments really started.

"Carlos not geeve a damn who da papa ees," Carlos said happily. "He marry Marga right now. Not wait!"

"Oh shut up," Craig told him. "Listen, Marge . . . what did you say to me in Marrakesh the day Zolotov was killed."

"I told you I was damned mad at you . . . writing all that garbage about me. Telling the whole world that the biggest mistake men ever made was to have ever given women the right to vote and that ever since, men have been cursed with the feminine mystique."

"Didn't you tell me to get the hell out of your life? Didn't you tell me that you had decided to be Ben Youssef's fourth wife. You were going to prove to me that living in a harem was no worse than living with a tyrant husband in suburbia?"

"Maybe," I grinned. "After all, your male ego didn't approve too heartily of what I had done! You wanted me to come crawling to you . . . and tell you how bad I had been."

"Okay," Craig said. "I just want to know one thing. If Zolotov were alive . . . what would you have done then? Did you marry him for better or for worse."

"For worse . . . and the hell with you," I said crying. "Thees ees seely," Carlos told Craig. "Marga ees not the woman for you. You not evair be happy that she sleep weeth Carlos. What Carlos do een bed bettair than me? . . . you ask her. You drive her mad all her life." Carlos grinned at me. "Deed you sleep weeth Zolotov? Deed you sleep with heem every night? Was eet any good weeth an old man?"

"Of course, I slept with Zolotov," I said hotly. I was determined no matter what, never to tell the truth to either of them. "I was married to him. What we did in bed is none of your damned business!"

Craig tried to put his arm around me. "Look, Marge . . . you know that I was angry with you. But for God's sakes, how did you expect me to react? I loved you. I love you still! I've grown up in the past few months. I've learned a lot, too." He sneered at Carlos. "I don't give a damn if it is his brat, I'll marry you and make an honest woman out of you, Marge!"

I suddenly realized that I was having my first labor pains. "Look," I grimaced as Zoltan joined the discussion. He started to offer his opinion on the merits of his potential fathers, "Zoltan is not a brat. And no matter who the father is, my baby is not a brat. I'll love them both and whoever I decide to marry better love them, too! If you don't love my kids, Craig, you can go hang!"

"Vairy good," Carlos agreed. "Carlos ees a vairy good papa. He love them . . . and ten more, too!"

"You can hang beside him!" I groaned.

Doctor Brightman had arrived and heard part of the discussion. He took one look at me. "Get up to your bedroom, this instant," he said disgustedly, "Unless you are planning to make a spectacle of yourself—or maybe you plan to deliver from that rocking chair." He scowled at Craig and Carlos. "Your 'husbands' can wait down here!"

He pushed me upstairs to my bedroom. "Marge Wentworth, I've known you since you were ten years old. I still can't believe it." He asked me if my water had broken. I told him no. He stuck a needle in my arm. "That's just to calm you down. How did you ever get in such a mess?"

I clutched the sheets as a wave of pain shivered through me. "There are worse messes. Look at Zolotov. No one loved him. They both love me." I chuckled. I was beginning to float as the injection took effect. Martha was wiping my forehead. "Maybe I'll marry them both," I sighed.

While I was conscious and I helped my baby poke his way into the world, half my mind drifted in and out of a dream. The President of the United States had invited Mrs. Margery Zolotov to Washington, D.C. The world had forgiven Zolotov. A committee had been appointed to build a statue in his honor—a statue of pure gold.

"Of course, gold is no longer valuable," the President said to me with a very kindly smile. "But we feel in this case it is a fitting tribute to a man who pointed the way for a better world."

"Not gold," I kept insisting. "Couldn't it be bronze?"

"We have considered other materials, Mrs. Zolotov," the President smiled. "Lead, for example . . ."

I laughed hysterically. Zolotov was dying again in my arms. "Make it of Zolotov's gold," I told the President. "I know the formula!"

As he did over and over again, in my dreams, Zolotov pulled my head down to his lips. "It was never stable, Margery," he whispered. "I tried for ten years but I never could make it stable. After about twelve months . . . something happens. The gold turns back to lead."

"It's a boy," I heard Doctor Brightman say triumphantly.

He slapped its behind. Before my baby cried, I distinctly heard him chuckle.

"No matter what his last name may be," I grinned at Martha, "I name him Horace!"